SEATED IN *Heavenly* PLACES

BOOK ONE

DR. RON ALLEN

Copyright © 2023 Ronnie C. Allen

All rights reserved.

ISBN: 9798882561221

DEDICATION

I dedicate this book to God's people everywhere. May the pages of this book inspire you to answer the call to bring heaven to earth. After 2,000 plus years of co-laboring with the Holy Spirit, we are still in need of increased revelation on the topic of *"Kingdom"*. May this book serve as an anointed supplement to your studies in God's Word, supplying deeper revelation and insight. May the verses used in this book bring God's people into agreement with scripture and alignment in purpose in these last days of the church on Earth. May our understanding of biblical identity, purpose and destiny be released in us as we study God's Word in this season of church history. May we *"say what the Father is saying and do what the Father is doing"* in a righteous attempt to get it right in this decade of harvest. May we learn from the past and seek not to repeat the same mistakes. May the Holy Spirit pour out on our generation; fresh wisdom, anointing and grace to lead the church into increased awareness of our authority and power. May we return to the Gospels and the Book of Acts to reclaim the original standard of the triumphant church. May we walk in Holy Spirit empowerment and authorization to defeat the works of darkness and establish Heaven on Earth…

A special thank you to *Scott Richardson* and *Anderson Grandini* for their creative input. I love you both deeply. I appreciate your friendship, passion for scripture and desire to tell stories that highlight the love of the Father. May the Lord Bless and keep you all the days of your life. May we live on the same street when we get to Heaven and continue to tell stories for a million years – together.

TABLE OF CONTENTS

DEDICATION 3
INTRODUCTION 5
CONVERSATIONS AT THE HEAVENLY PORTAL 6
CONVERSATIONS IN THE SECOND HEAVEN 12
CONVERSATIONS IN THE THRONE ROOM 23
THE VALUE OF A SOUL… 31
THE CONGREGATION OF SOULS… 44
DAILY MEETING IN THE THRONE ROOM 57
DAILY MEETING IN THE SECOND HEAVEN 71
DAILY MEETING IN THE THRONE ROOM (CONT'D) 76
THE COURT OF HEAVEN… 92
A SOUL IS RELEASED… 135
BEHAVIORAL RECONNAISSANCE… 185
THE EXCHANGE MARKET OF HEAVEN 195
THE ENEMY'S PLAN… 205
HEAVEN'S PLAN… 226
LITERARY REFERENCES 243
VIDEO REFERENCES 250
BIBLE REFERENCES 251
CREATIVE TEAM 251

INTRODUCTION

I have always had a deep love for stories. As a child, I couldn't wait to see the next Star Wars film when it was released, or the next episode of my favorite cartoon, to include He-Man and G.I. Joe. I have always been captivated by stories that inspire me to do better and be better, for my friends, family, and my God. I especially love to hear real life stories from people. As I have gotten a little bit older, my fascination has stayed the same. However, with this book, I ventured off into the wild unknown. It's not surprising. Recently, I was in a discussion with my wife, and I brought up a valid point to all my wandering and exploration in life. It occurred to me, probably for the first time, that I was raised on entertainment. For years I thought that being raised on entertainment was somehow a bad thing. Until I recalled the messages that God prophesied to me through the entertainment I was watching. He-Man taught me that *"I have the power"*, the power to make wise choices. G.I. Joe taught me that, *"Knowing is half the battle"*, therefore I love to learn. Star Trek taught me that I should never be afraid to *"Go where no man has ever gone before"*, therefore I have lived a life of firsts, as I have trusted God with each move or change of direction – even if no one in my family had ever attempted it. I joined the US Army at age 18, partly because the slogan spoke to me, *"Be All You Can Be"*. This is literally my first work of fiction. So, I had to write a story that encapsulates the topics I love most – the Bible and Human Development. May this story add value to your spiritual journey...

In His Service,

Dr. Ron Allen

Dr. Ron Allen

CONVERSATIONS AT THE HEAVENLY PORTAL...

It is written in the Word,

"Therefore, since we are surrounded by so great a cloud of witnesses, let us also lay aside every weight, and sin which clings so closely, and let us run with endurance the race that is set before us,"

"Is today the day?" **Asked Annabelle.**

"I think so". **George whispered.**

Annabelle smiled as they both peered through one of the many portals - where the citizens of Heaven gather as a *"cloud of witnesses"* - at the frantic pace of the Earthly realm.

This portal was established by the Father to encourage the gathering of Heaven's citizens, allowing them to check on their loved ones anytime they desire. The Father would never want one of His redeemed to worry about the family and friends they left behind on Earth. Heaven's inhabitants, who were officially declared a righteous citizen through public profession of faith in Jesus while on Earth, having their names written in the *Lamb's Book of Life*, have access to this portal all hours of the day or night. Inhabitants of Heaven are particularly excited when their loved ones establish dual citizenship. This allows them to make spiritual deposits to the layer of their soul now seated amongst the *Congregation of Souls*, which is located near the *Throne Room*. The portal itself is one mile in diameter, with exquisitely crafted ornamented bench seating around the perimeter. The table height edge of the portal is trimmed in gold and decorated with all matter of rare jewels – many not available in the Earthly realm. Each seat has a set of holographic controls where a citizen of Heaven can either speak to the operating system, or punch in the request by using the floating holographic keyboard located directly in front of the seat. The language found on the key boards, as well as all accompanying instructions found at each viewing station is written in the native language of Heaven. It's the same language downloaded to the soul of a believer in Jesus who is baptized in the Holy Spirit while on Earth. All citizens of Heaven understand this language, but they can choose their communication method depending on the situation. Communication between citizens can be in the native language of Heaven, or soul communication. Soul communication allows citizens to communicate without speech. It's the most intimate communication ever established by the Father. The enemy has no access to the thoughts of a redeemed one, therefore soul communication is the most common when details need to be safeguarded from the enemy. As with all spiritual abilities – spiritual discernment, prophecy, healing, authority over weather and authority over evil spirits - an introductory deposit of the capability is experienced while in the Earthly realm. The ability to communicate spirit to spirit is the foundational communication method humans were made with. This is because speech was originally reserved for creating. When the first human – *Adam* - spoke, he created the identity, purpose, and destiny of the animals. Speech is still the chief method for creating in the spirit realm. This is why *"life and death are in the power of the tongue"* even while still on Earth in bodily form.

    The initial experience, while on Earth, happens when your spirit bears witness with God's spirit that you are His child. It also happens when a believer meets another believer while on Earth. Their spirit bears witness to the spirit of God in another person.

Spiritual ability is downloaded in portions to the spirit of the redeemed, while on Earth, for practice. It's a down payment of ability to steward. Holy Spirit serves as the broker for this transfer of ability from Heaven's resources to the spirit of the believer. Through the prophetic act of *impartation*, believers can also transfer ability from one person to the next – by faith. When the abilities are stewarded well, more is given. Once a redeemed one comes home to Heaven, they are transformed into their fully restored and glorified version of themselves – which is able to live for eternity. They also walk in complete, unaltered, and unfiltered power and authority as a citizen of Heaven, complete with all fully manifested spiritual gifts. However, what they learn when they come home is simply breathtaking – they had access to this power and authority even while on Earth. Jesus imparted all power and authority when He rose from the dead and left them with the Great Commission…

    Annabelle went home to Heaven over one hundred years ago after leaving a heritage of love and devotion to her friends, her family, and her God. George has been in Heaven just over 20 years. Citizens of Heaven have access to this portal any time they desire. They use it to check in on loved ones and see their progress in Christ from Heaven's viewpoint. They also pick flowers from the near bye fields and shower loved ones with blessings of joy and peace by casting them through the portal, especially when they recognize Earthly life getting tough for them. In the Earthly realm, when someone feels as though their loved one is somehow near, it's because of this portal and the accompanying prophetic acts by their ancestors. Annabelle and George meet here often to make declarations and decrees over their family line through the portal. They were both experienced intercessors while on Earth, spending hours each day in prayer and meditation for the *ecclesia*. The ecclesia is the body of redeemed ones operating in the Earthly realm to bring about the will of the Father. Through the ecclesia, the governance of mankind is accomplished. The Father accomplishes His will in the Earth through them. They include every born again believer in Jesus, and the *Five-Fold Ministry Officials* assigned to lead them.

Annabelle and George's heart and passion is to see their loved ones walk with Jesus in Holy Spirit empowerment while on Earth and become a righteous citizen of Heaven. They also walk among the *congregation of souls* seated in Heaven to make decrees and declarations over their loved ones still present in the Earthly realm. When a person surrenders to Jesus, a layer of their soul is immediately seated in Heaven. New gifts, anointing for ministry and anything else a believer needs or asks for is deposited in this layer of their soul. It's an exact replica of their Earthly appearance but is transparent and flowing with life. The congregation of souls is at perfect rest at all times waiting to be reunited with their glorified body and the remaining layers. This layer of their soul is protected from the Earthly realm and is there only to receive the things of God that enhances their impact on humanity. Their seated position prophecies their identity, purpose and destiny. The congregation of souls also demonstrates the posture of the believer in Jesus - never having to strive for anything - accomplishing everything from rest...

Annabelle and George both keep records of every birth within their family lineage. They still bring requests to the Father, only now it is in person. They ask the Father, during the one on one time every believer has access to in Heaven, to Bless their loved ones and pour out favor on their family. Once an intercessor, always an intercessor. They work with Jesus personally to intercede for the nations as well.

Annabelle continues, *"This will be my great, great, great grandson's fourth child, and I hear it's going to be a boy. I didn't live long enough to be in this child's earthly life, but for now, I can celebrate this for him. This was one of my prayers while on earth, to bless my children with children who would demonstrate the love of Jesus. I prayed that their children would impact them as parents and help them to realize that the Father loves them more than they can imagine. This protects them from the spirit of religion running rampant through my generational line"*

George laughed and responded with, *"That's an amazing prayer. Children will always refocus their parents and give birth to revival with their childlike faith. I remember praying the same type of prayer for my children's children. Every family experiences trauma at the hands of religion because each generation continues to seek after God. This always teaches them what the Kingdom is not. One of my granddaughters was living for many years thinking that the Father hated her because she watched television, wore make-up or failed to wear a dress to church. My son and daughter are still in the earthly realm. They are in their 80s now. Through the lives of their children, they have experienced many breakthroughs in this area. I love how each new generation sees God's Word through fresh eyes and brings the Kingdom closer into unity with their childlike faith."*

"Exactly" Annabelle exclaimed. *"Jesus always allowed children to roam freely at his gatherings to highlight their value. They carry a measure of faith that often dwindles as they age. The cares of the world and the pride of life has a way of depleting them of joy and purpose. However, as they continue to grow in knowledge and grace, their impact on the world around them becomes something beautiful to watch from up here"*

Annabelle paused, then added, *"The only day I love more than days like today is when someone surrenders their life to Jesus. All prayers are collected in the golden bowls in the throne room as they are directed at the Father, Son and Holy Spirit. But when someone confesses with their mouth and believes in their heart that Jesus died for their sins, it is noised abroad throughout Heaven. Everyone hears it, even the demonic realm in the second heaven. That sound of celebration never gets old..."*

"I love it as well. If they only knew what that confession solidifies for them" George replied.

CONVERSATIONS IN THE SECOND HEAVEN...

It is written in the Word,

"*The thief comes only to steal and kill and destroy. I came that they may have life and have it abundantly.*"

"*Is today the day?*" said spirit of *Lust*.

"*I hope so. We get a fresh assignment to kill, steal, and destroy. I just hope I don't get this assignment. I hear it could be a new Pastor.*" Spirit of *Confusion* replied.

Spirit of *Lust* countered in disdain. "*Oh, I love assignments like that. Pastors are easy, but it does take time to circumvent their God given favor. I hate the way the Father protects them at any cost. Don't they know they are on the wrong side of this thing? Lord Satan has promised us power and glory beyond anything the Father can produce. When we accomplish our assignments to steal, kill and destroy, he rewards us with more authority. I want to be a Principality one day. Anyway, you can have the assignment to bring down a pastor. I'll take a new believer any day. They usually don't know their authority for decades and it's so easy to hit them with sickness, guilt, depression, or anything else I desire to unleash on them. They're clueless at best...*" Spirit of *Lust* pauses, then continues to explain to his less experienced disciple, "*And, you don't know my secrets. Taking down pastors is what I do best. It's my ticket to a fresh new promotion.*"

Spirt of *Confusion* looked interested, and asked, *"What is your secret?"*

Spirit of *Lust* paused while looking at the gigantic fortress that housed Satan and his personal assistants. From where they were standing, they had a view of the entire 6,666 acres of Satan's demonic headquarters. He gazed at the buzz of activity going in and out of the fortress entrances - there were many gates as large as an aircraft hangar door layered in gold and fine jewels taken from earth. They could also see the many portals linking the second heaven to all the cities of the world. Atop the main 66-foot entrance was a massive sign that read,

"All Hail Satan The Rightful King of Heaven and Earth".

Along the foundation were many symbols representing the ethos of his kingdom to include markings that bore the words - Belial, Leviathan and Asmodeus. Upside down crosses were used for the large door handles to remind all who entered about the ease with which they were able to steal, kill and destroy from the early church. Or so he thought…

In spirit of *Lust's* mind, he knew the kingdom of darkness was going to win. However, he longed to be accepted into the upper ranks of the demonic kingdom but knew that it would take something big to get Satan's attention. Satan would only show them attention if they did something to impress him, and this was no small task. Spirit of Lust would have to think outside the box. It was becoming harder to formulate creative solutions for his assignments. The truth was that he was dying a slow death. He simply didn't know it because Satan never told them the price they would have to pay for following him into disobedience. When they were kicked out of the Third Heaven, Satan assembled them all and soothed their fears for a season by telling them that everything was going to be just fine. He quoted the scriptures but twisted them to suit his vision for a world where he was in charge. He never told them that, from this moment, their glorified bodies would begin to wither away, forcing them to inhabit earthly objects, animals, and even people in order to survive. Inhabiting objects or animals is a worst case scenario for them. They are rewarded more for inhabiting a human. This is because inhabiting a human enables them to steal, kill and destroy the human's dominion. Every human is made in God's image and is built to rule and reign. When a human is oppressed by evil spirits, it makes it almost impossible for them to walk in their God given identity, purpose and destiny. When these three elements of a human are diminished, their earthly dominion becomes miniscule. They no longer carry the capacity to impact others for the Kingdom of God. They become a puppet in the hands of the kingdom of darkness. They become subject to whatever spirit is influencing their behavior. Spirits of lust, jealousy and envy drive their behavior making them a wrecking ball in their families, communities and even churches where they may attend. Believers in Jesus can even come under the influence of such spirits because they live in agreement with the enemy, and disobedience to the Word of God.

As spirit of *Lust* gazed at Satan's mighty fortress…

He thought about the first meeting he assembled after their abrupt departure from the third Heaven. Satan quickly assembled them to establish the culture of his kingdom. He didn't usually allow questions but in this instance, he wanted to establish a foundation of lies for them to unknowingly operate from. Several fallen angels asked about the end times and whether or not it was true that their destination was going to be the lake of fire.

Satan told them all with confidence, *"God is a liar! He was jealous of me and that's why He kicked me out. His end time strategy is not going to work as long as you all worship me regularly, serve my every command and never be disloyal to me. I saved you from the bureaucracy of Heaven, and the egotistical atmosphere of God's throne room. The Earth is my dominion given to me by God Himself."*

As spirit of *Lust* pondered this and continued to gaze at Satan's fortress from the outside, he instructed spirit of *Confusion* in a matter-of-fact fashion. *"What makes me so good at what I do is simple. I understand the power of trauma. Humans have a tendency to expect good things to happen to them. They came from God and therefore, they have already had a taste of Heaven before they are born into the earthly realm. Some of them miss heaven, supposing they have never been, and wonder why they are homesick. I love how completely clueless they are, by the way. From the time they are born until the age they finally start reading God's word and understanding the power contained in the name of Jesus, I will have made such a mess of their life, they usually give up hope and become religious. Religious people are of no consequence to the kingdom of darkness. They rarely display the fruits of the Spirit of God, and they live in constant fear of man. Their creativity is stifled because "where the spirit of fear is, there is bondage to tradition".*

Spirit of *Confusion* was confused and asked, *"Why are humans so cherished by God, but we can be thrown away like trash?"*

Spirit of *Lust* informed him, *"Lord Satan told us that humans came along after the fact. He had full dominion over the Earth but failed to cultivate it in the way that God wanted it. God created man and that is where the main competition began between them. Satan informed us that God was so jealous of him he never truly gave him a chance to cultivate the planet. Creating man was a slap in the face of Satan. He became very angry and went on a rampage throughout the earth. All the dinosaurs were destroyed in the chaos, and it left the earth "void and without form". God re-*

created the Earth to accommodate His new creature, made in His image. In my opinion, they are weak and frail to say the least. They may look like God, but they have no clue as to who they are. However, when they understand their biblical identity, purpose and destiny, they are dangerous to the kingdom of darkness. We will defeat the armies of Heaven in an all-out conflict someday, but for now, we must not allow humans to know who they are. This is why I chose you as my disciple to co-labor with. Lust and Confusion are a very powerful combination. We can make a great team and accomplish our assignment together."

Spirit of *Confusion* smiled and felt more comfortable having heard this from his mentor. What he failed to understand is that spirt of *Lust* was only going to use him for his talents and eventually take credit for all his accomplishments in front of the demonic council. This is the norm for demonic kingdom culture. They manipulate, bite, and devour one another regularly for power and position.

Spirit of *Lust* continued his instruction, "The only acceptable excuse for a demon to fail an assignment is if the name "Jesus" is utilized openly by a human in retaliation to our assignment. We all know that the Word was with God from the foundations of the world. However, when He took on the form of a man, He was given the name, "Jesus". Now, this name is above all other names and carries with it all power and authority in Heaven and on Earth. Satan told us that this "Jesus problem" will be worked out at some point, but for now, we are to obey any command given to us in the name of Jesus. Satan said that Jesus was just a prophet, and he is no more influential to human society than Buddha or Mohamed. Using the name "Jesus" is common among His own believers. However, His name has the same power even when used by unbelievers. Even if we have to flee the area, there is always another way - that's where experience comes in. When we hear the *name "Jesus" we must flee the location, but we often have a clear path of return because the human must also live in agreement with God's word in order to fully protect what they hold dear. If they live with open doors to our influence, leaving the area is just a mere inconvenience. It's quite funny to be forced to vacate the area, only to return in greater numbers because the human isn't living in agreement with the whole of scripture. I've only experienced one human that knew more scripture than me. He was a Brazilian Pastor and he refused to think in any way other than scripturally. If I attacked his thought life, his response was always, "It says in God's word..." If I attacked his body by co-laboring with the spirit of Infirmity, he would declare, "By Jesus' stripes we are healed..." This guy made me sick, and I eventually had to accept the punishment for my failure to steal, kill and destroy from his life. Never once did he come into agreement with any belief contrary to scripture. His thought life was impenetrable. This experience was embarrassing but it happened early in my career - I learned from it and thought about it while I was banished to Hades for my incompetence - for a season. I had to learn to use more than one tactic and work in a team. I now use several other weapons to my advantage and seek out up-and coming spirits hungry for recognition to co-labor with - like yourself."*

Spirit of *Confusion* looked confused and inquired deeper, *"I thought his name was Lucifer. Also, what does all this have to do with trauma?"*

Spirit of *Lust* looking bewildered by the question, replied, *"He refuses to be addressed by that name. It was given to him by the Father. As for your second question, quite simply, they always find a way to blame God or themselves for their trauma. It's the perfect internal storm. It's my go to move and it works almost every time because they won't study the scriptures concerning God's nature. Even if they do read their Bibles, the spirit of Religion has some amazing erroneous teachings concerning God's sovereignty that keeps them thoroughly confused. Many of them think God sends sickness to them to teach them a lesson. It's the most hilarious thing I've ever heard. Don't they know that God is literally "love". Their God actually desires to bless them, but their desire for justice makes them vulnerable to self-blame - for just about everything. They want to believe that goodness and mercy will follow them all the days of their lives, but they neglect the promise Jesus made to them that, "in this life you will have tribulation". However, what they don't want to understand is that disappointment and loss is part of living in the earthly realm. How they process disappointment and loss usually opens the door to growth or creates a barrier to their progress. Most people allow their trauma alone to steal, kill and destroy from their lives - it makes my job easy. Also, trauma is unforgiveness in diapers. Trauma is the seed, bitterness becomes the root, and unforgiveness becomes the fruit if they fail to receive emotional healing. Since the spirit realm is an exchange economy, humans who fail to forgive others develop roots of bitterness that often open the door to sickness and disease. If they don't forgive others, they naturally have a hard time forgiving themselves. They become judgmental and self-loathing. Most often, later in life they become religious to cope with their suffering."*

    Spirit of *Confusion* looked amazed at this new information and said, *"You mean to tell me, all that stuff happens in their life because they fail to deal with their trauma and believe erroneous teachings about their God?"* Spirit of *Lust* replied, *"Oh yes, and much more. By the time I bring in spirit of Guilt and Shame to finish them off, they are a shell of their true self. They almost always blame themselves for the bad things that happen to them, as Guilt and Shame bombard their thought and dream life with the fiery darts they themselves, or their friends and family create. They usually turn to religion to insulate their emotions from feeling anything. Once they are under the influence of the spirit of Religion, they are no longer a threat to our kingdom - that's when I leave them alone to die slowly and religiously. We don't care if they go to Heaven. We are mainly focused on making sure they don't take anyone with them. A traumatized, confused believer in Jesus isn't influencing anyone for Jesus. This is why we leave them alone, accept to continue to steal, kill and destroy from their life. Afterall, they think God sends all that stuff their way, so we are free to roam about their thought life and do whatever we want..."*

"Wow!" Exclaimed spirit of *Confusion*, *"I never knew the spirit of Religion's role in all of this. This must be why he so highly ranked. With the theology he manufactures, countless people are rendered powerless and unable to influence others for the Kingdom. You are teaching me so much!"*

Spirit of *Lust* turned his head and looked him in his eyes with sincerity and said, *"I'm going to teach you all my tricks, my friend."*

He said this knowing full well that he would never teach another demon all of his tricks. He was going to harvest all the talent and ability his inexperienced disciple had. Then he would hatch a plan to stab him in the back and take all the credit. Satan rewards such behavior. Sadly, spirit of *Confusion* would then have to take his place back in *Hades* where demons are demoted to tormenting duties. Only the most promising demons are called forth to take part in steal, kill and destroy missions. Spirit of Confusion had spent a great deal of time in Hades waiting for an opportunity to impress Satan. This was his chance, and he was taking every opportunity to ask the right questions. He wasn't aware that spirit of Lust was planning to use him in this manner. After all, he was inexperienced and rather naive. Spirit of *Lust* would use this to his advantage in the days ahead.

Spirit of *Confusion* had more questions and spirit of *Lust* was in the mood to answer them, for now. At least while they were waiting for this eternal soul to be formed and released into the natural realm.

"I thought our ultimate goal was to keep them from coming into covenant with Jesus. Is this not the case?" *Confusion* asked.

Lust continued to break down the strategy he uses and why, *"Just because an eternal soul confesses with their mouth and believes in their heart that Jesus died for their sins, doesn't mean they will live in accordance with their God given biblical identity, purpose, and destiny. The development of their identity, purpose and destiny are found in that book they are always quoting, but seldom live in agreement with. Satan told us that the bible is just a historical record of metaphorical principles. There is no academic weight or historical legitimacy to it. It's fine if they read it. Just as long as they don't understand or demonstrate it. Since few of them even study it, we can always twist the scriptures to accommodate their favorite doctrine. Since they love to huddle together around this book, we have a church for every kind of belief system imaginable. We even managed to convince countless teachers of scripture that the Holy Spirit and His gifts are no longer for them today. We convinced several others that only 144,000 people are going to be saved, subsequently stopping them from doing any type of evangelism at all. They are a pretty stupid creation to say the least. There are so many different interpretations of its meaning developed by people who are co-laboring with us and don't even know it. This is why Spirit of Religion and Spirit of Politics are so well respected in our kingdom. They are responsible for the first murder in human history as Cain brought a different kind of sacrifice than Abel because the spirit of Religion convinced him to. Cain's own jealousy drove him to murder his brother. However, Spirit of politics influenced him through his thought life to make this move to secure his dominion on the earth. Much of what we do is through the thought life of a human. We don't have the power to create, therefore we can use the fiery darts we collect from the words spoken by friends, family and what they read. Since life and death are in the power of the tongue, we have all the ammunition we need. You will be surprised at the ammunition available to us simply by collecting these fiery darts. Humans say things to their children like, "I wish you were never born" or "You will never amount to anything, just like your father." The list goes on and on..."*

Spirit of *Confusion*, looking interested fired off another question, *"How on earth did we convince them to have so many different ways of teaching this one book."*

Lust answered with a haughty look, *"They love to take credit for so-called revelation, and they build empires around themselves because they want power. This is when the spirit of Mammon begins to influence their decisions. If they have the right twist on scripture, and it makes the people feel special to carry a private interpretation, they know they have hit the jackpot. There was a man who claimed that he alone had an interpretation for the end times. Millions followed him and eventually, as he increased his control over their lives from the pulpit, many of them were hurt by his controlling leadership and would swear to never step foot in a church again. Private interpterion always gives birth to control and manipulation by the leaders of the movement. Since humans don't like to be controlled, they eventually leave this type of environment and they avoid any type of gathering where the bible is preached, often times for the rest of their lives. This man became very wealthy, and he was never in covenant with Jesus. He simply tapped into the carnality of the modern day believer and built an empire around one erroneous teaching."*

"Wow!" Exclaimed spirit of Confusion,

as spirit of Lust continued, *"These people are senseless. We have an advantage because we have had the Word for thousands of years. It was part of our training as angels to memorize it. When the Word became flesh, they celebrated the fact that Jesus died for their sins, but they never studied what He really said or exercised what He demonstrated. Imagine that... He is the Word, but they don't even know what He declared, and they won't practice what He demonstrated. You should be getting more confident by the second."*

CONVERSATIONS IN THE THRONE ROOM...

The throne room of God was buzzing with activity as usual. It was as the Apostle John described it in the Word,

"Then suddenly, after I wrote down these messages, I saw a heavenly portal open before me, and the same trumpet-voice I heard speaking with me at the beginning broke the silence and said,

"Ascend into this realm! I want to reveal to you what must happen after this."

Instantly I was taken into the spirit realm and behold—I saw a heavenly throne set in place and someone seated upon it. His appearance was sparkling like crystal and glowing like a carnelian gemstone. Surrounding the throne was a circle of green light, like an emerald rainbow. Encircling the great throne were twenty-four thrones with elders in glistening white garments seated upon them, each wearing a golden crown of victory. And pulsing from the throne were blinding flashes of lightning, crashes of thunder, and voices. And burning before the throne are seven blazing torches, which represent the seven Spirits of God. And in front of the throne there was pavement like a crystal sea of glass. Around the throne and on each side stood four living creatures, full of eyes in front and behind. The first living creature resembled a lion, the second an ox, the third had a human face, and the fourth was like an eagle in flight. Each of the four living creatures had six wings, full of eyes all around and under their wings. They worshiped without ceasing, day and night, singing, "Holy, holy, holy is the Lord God, the Almighty! The Was, the Is, and the Coming! "And whenever the living creatures gave glory, honor, and thanks to the One who is enthroned and who lives forever and ever, the twenty-four elders fell facedown before the one seated on the throne and they worshiped the one who lives forever and ever. And they surrendered their crowns before the throne, singing: "You are worthy, our Lord and God, to receive glory, honor, and power, for you created all things, and by your plan they were created and exist."."

Within the bustle of activity, The Father, Son, and Holy Spirit were having their daily meeting. At least, what we would consider a daily meeting. Time is an earthly concept. The Father created time to govern the affairs of man. He rolled out a duration of time in order to accomplish His will in the Earth. Heaven is on another time zone and time stamp altogether. In accordance with the prophecy revealed to Daniel, one day on earth is the Heavenly equivalent of 4 minutes. The messenger Angel declared this supernatural time difference in the Word,

"Seventy weeks are decreed about your people and your holy city, to finish the transgression, to put an end to sin, and to atone for iniquity, to bring in everlasting righteousness, to seal both vision and prophet, and to anoint a most holy place."

This angel spoke in terms of *Heavenly Standard Time* (HST) expecting us to do the math for ourselves. 70 Heavenly weeks is the equivalent of 490 earth years. From the time the decree went forth to rebuild Jerusalem in the book of Nehemiah, to the historical date Jesus rode into the Eastern Gate of Jerusalem on Palm Sunday prior to His crucifixion, 483 years passed, leaving 7 for the Tribulation yet to be fulfilled. When the *Age of Grace* has been fulfilled, this earth timeline will begin again with the Rapture of the Church. God has the ability to start, stop, slow down or speed up time in accordance with His perfect will...

This means that a messenger Angel battled the Demon *Principality of Persia* for 21 earth days. It also means that, with the eventual help of Michael the Archangel who is in charge of the angel armies in Heaven, the prophecy was delivered to Daniel after 84 Heavenly minutes of battle. The messenger Angel almost apologetically mentioned the reason it took him so long. Ironically, the deepest, most accurate prophecy ever released to a *Prophet* concerning the future of God's cherished people took only 84 (HST) minutes to discuss, release and deliver to Daniel. Even with a high ranking demon *Principality* oppressing an entire nation, responsible for millions of inferior demons, who was personally involved in the fight - Heaven took only minutes to break through.

The Word declares,

"Fear not, Daniel, for from the first day that you set your heart to understand and humbled yourself before your God, your words have been heard, and I have come because of your words. The prince of the kingdom of Persia withstood me twenty-one days, but Michael, one of the chief princes, came to help me, for I was left there with the kings of Persia,

This is why Heaven has the ability to stay ahead of any attack sent by the kingdom of Darkness. Time moves slower in Heaven, giving them ample time to collect, discuss and execute the prayers, declarations, and decrees of the Saints. Heaven is never behind in the fight. When we pray, declare or decree from the Earthly realm, Heaven has more than enough time and resources to bring it to pass. We never have to fear that our prayers, declarations, or decrees aren't heard, because they are stored in golden containers located directly in the throne room of God. From there, they are taken out and discussed at daily meetings with the Father, Son, Holy Spirit, the Guardian Angel assigned to the eternal soul being discussed, and the Guardian assistants. When Prayers of agreement are collected, every Guardian Angel must represent their eternal soul at the daily meeting along with their assistants. Since 1 earth day is equal to 4 (HST) minutes, meetings last roughly 2 (HST) minutes or 6 earth hours. This is why Jesus taught His disciples to pray "give us this day, our daily bread". We are already living in the day that Heaven planned. Therefore, our prayer for provision is a release of tomorrow's bread, today. This is also why obedience is crucial to Kingdom citizenship. Holy Spirit releases direction and inspiration in real time, often during the meeting, as they streamline the life plan.

This is why, the bigger the prayer on Earth, the longer the process in Heaven can seem to us. 4 minutes of Heaven's time concerning 1 eternal soul is worth 1 day on Earth. This is also why we are encouraged to spend Earth time in prayer and fasting. If we pray and meditate for 1 whole earth day, we are still only bombarding Heaven for 4 heavenly minutes. If we pray and meditate for 10 earth minutes, our engagement with Heaven is measured in mere seconds. Sometimes, Heaven wonders why we would call a meeting that only lasts seconds. They will honor the request, but without our time participation, they are often left to fill in the details for us. This works in the beginning stages of a believer's life. However, as our requests become more detailed, we are better positioned for breakthrough.

Breakthrough comes when we learn to co-labor with Heaven's process. Why does it often take so long on Earth to see a prayer answered? Quite simply, when the request is big, the variables surrounding the execution of the request on the part of Heaven takes more planning. It isn't about possibility because for Heaven, nothing is impossible. However, the Heavenly planning it takes to manifest a gigantic aspiration or request by a Kingdom citizen in the Earthly realm is detailed and methodical beyond our comprehension. Even if we could fully understand the mechanics of our own life plan, the attacks of the enemy through other people, or our own self-will can make it complicated - for us but not for Heaven. Heaven often readjusts the plan through an act of *Grace*. Mainly because humans are created with a will, and we don't always understand how to cooperate. People placed in our lives to nurture our life plan don't always know how to cooperate either. This is why Prophecy is so important to the New Testament Kingdom citizen.

Often in Old Testament, Angels had to be sent directly because there was no one operating in the inner circle of the eternal soul to co-labor with. Every believer now has the ability to Prophecy what is decided at the daily meeting on behalf of the eternal soul in question - this wasn't the case in the Old Testament. Israel would often kill the Prophets, subsequently stopping the flow of information to eternal souls. Messages we now take for granted had to be sent directly from Heaven and personally declared by a messenger Angel. Now, when a Holy Spirit filled *Prophet* is operating in the inner circle of an eternal soul, messages from Heaven can be immediate, bringing them into alignment with Heavens plan much faster. Since time moves faster on Earth, Prophecy can keep us in perfect alignment with Heaven, allowing our life plan to keep pace with the perfect will of the Father.

Heaven does not infringe upon the will of man - we are free moral agents at our core. We only get what we ask for. Heaven responds to our prayers, declarations, and decrees. Since language is reserved for creating in Heaven, we are trained in this aspect while on Earth, in preparation for eternal life. *"Life and death are in the power of the tongue."* Daniel's request was enormous. He was asking for a revelation concerning the future of an entire nation - the nation of Israel. It is possible that many in his time had the same request. However, Heaven accepted his request for revelation because by that time, he had proven himself trustworthy to use it for the good of his people. The time it took to plan the delivery of this revelation was immediate. It only takes a second to send a messenger Angel to Earth. However, this revelation was so hope filled and powerful, and since the prayer originated geographically in a region controlled by the kingdom of darkness, the *Principality of Persia*, the highest ranking demon in the region was alerted and fought to keep it from ever reaching Daniel. The *Principality of Persia* was alerted because, very simply, prayers, decrees and declarations released into the spirit realm are heard by every spirit realm resident, to include the kingdom of darkness. This is why the kingdom of darkness also has access to our words. Words are weapons and tools in the spirit realm. Daniel waited 21 earth days. Heaven planned, released, and fought to get the message to Daniel, finally delivering it 84 (HST) minutes later.

"Is today the day?" Holy Spirit asked Jesus.

"I believe so". Jesus replied.

Holy Spirit continued, *"The Father had several things on his agenda today, but I believe today is the day. I hope this one is another businessperson, or maybe a congressman, or maybe even another athlete. These types of people carry so much influence in their earthly society. I get so excited on days like today. When the Father brings another soul into being. He carefully and wonderfully fashions their eye color and hair color. I just can't stand it right now! I'm pumped!"*

Jesus laughingly responds with a simple, *"I know, right?"* and then went on to say, *"If people only knew the detail that the Father puts into each molecule of their structure, they would never suffer from jealousy. I remember a man, a political leader, that the Father fashioned so well in regard to public speaking, people thought he was a god when he spoke. It did not end well for him. However, had he only come to the realization that every bit of favor on his political career and public speaking ability was placed within him when he was conceived in the womb, he may have accomplished greater things. It's astounding the attention to detail the Father puts into every characteristic, talent, ability, and gifting in a single soul."*

"I remember him", said Holy Spirit. *"He won every election as he climbed the political ladder, and never once stopped to think about why he was so successful, beyond thinking it was by his own effort. Sure, effort played a part, but favor is the lubricant of the Kingdom."*

"It is unfortunate. I love him dearly…" Jesus said.

"That's part of the journey, isn't it? Coming to that realization as a human being as to where all good gifts come from. Some think all their success is the result of working hard and somehow being in the right place at the right time. It's all about the Father's favor."

On a day like today, all of Heaven's citizens wait in wonder. Every child conceived has admirers long before they are birthed into the natural realm. All the grandparents and ancestors stand in awe and anticipation for the new arrival. They discuss the opportunities afforded to their new relative as they reminisce about their own earthly development. Now that they left the earthly realm, been issued their glorified bodies, and have joined the cloud of witnesses, they have an up-front view of the process - and they know it well. They love to talk about the plans God has for them to prosper and how He places within each new soul the ability to accomplish everything written in their book. They love to guess when and where their new relative will believe in their hearts and confess with their mouths that Jesus died for their sins. Partially because, when a person confesses with their mouth that Jesus died for their sins, its noised abroad throughout Heaven. It's the loudest announcement in Heaven, and for a reason. Another soul has come home and entered the Kingdom.

Another soul, at least a layer of their soul, becomes seated in Heaven. It's a joyous occasion that can last for days on end. Every ancestor is present, especially parents who had the opportunity to live on earth at the same time as them.

THE VALUE OF A SOUL…

It is written in the Word,

" Look at the birds of the air: they neither sow nor reap nor gather into barns, and yet your heavenly Father feeds them. Are you not of more value than they?"

Whisps of brightly lit activity flowed in an out of the Father as He sat on His throne in Heaven. Eternal souls all begin in this way. Like little fireflies floating and gleefully playing in the Glory of the Father's essence. He was planning on releasing the soul of a young man today, but was waiting on the consummation of love in order to knit the soul to the single cell of flesh that would form in the womb of a young woman name Sarah Johnson - currently living in Dalton, GA. It was customary to have the identity, purpose and destiny of a soul solidified prior to the earthly protocol of being conceived in a womb. The womb is simply the place where the physiological features of the person are formed in accordance with their unique DNA code.

The soul is protected while in this season of life because the soul has no choice of environment. The Father has the ability to make spiritual deposits in the soul during this time as well. As the fleshly component of the person is developed, to include hearing, the Father gives the embryo the capacity to hear the voice of their earthly father. This is the initial step in training the person to recognize love and authority in the voice of their earthly parents. When a child is born, they will recognize the most commonly heard voice while in the womb. This is a protective feature planted within us by God the Father that enables a child to feel safe during a rather dangerous transition from womb formation to birth.

Inside the DNA is the identity, purpose and destiny of an eternal soul. The DNA provides the creative direction for the cells to move into alignment and manifest the physical image God had in mind for the person. This process can also take place without the fertilization of an earthly father due to the life-giving properties found in DNA. When God speaks, He creates. However, God doesn't just speak language that ears are trained to recognize. He can also speak to a single molecule. DNA is simply God's biological voice that moves and manages fleshly cells into action. His voice can move molecules into action to fertilize an egg produced by an ovary, with or without the help of an earthly father.

Adriel, the guardian angel assigned to this soon to be released eternal soul was standing watch, ready to take on the assignment. His name means, *"My Help is God"*. He was aware of the timing, and the dilemma already present in the life plan for this eternal soul. Sarah had never heard about Jesus as a young woman. She had already developed a highly destructive drug addiction that plagued her life. It was impossible to form healthy relationships in her circle of influence because, after all, they had the same problem she had. *Pharmacia* or spirit of *addiction*, the addictive spirit oppressing Sarah was also standing by peering through a portal from the second heaven, ready for the conception process. It would be an opportunity to steal, kill and destroy from her on another level. He was aware of the assignment cancelation order issued by Gladys concerning the child. Gladys was a believer in Jesus and prayed often for Sarah.

She prayed this prayer and declared blessings on Sarah often, especially since she moved in with her boyfriend against her counsel,

"Father, I plead the blood of Jesus over my daughter's life,

and I repent on her behalf of all sin and disobedience. Have mercy on Sarah and give her a mighty encounter with your love. I cancel all enemy assignments against her, in Jesus name."

It was an inconvenience when a Saint canceled an enemy assignment, but it wouldn't stop the gathering team of demons from finding another way. If there were valid ancestral contracts with demons in Sarah's lineage, Gladys's prayer wouldn't carry much weight in the court of Heaven, since Sarah was no longer living under the spiritually authoritative covering of her mother's home. In the demonic kingdom, failure isn't an option. They would be punished if they didn't find a way, because their work is the only way to earn a promotion. If it weren't for Sarah's mother, there would be little hope for the future of this soon to be released eternal soul. Sarah was living in agreement with *Pharmacia*, so the cancelation order issued by her mother for Sarah's life had no real effect on his plan. He would simply target the unborn child through other means. Sarah was also living in willful disobedience to scripture, which restrains the much needed protective covering in the spirit realm. This wasn't Heaven's choice - it was Sarah's.

Sarah was defiant in her lifestyle and held no reverence for God the Father. The only reason she was still alive was because of Gladys' prayers. Sarah told her that she was trying to get pregnant and was going to raise this child whatever way she pleases, and she *"didn't need religion, or Jesus telling her how to live her life."* This was heartbreaking for Gladys to hear, but she continued to love her and pray for her regularly. Gladys was a seasoned Holy Spirit filled believer who refused to co-labor with the spirit of *Religion*. Many people looked down on her as a parent because of Sarah's openly defiant behavior. Gladys served as a Deaconess at her church, and she knew about the gossip. She simply prayed for those who were hurling accusations against her and asked the Father to show them mercy. She knew they were simply reacting out of fear for their own children. In recent days, Gladys turned her prayer focus to the greatly anticipated unborn child. She knew it was only a matter of time before Sarah would become pregnant due to her promiscuity. Sarah was also living in agreement with the spirit of *Disobedience*.

Gladys poured out her heart in prayer for her daughter and the protection of Sarah's child. Thankfully, a new eternal soul has yet to develop a connection to oppressive spirits through cognitive agreement. The only way addiction would pass to this new child is if generational curses are present and legally binding. These were all canceled years ago by a Prophet visiting Glady's church. For this assignment, *Pharmacia* would use his usual tactics by co-laboring with *fear* and other inferior spirits to remind the family often about the *"high probability"* of addiction in the child. Once the family comes into agreement with a declaration such as this, *Pharmacia* would have free reign to steal, kill and destroy - at least for a season. The demonic team assigned to this child was growing. There was an anticipation in the demonic kingdom. Word was spreading and questions were being asked, *"Is this one of the Five-Fold ministry?"* From the kingdom of Darkness's perspective, all evidence was pointing in that direction, and it was easy to make that assumption.

It's not that a member of the Five-Fold ministry is more loved and cherished by the Father. Every eternal soul is fearfully and wonderfully made with divine identity, purpose and destiny. Five-fold ministers are simply created to gather and lead others. Consequently, as they go, so does the church and all humanity. One *Pastor* can change the culture of an entire city. One *Prophet* can shift the destiny of nations. One *Teacher* can bring generational revelation of scripture to the church that empowers people and builds momentum for God's plan to unfold. Many generations after they leave the earthly realm, their followers will still be better equipped to defeat the kingdom of Darkness. This is all out war, and these people are considered extremely dangerous to Satan and his followers. Every eternal soul is special. However, a Five-Fold minister is dangerous to the demonic realm, and they carry favor and anointing from birth.

A typical demonic team assigned to a Five-Fold minister is much larger than normal. It is usually comprised of one experienced overseer, usually a spirit of *Lust*, and three lower level demons who have successfully graduated from training. Demons are trained in the art of influence and manipulation of natural human tendencies in schools separated by specific disciplines. They are given little creative freedom and are expected to conform blindly or suffer ridicule from their peers. Getting kicked out of training for failure to conform gets them a ticket to *Hades* for tormenting duty. Many demons have been on tormenting duty for hundreds of years due to a simple momentary lapse in judgement in their assignment. There is no forgiveness in the kingdom of darkness. If they are given another chance to prove themselves, it is only because Satan needs their gifts and talents to accomplish his schemes. He isn't at all interested in their development or future. It's purely a transactional relationship.

Under the umbrella structure of the *Kingdom of Darkness Training Institute*, The school of *Fear* graduates demons trained in the art and science of *Fear*. They are trained to work within the limitations of their created identity. Demons or "Fallen Angels", have divine limitations set forth by God when they rebelled. They don't have access to future knowledge, they only have access to your past. They have a will; therefore they aren't always obedient. They can manifest in the natural realm, but only momentarily due to the physics of the seen realm. They lose energy when they manifest bodily. This is why they would rather inhabit a person or object.

This enables them to stay engaged with the natural realm through the actions of their host. Prior to admission into the KDTI the most promising demons are organized into two main categories of demon - *scorpion* or *serpent*. The needs of the kingdom of darkness and the nature of their life long assignment enables Satan to focus their training in these two very specific areas of expertise for prolonged infirmity. It is the goal of every demonic team to pave the way for a spirit of *Infirmity* to inhabit the target. *Serpent* spirits operate in the psyche of humans causing all manner of mental, emotional and intellectual impairment to include Bipolar disorder and Schizophrenia. Lower level Serpent spirits, like spirit of *Lust*, simply manipulate the senses paving the way for a higher ranking demon to move in for habitation. Lower level demons are rewarded for finding a way in, but the higher ranking demon always gets the credit.

Scorpion spirits operate in the fleshly realm causing all manner of physical impairment to include Diabetes, blindness, and deafness. The most gruesome combination is when scorpion and serpent spirits combine to cause low functioning Autism, robbing the human of identity, purpose and destiny - all at once. God's grace covers a human in this condition because it is generally handed down through no fault of their own as a result of generational ancestorial curses. God is gracious and kind... In the Gospels, the disciples encountered this combination and could not deliver the boy from the demonic influence. Jesus informed them, *"This kind comes out through prayer and fasting."* Jesus did not elaborate on how much prayer and fasting, so the ecclesia is still in pursuit of a revelation on this topic. When this revelation is released and we see wide spread healing of low functioning Autism, the church is officially entering into the days of the triumphant church. When the church finally carries the solutions for society, the nations will be drawn to Jesus in a way we haven't witnessed in human history.

Demons can't read the mind of a human, but that doesn't hinder them all that much. They simply observe human behavior meticulously. Human behavior is a direct reflection of their thought life and the mental constructs built through instruction. This is because every human becomes what they desire the most and what they spend their precious time doing. Spirit of *Lust* will war against the human desire to serve and know their creator, which is implanted naturally from conception. Many humans regularly attend church, but their time and affection is anchored in work, sports, hobbies, or even food. Of course all these activities are acceptable, fun and enjoyable. However, spirit of *Lust* wants these activities to become the human's primary source of vivacity and satisfaction. Spirit of *Lust* isn't afraid when people drop in for the once per week visit to a church. He is working overtime to anchor the human's affections in the seen realm the rest of the week. He is willing to make an exchange - 1 hour of church time as long as he gets 30 hours of hiking or listening to the news.

Once the affections are anchored in the natural realm, the desire for the supernatural will weaken. Since humans are first and foremost eternal spirits, the desire for the supernatural will fade away leaving the human uninterested in seeking after their eternal creator. Standing ready at all times to co-labor with *Lust* are spirits of *Confusion* and *Fear*. This deadly combination worked on Eve and continues to work many generations later. Eve made her decisions based on her natural affections, rather than being anchored in covenant relationship with her creator and obeying His guidelines. Ironically, The Father only gave them one rule to follow in *the Word*,

"And when the woman saw that the tree was good for food, and that it was pleasant to the eyes, and a tree to be desired to make one wise, she took of the fruit thereof, and did eat, and gave also

unto her husband with her; and he did eat".

Spirit of *Lust* influenced her decision to spend the time to go closely examine the tree she wasn't supposed to eat. Her natural affections took her places she was cautioned to avoid. Spirit of *Confusion* provided the fiery darts of doubt concerning what God originally said. Spirit of *Fear* influenced her decision to hide from God after the fact, rather than approach Him for forgiveness. This deadly combination has been in existence for thousands of years. The demonic kingdom has no reason to change the structure of this team - they work so well together. God has the Five-Fold ministry team to equip the Saints and bring down the works of darkness - globally. Unfortunately, demonic teams are more devoted to their cause, and they insist on working together. They may fight over who gets the credit once the assignment is complete, but while they are in the fight together, they will stop at nothing to do their job well as a unit.

Gladys, a 50 year old woman of African-American descent, who gave her life to Jesus many years ago, prayed this prayer one day during her quite time with the Lord.

"Father, I declare that if Sarah were to become pregnant, the child will serve you all the days of their life. I repent on Sarah's behalf for her disobedience to your word. The addictive spirit oppressing my daughter will have no hold on the child. I cancel the enemy assignment to kill, steal and destroy from this child's life, in Jesus name."

Like many believers in Jesus, she prayed this prayer so many times, as if to think it wasn't heard the first time. Adriel was given liberty to protect the child the first time she prayed it.

Each time she prayed it, Adriel would sigh and say, *"I wish more believers would pray this way. If humans only knew the power in the name of Jesus. If they only knew how their prayers are collected and stored away in the golden bowls in the throne room. If they only knew how detailed the Father is about these things. If they would read and understand the book of Daniel, they would see a glimpse into the spirit realm and the mechanics of how prayer even works."*

Adriel was in love with God's word. He quoted it often because he had it memorized. He took his job very serious and knew the ramifications of operating without a sense of duty. He is a soldier, like all guardian angels, who carries a sense of soberness and thoughtfulness about him. He likes to have fun, but he takes his assignments very serious. Especially on a day like today. He felt privileged to be selected for this assignment. Only the best are selected to be guardian angels. This is because a guardian angel has the capacity to manifest in the earthly realm in their glorified body without losing power, for as long as they need to. They are given liberty to display the power and authority of the Father to accomplish their duties as long as it doesn't interfere with the human will. They are also commissioned to fight all threats against the life plan and take charge in the moment, even if it means causing temporary blindness or canceling a human's ability to speak. They operate like the Special-Forces, having the authority to make command decisions in real time, without having to consult *Michael* or *Gabriel*.

They are the most highly trained and cunning of all the angelic host. They understand human behavior specifically and spend a great deal of time in the *Hall of Learning* - Heaven's library and source of all knowledge. They are experts in the hierarchy of the demonic kingdom and understand enemy devices, schemes and plans to perfection. Often, the only thing that delays their actions is our lack of prayer. Our Prayers, decrees and declarations provide the ammunition they need to operate. It's discouraging for a guardian angel to approach the assigned golden bowl in the throne room only to find it empty. Without the authorization to act, the guardian angel is left without ammunition. It is then, their assignment becomes defensive in nature. This is not their primary role in accordance with the anointing they carry. Heaven is never on the defensive. God's plan always marches forward - if we pray.

As Adriel stood in the throne room waiting and contemplating the days ahead, he looked down at the sword hanging from his belt. Written on it were the words, *"Prayers, Prophecy, Decrees and Declarations"*. This weapon becomes stronger as he dips the sword into the golden bowls in the throne room of Heaven. The sword is sufficiently strong enough to get the job done. However, it breaks his heart to think that this child literally has one person praying for them. He hadn't experienced that very often in his career, but this was a huge assignment, and he was going to get extremely creative throughout the process of protecting this child's life plan. The cards were seemingly stacked against the child, but he had experienced worse. Being a guardian angel wasn't easy. It was a busy job, but it was what he was built for. The Father creates every creature with a specific identity, purpose and destiny. It's what he was born to do - and he loves every minute of it. Having served as a disciple for many decades under the training of Kemuel, whose name means, *"Helper of God"*, he felt well prepared for this new season in his career. He knew that Kemuel would be available if he found himself in a tough situation. This is the culture of Heaven. Covenant discipleship is for eternity. Even though Adriel was released to his own assignment, Kemuel was ready and willing to come to his aid at a moment's notice.

Pharmacia stood beside his disciple and peered through the portal from the second heaven. His disciple didn't have a name quite yet, but he was being trained to be a *Wicked Spirit*. Identity isn't given freely in the demonic kingdom like it is in God's Kingdom. Everything is earned in the demonic realm because Satan refuses to operate like the Father. Identity, purpose and destiny are all worked for tirelessly. They aren't allowed to think freely for themselves, and they are controlled and manipulated every step of the way. Disciples are treated unfairly, unjustly and demanded to work regardless of how they feel. *Principalities* who oversee countries and *Powers* who oversee states, provinces and cities all have disciples who are taught to steal, kill and destroy. *Wicked* spirits operate at the neighborhood and house level in teams, but always have someone in charge of the overall management of the group as they co-labor. Since they operate at the mind, will and emotional level, scripture categorizes their influence as works of the flesh. Spirits of *Adultery, Fornication, Uncleanness, Lasciviousness, Idolatry, Witchcraft, Hatred, Variance, Emulation, Wrath, Strife, Sedition, Heresy, Envy, Murder, Drunkenness* and *Reveling* all co-labor together in teams to steal, kill and destroy from people.

Jesus would categorize demons into two major categories in the Gospels - serpents and scorpions. *Serpentine* spirits attack the mind, will and emotions. *Scorpion* spirits attack the body with infirmity. Since the physical body manifests the condition of the mind, will and emotions - they work hand in hand often. Demons are taught how to manage those under their authority as they progress in rank through their works of service to the kingdom of darkness. They are assigned names in accordance with their work at the lowest level. Their work is their only identity. The only way they can earn a name is through their works…

Every demon, no matter their rank, has a disciple. This ensures the success of generational plans already in progress since the fall of man. This generational concept was stolen from the

Father's Kingdom. A disciple's gifts are harvested and used to bring glory to the one they are receiving discipleship from. Their expertise in an area is gained through being discipled by a higher-ranking demon, but something in return is always expected. Information and promotion isn't given freely in the demonic realm. There is always a cost attached. Low ranking demons stop at nothing to get the attention of a higher-ranking demon, with the hopes of being discipled well. This is their only chance for advancement.

When a demon shares information with their disciple, there is an expectation of service and loyalty in return. Two *Principalities* in particular, The *spirit of Religion*, co-laboring with the *spirit of Politics* were given the assignment to create the structure, strategy and advancement techniques of the demonic kingdom. They stand at the right and left of the throne of Satan in his palace. They don't have thrones because Satan refuses to share his glory. The only reason they are still there is because Satan refuses to share any more information with them that would enable them to know what he knows. Satan filters all information and demands blind obedience to his word.

Pharmacia is a high-ranking *Principality*, who works directly with Satan, but has several *Powers* under his charge. The structure of the second heaven and the demonic kingdom are patterned after the Father's original ideas. It's simply a copy of what Satan knows well, with subtle differences. Every demon has a generic identity, purpose and someone to disciple. However, their identity is earned through works. Satan doesn't carry the same measure of creative capacity as humans for governance because he was created for a specific purpose - to lead worship in the throne room. This is why he has to copy and steal ideas. Powers have entire cities under their authority and work closely with inferior spirits to do the grunt work for them throughout their assigned territories.

When a demon fails an assignment, they are demoted and then fall under the authority of the established principality in their area of operation. Principalities also work very closely with the church of Satan and its leaders to carry out specific assignments at the ground level in the earthly realm. Demons who disobey are locked away in Hell until they have learned their lesson and become willing to take part in expanding the kingdom of darkness.

Working directly with Satan is the highest honor in the demonic kingdom, but the stress that comes with it isn't for the faint of heart. *Pharmacia* has been in this position for thousands of years but is often overcome with the desire for more. He wants the glory and honor that Satan has as their leader. The only way for him to receive a promotion, is to somehow unseat Satan from the throne. He has to be careful because the demonic kingdom is full of jealousy, which fuels the occasional all-out war between factions. When this happens, Satan always promotes the winner. He rewards those who show the most aptitude to steal, kill and destroy. Losers are locked away and tormented for their failure and inability to think on their feet, and then they are demoted to entry level work. Mistakes, blunders of judgment, and losing in general are all punishable in the second heaven. Especially when it comes to days like today.

THE CONGREGATION OF SOULS...

It is written in the Word,

"And He raised us up together with Him [when we believed], and seated us with Him in the heavenly places, [because we are] in Christ Jesus,"

George and Annabelle decided to go for a walk together. They decided this as they wrapped up their daily visit to the portal. They walked past the beautiful rivers of living water that flow throughout Heaven. These rivers flow forth from the Father's spirit, providing life for all Heavenly inhabitants. The landscape of Heaven is breathtaking. Mountains, rivers, valleys, and all wildlife radiate the love of the Father, demonstrating His beauty and excellence. Flowers range in size from tiny to enormous. Flowers of every color and variety sprinkle themselves amongst the hills and plains as far as the eye can see. Mountains in the distance, if measured by Earthly measurements, stand 30 miles tall. If a mountain this tall were to be seen on Earth, while standing at sea level, its peak would be bursting through the ozone layer.

As George and Annabelle casually pass by, the flowers sing praises to the King of kings and Lord of lords. As far as the eye can see, citizens are sprinkled throughout the landscape, walking, talking, laughing, enjoying the Father's creation. Citizens are free to roam, explore, and do whatever they desire. Groups of citizens can be seen congregating around a prominent Teacher or Prophet, learning about the ages to come. Smaller groups gather to witness an artist, painting with light, on a floating canvas. Children can be seen running, playing, and climbing trees. Should the child need help climbing, trees are seen gathering children with their branches, gently lifting them up, and assisting them in the fun.

Annabelle said, *"The scenery here never gets old. I'm blown away by it, over and over."*

George nodded his head in agreement and replied, *"I'm amazed as well. There is never a dull moment in Heaven. I love seeing the children play and enjoy themselves."*

Annabelle momentarily stopped walking, turned to George, and said, *"Many of these children died before their time. The Father allows them to stay at their current age until their parents arrive. He does this because He is the God of Recompense. He loves to give back all that the enemy steals, kills, or destroys from the life of his innocent ones. They will then be raised by their biological parents here in Heaven. Abba never ceases to amaze me..."*

They continued their walk through the *Valley of Flowers and Fun*, eventually arriving at a sign that read, *"Congregation of Souls"* and a giant arrow pointing west, brightly lit, and floating in midair. They took the path pointed west and continued their conversation.

Annabelle asked George, "What is your fondest memory of Earth?"

George replied casually, *"That's a tough one. I have so many."* They shared a laugh, as George prepared his reply, *"I met my wife in a bar. We were both unbelievers at the time. Life was enjoyable, but we knew that life was somehow incomplete. We studied mysticism, spiritism, atheism, humanism, and just about any type of "ism" we could find. We were seekers to say the least. A friend of ours invited us to a gathering. It was a giant tent, in the middle of a field. As we approached the tent, we heard singing and joyful clapping. I figured it was another cult of some sorts. There were several popping up throughout the region we were living in."*

Annabelle gently interrupted, *"It was California, correct?"*

George answered, *"Yes. In the suburbs of Los Angeles. We were the creative types, just looking for something new. As we arrived at the tent gathering, there was a different vibe in the tent than anything we had experienced. We walked in and we were greeted by some people with huge smiles. They directed us towards the open seats, and we sat down. The band was playing something slow and melodic. It was so peaceful. I never felt peace like that before. It was as if I found what I was looking for. After about an hour of that, the main speaker took the stage and began to talk about Jesus. From my studies of world religions, I knew Jesus was a Prophet and was a prominent historical figure. However, I had no idea that He died for my sins. I wasn't aware that I had any sin up to that point. He explained that Jesus was God's only Son, and He loved the world so much that He gave His Son to pay the price for my sin. No other religion claimed that. I was searching for which religion was the actual Way to eternal life. I was convinced that there was some being out there who created me."*

Annabelle gleamed with joy, and said, *"That part of the journey is the most pure and simple. The day we surrender to Jesus is the day we started truly living."*

George smiled and said, *"Amen. However, I didn't surrender that evening. I was skeptical. My wife, Diane, raised her hand when the speaker asked if anyone wanted to surrender to Jesus. She prayed what the speaker called the "prayer of salvation" while I bowed my head and poured over the details of the message internally. As we left the tent that night, she was given a copy of the Bible. I watched her life in the subsequent weeks following her encounter and saw that she was very different. She had a new sense of identity and peacefulness. In our conversations, I asked her if she was certain that Jesus is the Way. I wanted what she was experiencing, so I prayed a simple prayer on my own on the way to work one day."*

Annabelle, looking completely engrossed in the story, said, *"Was the prayer to Jesus?"*

George countered lightheartedly, *"It was actually a weird prayer. I just said, "Mighty creator, or whoever you are, please show me that you are real, because whatever my wife is experiencing, I would love to experience it as well." The next night I had a dream. Jesus walked into our bedroom and gently woke me up from sleep, but I was still asleep... I told you it was a weird experience."*

Annabelle laughed and said, *"Never a dull moment with Jesus!"*

George continued, *"I know, right? So, I got up from the bed, in my dream, and followed Jesus down the stairs and outside to the back yard. He took me by the hand and pointed to the night sky. As I looked up at the sky, millions of stars began to move and form words. When the words were finally formed, it read, "I am the Way, the Truth, and the Life..."*

Annabelle gasped, *"That must have been spectacular."*

George exhaled, *"Yes it was. In that moment, I crumpled under the weight of my own sin and shame, for the first time. I actually asked Jesus to save me, while in a dream, on my hands and knees. It still messes me up when I think about it. Jesus, the Son of the Living God, took the time to give me an encounter that changed my life, for eternity.*

He reached down,

took me by the hand and helped me up,

and told me to wait a minute.

Seconds later, I could see Him placing a new heart inside of me. It was shaped like a real heart, but was luminescent shades of blue, and it was on fire.

Then I woke up..."

Annabelle was crying tears of joy at this point. She collected her thoughts and said, *"That's one of the most beautiful encounters I've ever heard. I'm always interested in hearing the testimony of others. So many of my generation gave their lives to Jesus by hearing the Gospel Message from a preacher. We ran to the alters and surrendered right there and then."*

George replied, *"Yes. I studied your generation of church history later in life. Los Angeles was still buzzing with the supernatural empowerment released during the Azusa Street revivals. Tents were packed out all through the region, throughout the week and on the weekends. The speaker at the tent revival was Aimee Semple McPherson. She built a church building in 1923, and we attended there for the rest of our lives. Diane and I had our challenges. However, our faith was strong, and we continued to serve Jesus on the intercessory team at Angelus Temple until the day I was called home."*

Annabelle looked thrilled to hear that they shared a connection, *"I love Aimee. I was with her just last week at her mansion, catching up with her and listening to her latest song she was in the process of writing."*

Then suddenly, Annabelle eagerly pointed to the enormous coliseum about 3 earth miles away. It was massive, stunningly adorned, and excellent in every way. Giant pillars, one every 12 feet, were positioned around the perimeter, with as many doors to accommodate the traffic. A ministering Angel was present at each door as a greeter. They greet every visitor with the greeting of the day,

"Hello Precious Saint! His righteous judgements endure forever."

The roof was dome shaped, similar to a giant soccer stadium, but much, much larger in area. The square footage would be hard to calculate due to its ability to enlarge itself to accommodate capacity, but it was enough to house at least 40 billion seats. It was a busy place, teaming with activity,

citizens coming and going,

chatting, and fellowshipping at the café style seating around the perimeter,

walking in to visit and leaving again.

As George and Annabelle approached the stairs leading up to the porch, 12 stairs in all, they began to discuss the business of the day.

George began to divulge his reason for the visit today, *"My plan is to make a deposit of peace and joy for my great, great, grandchild today. His name is James, and he is currently in Middle School. He is an amazing young man who cares for people. Middle school can be tough, and I want to help in any way that I can. He surrendered to Jesus and was Baptized a few years ago. However the pressure to be like everyone else is often times overwhelming for him. Some peace and joy always helps."*

Annabelle shook her head in agreement, *"Great idea. I'm actually going to be present for an impartation for one of my great grandchildren today. His Guardian Angel is ensuring that he is present to be ministered to by an itinerate Evangelist at a local conference."*

George asked, *"Anyone I know?"*

Annabelle answered, *"I believe so. Are you aware of the work that Reinhard Bonnke is doing in the Earth?"*

George replied, *"Yes. A million times yes. He is on pace to preach to millions and lead them to Christ in waves. It's been years since I witnessed an impartation. I'm glad we decided to fellowship today."*

They reached the top of the stairs and approached one of the many entrance doors to the coliseum. A ministering Angel greeted them with the greeting of the day,

"Hello Precious Saint! His righteous judgements endure forever."

They smiled and walked through the door as the Angel held it open for them. Honor and respect is the culture of Heaven. Everyone is valued and honored for who they are and what they carry. The Redeemed carry the power and authority of Heaven in their veins. They are held in the highest esteem by the Heavenly creatures great and small. Angels are always present should the Redeemed need anything, anytime, anyplace amongst the vastness of Heaven. This particular Angel has been serving on the welcome team at the Congregation of Souls since the very beginning. Since the first human to openly declare that Jesus is their Savior. Since the first human made their public profession of faith, and asked Jesus to forgive their sins. This Angel loved his job, and he does it with excellence.

He gazed at George and Annabelle with respect and honor as they passed by. Their robes of white flowing in the gentle breeze of Heaven. The beautifully ornate robes of the Redeemed are beyond anything humans can craft. The technology simply isn't available in the Earth quite yet. Rubies, sapphires, and several gemstones not available in the Earth, outlined the robes stunningly.

They aren't even permanently attached – the jewels seem to just stay there but have the ability to shift and create different designs. In Heaven, many possessions like this are free to change and create at the direction of the Redeemed, or on their own. Clothing, hair styles, mansion exteriors, are all alive and filled with the Love of the Father and Holy Spirit creative anointing. The golden crowns of the Redeemed were yet another masterpiece to behold. They were wearing their everyday crowns which were smaller versions of their official crowns. Official crowns were to be worn for special events. *The Release of a Soul* would be one of the many events where official crowns can be seen by the millions… On an official crown, the words, *"Crown of Righteousness"* can be seen in a gorgeously engraved font. On an everyday crown, the words, *"Crown of Life"* are written. Both are stunning and usually command the attention of Heavenly creatures. As the Redeemed pass by, Heavenly creatures can be seen talking amongst themselves, saying, *"There is one of the Redeemed!"* The Redeemed are famous in Heaven…

George and Annabelle cleared the threshold of the door they were ushered into.

They set their gaze on the hustle and bustle of activity taking place.

Billions of blue transparent versions of human form were seated, evenly spaced, on throne like chairs. Each carbon copy of a human form still operating in the Earth realm, sat perfectly at peace, unless engaged in some type of activity. Many could be seen with hands raised in worship. Some could be seen with their head slumped over forward, indicating that some type of anguish was taking place. Instantly, ministering Angels rushed to make a deposit of peace for these souls, enabling the soul to regain composure and confidence in their God. Since the human soul is layered, each blue transparent version of human form represents a single layer of their soul, safe and protected from harm, able to receive deposits, impartations, gifts, and talents, all under the watchful eye of the *Ministering Angels*, under the direction of Jesus.

George and Annabelle were fully aware of the purpose of the *Congregation of Souls*. They received this information when they arrived, after leaving the Earthly realm for good, and taking part in their seven day *Orientation to Heaven*, which is taught by Jesus Himself.

When asked why this type of system was needed, Jesus explained in detail at the orientation, *"This enables me to safeguard a single layer of their soul while they operate in the Earth. It's a tough place down there, especially on the soul. No matter what they experience in the Earth, tribulation, persecution, peril, poverty, trauma, I have access to this layer. They are mine now, bought with a price. The enemy has to gain access to their soul through their senses in the Earthly realm. I have direct access to facilitate their growth in the Kingdom because they have been redeemed. This is why a believer in Me cannot sell their soul to the enemy. It would be spiritually impossible and would contradict the physics of Heaven. Even if they make this kind of covenant with the enemy prior to surrendering to Me, once a covenant is made, a layer of their soul is permanently seated among the congregation. I didn't just purchase their soul; I now stand as their Guardian. The Apostle Peter said it best when he declared this revelation in the Word, to those following him,*

"Once you were like sheep who wandered away. But now you have turned to your Shepherd, the Guardian of your souls."

It's especially helpful when you understand dual citizenship. On Earth, the laws and customs of each region are different. For example, You could be carrying a fire arm in Texas, with all the appropriate paperwork to ensure you are legal. In this case, you are considered a righteous citizen. This is legal terminology to officially describe your standing. Your actions, having the appropriate paperwork, solidifies your standing as a righteous citizen. You are also declared blameless in a court of law concerning the carrying of said fire arm, while in Texas. If you were to carry that same fire arm onto an airplane, having the same paperwork that was appropriate for Texas, you would be in violation of several international laws, placing your righteous standing in jeopardy. The Laws of one region don't always accommodate the righteous standing of a traveler.

Placing one layer of a person's soul here in Heaven, ensures they carry the authority and power of Heaven into the Earth. Their seated position prophecies their authority to govern. Their location in Heaven ensures they are in proximity to receive from Me in the spirit realm. Their righteous standing in Heaven ensures they carry the level of power and authority they need to bring Heaven to Earth. This also trains my followers to think from Heaven's perspective, since they are already here... The Apostle Paul instructed them on how to navigate dual-citizenship. Obey the laws of the Earth and pray for their leaders. However, as the ecclesia moves into their season of triumph, the laws of Heaven will become the laws of Earth..."

Annabelle looked at George and said, *"Can you go with me for the impartation first, and then we can drop by and bless your great, great, grandson?"*

George replied, *"No problem. Sounds like a plan."*

They made their way up the aisle towards the section marked, E - 1,200,324,194. Ministering Angels were busy, rushing to the aid of the souls crying out in anguish. The millions of souls sitting with hands raised were receiving fresh waves of peace of joy. It's remarkable how one soul can be seen worshiping in Heaven, even though their physical body is located in Brazil. Two souls can be seen worshiping in this congregation, sitting beside one another amongst the congregation of souls, but be present physically on completely different continents. When two believers meet on Earth and share a deep connection, it's because they are seated together in Heaven. When the Saints worship on Earth, their soul worships here, seated amongst the Congregation of Souls. It's how Heaven can recognize true unity of faith. It's how the ecclesia can worship in spirit and in truth filled unity, even while operating in different geographic locations on Earth. It's a beautiful site to see. The Father makes His way for a visit to the Congregation of Souls often, to check on the progress of the ecclesia. He is waiting for the ecclesia to come into agreement on many things, with patience. Visiting the Congregation of Souls and seeing if they are in any way worshiping in unity, is one of the benchmarks for the release of revelation of scripture and additional resources to bring about His will in the Earth. What is bound here, is bound on Earth. What is loosed here, is loosed on Earth. What is allowed here, is allowed on Earth. What is disallowed here, is disallowed on Earth. What is deposited here spiritually, manifests in the life of a believer on Earth. The Congregation of Souls gives a full revelation of what one giant governing body looks like. Once a human comes home to Heaven, this layer of their soul is reunited with the rest of their being. Until then, they operate with dual-citizenship, to bring about the will of the Father. His will hasn't ever changed – *"on Earth as it is in Heaven."*

Once Annabelle arrived near to the section where her grandson's soul was seated, she motioned to George and said, *"There he is!"* George replied, *"Wow. The Ministering Angels are already at work."*

On Earth, at the conference located in Lawton, OK, at a

medium size church gathering, James, who is 25 years old, was standing in the front near the alter, waiting for the Evangelist to make his way down the line to minister to him. When it was his turn, he asked the Evangelist to impart something he would need for ministry. The Evangelist prayed a simple prayer, *"Father, I impart and awaken the gift of Prophecy in this young man, for the purpose of serving your people well, all the days of his life, in Jesus name."* Then, the Evangelist laid his hand on James' head and declared, *"Receive the anointing!"* To which, James fell backwards and lay flat on the church floor for what seemed like the next 30 minutes – with a smile on his face.

Concurrently, his soul seated in Heaven received a special delivery from the Holy Spirit. Impartations, spiritual gifts, and special anointings for ministry are hand delivered by Holy Spirit. Ministering Angles are authorized to comfort only. Holy Spirit does the equipping for ministry. Holy Spirit breezed in carrying a small gold treasure chest. Once arriving at the location where James was seated in Heaven, He opened the chest, pulled out a brilliantly crafted shimmering key, and placed it in James' right hand. This is considered one of the many keys to the Kingdom. With this impartation, James would now carry the capacity to speak words of wisdom, knowledge, and prophecy. He would be able to shift atmospheres with powerful prophetic utterance. He would carry the ability to declare the identity, purpose, and destiny of anyone he decided to minister to in the Earthly realm. As he learns to steward this impartation of power, he will be able to guide nations and declare their future into existence, in accordance with the will of God. With this key, he will have access to the Books of Destiny for anyone he decides to minister to, both believer and unbeliever, which covers all of humanity…

James wasn't quite aware of all the details surrounding what just happened. He was simply enjoying the moment, as he lay there experiencing waves of peace and joy…

Holy Spirit smiled and winked at Annabelle, and then He was off to His next appointment, deliberate, but never in a hurry.

George said emphatically, *"That never gets old! Wow! The things we had access to while on Earth, all because our soul is positioned right here, where the action really takes place."*

Annabelle replied, *"I agree. Had I been taught about this; I would have made my way to every conference in America. The ecclesia must understand that a layer of their soul is already here. If they will understand the protocols of Heaven, and how impartation works, they will become better equipped to bring Heaven to Earth in the coming decades."*

George was still gathering his thoughts, *"I'm simply undone by all this. You'll have to give me a moment…"*

DAILY MEETING IN THE THRONE ROOM...

It is written in the Word,

"Righteousness and justice are the foundation of your throne; steadfast love and faithfulness go before you."

The Father looks intently at Jesus and Holy Spirit from His throne. Jesus standing on His right and Holy Spirit to His left. The melodic cadence of

"Holy, Holy, Holy, is the Lord God Almighty, Who was, and is, and is to come"

sweeps through the throne room in waves.

The brilliant radiance of the Father's Glory ingulfs the Heavenly creatures with layers of love and joy. The twenty-four elders respond with worship and praise as they stand ready to discuss the matters at hand. The names of the twenty-four elders are the original 11 disciples plus Paul of Tarsus, and the 12 patriarchs of Israel. They are all present for the meeting as The Father takes a brief attendance. Peter, Andrew, James, John, Philip, Bartholomew/Nathanael, Matthew, Thomas, James son of Alphaeus, Simon the Zealot, Judas the Greater, and Paul of Tarsus who replaced Judas Iscariot are all present. So are Reuben, Simeon, Levi, Judah, Dan, Naphtali, Gad, Asher, Issachar, Zebulun, Joseph, and Benjamin. The Father stands and begins to walk closer to Peter desiring to engage him in conversation.

Peter greeted the Father with, *"I Bless your name Father. What would you like to talk about?"*

The Father looked at him with a smile and said, *"Today is the day! Are you ready?"*

Peter responded with a resounding, *"Amen! Father, you know I'm always ready to stir some stuff up for the Kingdom. I wouldn't miss days like today for anything in the galaxy."*

The Father responds with a chuckle, *"You don't have a choice, you work here my friend."*

They both shared a laugh that sounded like joyful thunder. The laughter of Heaven began to spread through the other elders as they joined in. Soon after, all the angels and creatures great and small began to laugh and praise the Father for His grace and mercy. Laughter is a wave of medicine for the soul. In Heaven, a soul has come home and therefore doesn't need medicine. However, the laughter in Heaven becomes so contagious that it sounds like a sonic boom as it increases. From one citizen of Heaven to the next, the laughter continues to remind every redeemed human being and every angelic creature great and small that joy was the reward for the suffering Jesus endured at the cross. Laughter always turns into declarations of thankfulness and gratitude in Heaven.

The Father declared to all present in the throne room, *"Today we have a guest for our meeting. She just arrived today. She was a Public School Administrator before she retired and then she volunteered at her church for many years as a Children's Pastor. She is with me to learn about the planning and preparation for the soul creation process. She finished many years of formal education in instructional teaching and Psychology, and she used her gifts to the best of her ability to make the world a better place. As is our custom, we are asking her to share her wisdom and knowledge, coupled with her newly deposited revelation of scripture. As you all know, since her body has been glorified, she now has access to 100% of her brain's capacity. Go ahead and share from your heart precious Bethany."*

Bethany was still in awe at the Glory of Heaven. In essence, Heaven is a person. Nothing in Heaven is separate from God Himself. His light and breath sustains everything. His light is displayed through every plant. Even the flowers dance and sing Praises to God as they respond to waves of His Glory. She was thinking about her loved ones who cared for her in her last days on Earth. Like most believers, she thought when she got to Heaven, she would somehow be retired and able to sit on the porch of her mansion for eternity. She is quickly finding out that Heaven is a busy place. There is something to do for everyone. Everyone is honored and cherished. Whatever gift was deposited in you, is to be utilized to advance the Kingdom agenda set by the Father. Since Heaven responds to Earth in a co-laboring relationship, they all wait for the prayers of the Saints to be collected and stored in golden bowls. Since man is governed by the will, Heaven seldom interrupts unless called upon. The only way Heaven interrupts the will of man is in dire situations where man refuses to live in accordance with the Father's Word. In cases like that, Heaven must advance, so Heaven invades, whether man asks them to or not. Heaven would rather co-labor with man. However, man isn't always tuned in to what the Father is saying and doing.

Bethany looked at everyone present in the throne room with intentionality and respect...

She could feel wisdom flood her soul. She had so much to say, because of all she experienced in the Earthly realm. The angelic beings looked at Bethany with wonder and admiration. Heavenly creatures are not entirely familiar with the culture of Earth. They also have no idea what it feels like to be *Redeemed*. The only time disobedience was present in Heaven, Satan was sent hurling through the spirit realm. They looked at Bethany with great veneration and admiration for all she accomplished for the Kingdom, because she walked in faith. Bethany was actually a Methodist and never even knew there was a spirit realm or Holy Spirit empowerment for her life on Earth. She lived an entire life simply knowing that Jesus died for her sin, but never experiencing the supernatural. The angelic creatures marveled at this.

Jallel, a seasoned cherubim asked his friend standing next to him, *"How on Earth can this be? Her testimony is blowing my mind right now. We live in the presence of the Father, and we understand that through Him all things exist. How did she make it all those years without Holy Spirit empowerment?"*

Jallel's friend responded, *"She was devout concerning what she was taught from God's Word. She was only held accountable to what she was taught and revealed to her. This is the Father's way. He is kind, peaceable and gentle with the Redeemed. He understands where the ecclesia is at concerning revelation of scripture and will never hold an individual accountable to a truth that wasn't properly revealed through Teachers."*

Jallel chimed in with a chuckle, *"This is why I love the Hall of Knowledge. I was studying there yesterday and was in awe concerning the Father's plan for mankind. Occasionally, an Anointed Teacher sits down and attracts a crowd. The Apostle Paul is one of my favorites"*

Jallel's friend interrupts, *"I love me some Oswald Chambers and C.S. Lewis. I've sat with them several times. They are always studying, writing and teaching. If they stroll into the Hall of Knowledge, they get bombarded with questions, but it's what they were built for. They love it!"* Have you ever noticed that most

Teachers begin their sentences with, "Did you know?

Jallel nodded his head up and down as if to say, *"Yes. It's how the Father made them…"*

Bethany began to speak from her heart, because in Heaven logic is inferior to the natural emotions present in the heart. It is with the heart, man should believe, but Religion teaches to suppress emotional response and lean toward logic and reason creating an almost, *"Christian humanism".*

Bethany was finally free to be herself. *"Thank you Father for inviting me to this meeting, on a day like today. Also, a special thank you to the twenty-four elders. We appreciate all you do as you serve on the governing council of Heaven. All heavenly creatures great and small, I am so pleased to finally see and meet you. You are precious in the Father's sight. I would like to begin by answering some questions you may have."*

Simeon stood up from his throne and bowed in respect to Bethany, and said, *"Blessings upon you Precious Bethany. Thank you for being with us on short notice."* The entire throne room erupted with laughter yet again.

Peter immediately interjected, *"I'm at a loss as to why the ecclesia hasn't advanced the Kingdom further than it has. It's been 1,975 years since Jesus paid the price for sin, redeemed mankind, released the Holy Spirit to empower their mortal bodies, and established their dominion on the Earth. Jesus demonstrated the life of a born-again believer and trained us to bring Heaven to Earth. There are currently sixty-six books of information contained in the Bible and we aren't much further than we were in the Book of Acts. What is your discernment on the matter?"*

Bethany smiled and closed her eyes preparing to give her response. She knew that Peter would never ask her a question that he didn't already know the answer to. Bethany didn't feel any pressure to perform. She was now walking in her true identity, fully aware of things past, present and to come. Peter had now been serving on the Heavenly council for at least 1,900 years. He was looking for honesty and transparency. However, It felt amazing to be honored and appreciated in this way. She was never allowed to be a Pastor at her church because they said it was against the bible. She was never asked to participate in the governance of the local church body. Now, she was standing in the throne room of Heaven being asked her opinion by Peter himself.

Bethany opened her eyes and said, *"Quite simply...we became unbelieving believers. We failed to see scripture as something that revealed what was possible. We celebrated the amazing deeds of Jesus and the disciples, but we didn't think it was possible for us to walk in such a supernatural way. We huddled around the scriptures on a weekly basis but didn't apply them to our societal ills. We created medical terminology to explain emotional and intellectual sickness, rather than calling it for what it is - demonic oppression. The doctrine of devils was released at some point during early church history, and it stunted our growth tremendously as well. It was called Cessationism."* Joseph raised his hand wanting to make a statement.

Bethany noticed and said, *"Blessings upon you Joseph. Would you like to add something?"* Joseph stood and said, *"I agree that Cessationism held the church back. However, I demonstrated that is was possible to become Prime Minister of Egypt with one aspect of Holy Spirit empowerment. I simply had the anointing to interpret dreams, which informed my governmental decisions. The ecclesia has the ability through Holy Spirit empowerment to do so much more than this. Gifts of Wisdom, Knowledge and Prophecy are all deposited in you through the baptism of the Holy Spirit. Any one of you*, who the Father has empowered, has the capacity to rule and govern your people well. *In the Old Testament, the Holy Spirit would come upon us for a specific purpose, for a season. The ecclesia holds the keys of death, hell and the grave. The ecclesia carries the capacity to take all the territory on Earth, kick the enemy out, and establish Heaven on Earth."*

Bethany displayed no insecurity because those spirits are not active in Heaven. For the first time in her life she could stand in confidence and declare truth without any hesitation. She was now involved in a deep theological discussion with Peter and Joseph in the throne room of Heaven, and she loved it. Power and Authority was surging through her veins like never before. She could clearly see the failures of the ecclesia, but in Heaven, failure isn't dwelt upon. Solutions are the only important thing. Since there isn't any guilt or shame, solutions flow freely.

Peter sounded off once again because, after all, you take your personality with you into eternity. He said, *"Our time with Jesus was amazing and well documented. We couldn't write it all down, but the Holy Spirit instructed us to include specific accounts to demonstrate the life of a believer and what was possible for you. The Book of Acts was written to further influence your thinking concerning Holy Spirit empowerment. My shadow healed people of all sickness and disease as I walked past them on the way to the temple for daily prayer. I didn't have practical language to impart as a teaching on this, but I knew the ecclesia would press in for breakthrough in this area through prayer and fasting. Jesus taught us how to heal the sick, raise the dead, cast out demons and cleanse lepers. He also taught us how to rebuke and calm the weather. I even walked on water...do you see our point?"*

Bethany responded with, *"I see it clearly now. My question is what is our next step?"*

Judah stood up from his throne to address the elder team.

Honor and respect is the custom in Heaven because everyone is valued and cherished for who the Father made them to be. Self-will and self-promotion are nonexistent because everyone has a distinct identity, purpose and destiny. The twenty-four elders are themselves filled with appreciation for the Father's Grace. They all made mistakes while on Earth. They all failed in some way to demonstrate the Glory of the Father and bring Heaven to Earth. However, they aren't chained to their past or stuck in regret. They all repented while on Earth, picked themselves up and continued to walk with God. Each elder carries a unique perspective developed during their lifespan. This is why meetings in Heaven are so efficient. There is no striving or competition among elders. They seek only to find solutions. If someone shares an idea with the team, it becomes the team's idea.

Judah declared, *"The ecclesia must step into a full revelation of their identity, purpose, and destiny. Jesus released many teachings to the disciples and was very clear concerning their identity, purpose and destiny. He told them to pray - Your Kingdom come, your will be done, on Earth as it is in Heaven. He also told them that they were light and salt. Salt is to be sprinkled evenly throughout the meal and light can't be hidden when its displayed in pitch black darkness. The ecclesia carries the capacity to rule and govern like no other group of humans ever created. They have the power and the authority to take over regions in the spirit realm and advance the Kingdom. In your opinion, Bethany, why hasn't the ecclesia recognized this sooner?"*

Bethany was ready for this question. She had lived a life of faith in Jesus without knowing about the power and authority she carried. She attended church and served with such devotion for many years before her passing from the Earthly realm to receive her glorified body.

She looked at Judah and said, *"That is a great question Judah. I believe, once again, the doctrine of devils mentioned by Paul hindered our growth in such a devastating way. The Christian Crusades were a direct result of Cessationism. Without Holy Spirit empowerment, we used only our logic to make decisions as a church body. We saw the widespread effects of the spirit of Religion through the teachings of Mohamed and we aggressively converted millions to our way of thinking - while co-laboring with fear. This also hindered our testimony as a body of Christ followers and many generations avoided anything we had to say. If anything, we pushed even more people into Islam creating a generational offense. Since the Bible is a spiritual book, to be studied utilizing our empowerment, we misinterpreted most of it."*

Judah loved her honesty. Bethany's fresh way of thinking was helping the elder team immensely. They all looked intently and hung on her every word. Since Heaven operates through the prayers of the saints, they were developing fresh ideas from her statements. Since she just arrived in eternity, her ideas were revelatory for the team.

Judah asked her, *"What do you feel our next steps are? What should we impart to the ecclesia that they don't already have. Do you see our conundrum?"*

Bethany responded with, *"I do, Judah. I understand the danger of revealing too much information to the ecclesia because we usually take it and build a mega-ministry with it. We didn't bother to invade society and change it from the inside out because we were afraid. We think revelation is to build a following and create systems of religion so we can sit around and talk about it. It wasn't too long ago that millions of believers pulled their children from public schools, rather than teaching them that they are salt and light, empowering them to bring change. We lost a few generations because of it. We made our decisions from a place of fear, even though Jesus declared that we would never have to. Jesus positioned us to invade society and take over with love and wisdom. We also lost several generations of leaders when we were taught to avoid running for public office or pursuing secular careers."*

Joseph responded with, *"That blows my mind. I was a Prime Minister of Egypt - a pagan nation. At the time we were the modern day equivalent of America. Daniel was so highly respected and protected that he outlived four kings and managed to influence Nebuchadnezzar to the point of conversion to God. They tried to get rid of him, but never could. Don't these examples carry any weight with the ecclesia?"*

Bethany shook her head from side to side as if to demonstrate the word, *"No…"* then she countered, *"We saw the Old Testament for many generations as good stories about imperfect people. We read about the miracles the Father did for us, but theologically we knew that these were mighty outpourings of God's power on specific people for specific purpose."*

Judah continued, *"Yes, exactly. After the day of Pentecost recorded in the Book of Acts, your empowerment was complete. This enabled you to walk every minute of every day in the same measure of wisdom, knowledge and power that the Old Testament saints were given access to for only a season of their lives. If you put it all together, based on what the Old Testament saints demonstrated, you will see that they raised the dead, healed the sick and cleansed lepers. You will also see that Samson killed 6,000 Philistines while operating with only periodic Holy Spirit empowerment. Elijah even controlled the weather. The Day of Pentecost was the complete package of authority and power to equip you to go into all the world. Of course, through discipleship you were supposed to train each* *generation to do the same things you saw Jesus do."*

Bethany agreed with everything Judah was saying. She got it now.. as she said, *"Most of the people who reached that level of anointing were disgraced publicly for their ministry by the religious and did not think to train the next generation. Our seminaries only focused on Exegesis and textual analysis, instead of simply reading it and applying it. We had entire generations of Pastors and Teachers who could tell you what was in the Bible but could not demonstrate it. We fell in love with oratory, instead of the application of God's Word. We have church services filled with thousands of people who have never witnessed the miracles and power of God over sickness, disease and spiritual oppression of any kind. They were taught that it is God's will for them to be sick."*

Jesus looked patiently at all who were present for the meeting. This wasn't the Jesus that Bethany was familiar with in the Gospels. It was the Jesus we see in Revelation. Of course, all His characteristics found in the Gospels were present in His behavior in the throne room - love, joy, peace, patience, kindness, goodness, faithfulness, gentleness and self-control. Bethany recognized, however, that He was different. He was more intent on the topic of building His church. She could see Him thinking more in terms of advancement and strategy. Afterall, His death and resurrection provided the ecclesia with all the power and authority they needed to accomplish the Great Commission. Bethany asked Jesus if He had anything to add.

Jesus stood up and said, *"Thank you precious Bethany for all you have to share with us. I appreciate your honesty and as you can see, Heaven is a team. We think and operate as one. I want to give you some fresh revelation, so you understand my overall vision for the ecclesia. Of course I started with the foundational teachings found in the Gospels. My Earthly ministry, as you know, was very* difficult, but I deposited the right information coupled with timely demonstrations of Holy Spirit empowerment. I was careful to teach about the importance of loving one another and serving the community. I understand that many teachings have been misinterpreted and misunderstood. The miracles I displayed were seen as acts of God, rather than what was possible for every born-again believer who walked in right relationship with the Father, empowered by my Spirit. This is why it is crucial that in the last days I pour out my Spirit upon all flesh. Sons and daughters will prophecy and usher in the 3rd Great Awakening. We must make up for lost time and put my Spirit on full display in the lives of ordinary people. These people will not be asked to give up their careers, they will be directed to pursue the dominion given to them in the societal spheres of influence they have entered. Business owners, educational professionals, coaches, mental health counselors, physicians, politicians and entertainers will be directed to take over their specified profession through Holy Spirit empowered love and service to humanity. They will walk in a full revelation of my plan for mankind and be allowed favor and grace to operate at the highest levels of societal influence. The ecclesia was supposed to notice that these were the types of people I selected to be my Apostles to begin with."

Bethany looked with amazement at the authority with which Jesus spoke. She responded with, *"My Savior, This sounds amazing."*

Jesus continued, *"You see, Bethany, the ecclesia wasn't supposed to be a weekly meeting only. Meetings for prayer and worship were supposed to be a time to celebrate the breakthroughs already happening in society, through my Redeemed Ones. Home groups were supposed to meet for the same reasons. Since every Holy Spirit filled believer is empowered to heal the sick, raise the dead, cast out demons and cleanse lepers, the weekly meeting was simply to give Praise to the Father for what He was doing through His people. When I ascended to Heaven to take my place at the right hand of the Father, I gave gifts to mankind. This scripture was also misinterpreted to mean only within the walls of the local church. It's so much bigger than that. Apostles were to rise to the societal position of City Mayor, Governor of a State, and even President. The local Pastor was to facilitate, train and shepherd the people as they walked in the anointing I poured into them to effect societal change. It may be too big to understand right now, but imagine a world where my Apostles, Prophets, Teachers, Pastors, and Evangelists are in charge.*

Imagine a world where the Prophets are in charge of the news stations and political podcasts. The only news you would receive would be what the Father is saying and doing, filling the Earth with hope. Imagine a world where the Apostle establishes the culture of Heaven over an entire city or state through Kingdom policy. America is already established as a place where a Sate can pass any law they agree on, as long as it's not unconstitutional. Imagine a world where every business owner is an Evangelist. They already carry the anointing to be with people all-day, every day. Imagine a world where all literature and instructional teaching is circulated by Teachers with one purpose - to increase the revelation of the people for Kingdom expansion. You see, I gave these people to mankind. I didn't simply give them position within the walls of the church; I gave them to the human race. It's time for them to rise up and bring Heaven to Earth. Of course, there is more to this. However, I wanted you to begin to catch this vision now that you are here with us. This won't be your last meeting. We are adding you to the team as a consultant."

Bethany was speechless. She was overwhelmed with

gratitude. She took off her crown and cast it across the throne room at Jesus' feet. This is the custom for those assembled for meetings of this magnitude. An overwhelming emotional flood of thankfulness and appreciation causes them to be undone in the presence of the King of kings and Lord of lords. Especially when He reveals fresh revelation. Not out of fear, but reverence for the majesty and wisdom they are privy to. She was beginning to understand it fully. She didn't have guilt or shame for the condition of the ecclesia or her personal past failures in understanding scripture. However, her awareness of where the ecclesia was, currently in human history, couldn't have been more clearly revealed to her spirit. This revelation birthed something within her.

Now she had questions.

She asked emphatically, *"Jesus, what is our next step?"*

Jesus smiled and said, *"Its beyond anything you can imagine."*

DAILY MEETING IN THE SECOND HEAVEN...

It is written in the Word,

"For we do not wrestle against flesh and blood, but against the rulers, against the authorities, against the cosmic powers over this present darkness, against the spiritual forces of evil in the heavenly places."

Satan and his top leaders attempt to stay ahead of what the Fathers is saying and doing, but it's impossible for them. Everything they do is reactionary, since his disconnection with the Father destroyed his capacity to see what is to come. The demonic kingdom only has access to past events. The future is declared only through Holy Spirit empowerment by the Father's sons and daughters. And they don't simply predict it, they shape it. Satan, to include his subservient Principalities and Powers ruling under him from the second heaven don't have this privilege. They are disconnected from the store houses of Heaven where all wisdom, knowledge and prophecy are kept. As he peered around his throne room, he was filled with disdain for his subordinates. His own insecurities were apparent as he worked to devise another plan for this season. The *spirit of politics* and the *spirit of Religion* were both present standing to his right and left, having no thrones. No one else was allowed in the meetings in order to compartmentalize information and keep subordinates in the dark.

Satan impatiently questioned his leaders, *"What is our plan* to combat the current revival that is breaking out across the planet? I want answers as to why it isn't being contained."

Spirit of politics spoke up in a submissive manner, *"My Lord, we are planning on using the same tactics we used after the Azusa street revivals. Man is proud and loves to take credit for what the Father is saying and doing. As you know, many new denominations were created for this reason. I sent millions of fiery darts through the thought life of the leaders of the ecclesia, and they responded as expected. I entered these organizational structures with my usual teams and convinced them that they did not need to teach about Holy Spirit empowerment or gifts of the Spirit. This depleted them of all authority and power to effect change in society, leaving them fruitless and ineffective. Except for the occasional person who confesses Jesus as Lord - which we really can't stop because that is a gift of faith deposited in them from the Father - their churches are pretty much filled with works of the flesh."* Satan responded in anger with, *"Not good enough! I could kill both of you and promote someone else. I only keep you around because of your devotion to the cause. I don't even need you."*

Spirits of politics and religion looked at each other. They knew that Satan didn't have the power to kill a spirit. However, they also knew full well that he could demote them and relegate them to tormenting duties in Hell - which in their opinion was worse. This wasn't something they wanted at all. If they were demoted they would be stuck there for decades.

Spirit of religion said, *"My Lord, Denominations are dwindling so, we must take a different approach. More and believers are rallying around God's word, and not a doctrinal statement. For many years doctrinal statements separated believers into small groups that we could easily manipulate."*

Satan countered, *"So why isn't this tactic working*

anymore?"

In response, spirit of religion said, *"The internet has made it possible to learn from the five-fold ministry leaders in the Father's Kingdom at an alarming rate. Revelation is being freely given and received among the followers of Jesus. People are leaving their churches in search of more because, they have immediate access to revelation of scripture for the first time in human history. With technology, it is much easier to gather mankind for events. They are becoming more aware of the spirit realm and usually have intercessory teams poised and ready for us, canceling our assignments. People are watching less news and reading God's Word at an alarming rate."*

Satan looked interested now but hid his insecurity with anger. He didn't often ask for advice, but he knows that his time has been shortened somehow.

Satan asked with a loud and angry voice, *"What is your plan? I don't want any more excuses. They are weak and useless creatures. You know the average believer in Jesus doesn't even study God's Word. They attend church out of tradition, shame and guilt. They have no idea what their identity, purpose and destiny is according to scripture."*

Spirit of Religion began to walk around the throne room submissively thinking of something to say. However, he knew that he had some leverage to be creative. At least, the measure of creativity he now carried. Since being cast out of Heaven, hurled through the spirit realm and relegated to the second heaven, the demonic kingdom has been depleted of their divine creativity. They simply repackage and repurpose ideas that have been in existence for thousands of years. They recommission the same demons and release them into the Earth to influence humans through literature, old wives tales and main stream media. Some of these demons are still in operation within the structure of the nominal church. However, something new has to be done in this current age of technology.

Continuing to stroll, and after reaching the *wall of tribute* in satan's throne room, where Satan hangs trophies celebrating the legacies of men he has tarnished,

he turned around with confidence and said, *"I will turn the church against the church. I will bombard them with negativity concerning anything they hear or see in this current revival. For every anointed five-fold ministry leader who has a large public following, I will raise up a religious leader to attack their teachings. Leviathan and Jezebel will be released, with their teams, to create confusion, offense and malice towards the ecclesia that is walking in Holy Spirit empowerment and freedom from guilt and shame. The nominal church will spend time and resources to fight against the revival and spread mass confusion for God's children. For every teaching that leaves the throne room of God, there will be hundreds of teachings to tear down and confront the truth of God's Word declared by God's Anointed Five-fold ministry leaders. This will strengthen the nominal church and they will grow, thinking they are protecting the purity of the Gospel message. This is the beginning stages of the great delusion to be spread throughout the Earth concerning God's truth."*

Satan, who is hard to impress - looked impressed.

He said to spirit of religion, *"I like this plan. It's similar to what we did when Martin Luther was given his revelation about Grace. The only problem is that there are many believers walking in fresh revelation of scripture because in the last days, God said that He would pour out His spirit on all flesh. With this upgrade in the spirit realm, they will be prophesying more often, shaping and bending the future to fit God's perfect will. It's the most dangerous gift they have."*

Spirit of religion agreed, but interjected, *"This is why we need more false prophets to counteract the declarations and decrees they are prompted to release into the atmosphere. The nominal church will declare that anything not suitable to their doctrinal statement is false, thereby labeling them publicly as a false prophet. In essence, we will use false prophets to shame and humiliate the real prophets. It will be mass confusion because the nominal church doesn't walk with the Holy Spirit, but still has a large following."* Satan laughed and countered, *"Its brilliant. The nominal church is afraid of false prophecy. They will not recognize the touch of Heaven on the words of the real prophets because they have no discernment. As they name and shame the prophets and their prophecies, they will be brought deeper into our control."*

DAILY MEETING IN THE THRONE ROOM... (continued)

It is written in the Word,

"The Lord has established his throne in the heavens, and his kingdom rules over all."

The Father gazed around the throne room with love and amusement, taking the time to momentarily engage with each meeting participant through discernment. In Heaven, we can carry on full conversations in this manner. It's possible to do this in the Earthly realm when empowered by the Holy Spirit as well. God's people carry the capacity to recognize truth and share it through a discerning glance - without a word spoken. In the Earthly realm, language is used for communicating. In Heaven, language is used for creating. The Father was sharing His joy concerning the discussions they were having. He was also setting them up for what He was about to say. All of Heaven stands ready to listen to what the Father creates with language. When He speaks, His words become law immediately. When He speaks, words become spirit, and Kingdom is released into the Earthly atmosphere...

Since this was a day scheduled for the conception of a soul, He allowed the conversation to continue as He listened. He was amazed at the faith and devotion of Bethany. He had her Heavenly assignment planned out for many Earth years prior to bringing her home. Bethany died in God's timing, unlike many who came into agreement with sickness and disease as their portion. There is no guilt or shame in Heaven. Therefore, when a Saint comes home early, the welcome is the same - unless the Father decides to send them back with testimonies of Heavenly experiences. Dying before our time simply means that we had more to accomplish on Earth if allowed to continue. Since the work will always be there, assignments are most often passed down to the next generation when a task is left unfulfilled.

Often, the Father sends a person back to Earth when a premature death occurs. Especially, if they are being prayed for regularly. Some lay on their death bed without anyone uttering a prayer on their behalf. In this type of situation, the Father simply allows them to come home to receive their eternal reward. However, the unfulfilled dreams they carried must be accomplished. Especially if it was declared from a throne room conception meeting or through Prophetic utterance in the Earth. This usually happens through their descendants still positioned in the Earthly realm. The Father thinks generationally concerning the individual assignments He endorses. Their Guardian Angel is given a new assignment. Usually, it's their descendent. This is done in order to maintain continuity of the generational life plan. Guardian angels watch over the entire lineage of a person due to the intricate details of a life plan. It's never about one person by themselves. The Father thinks in terms of generational blessings and assignments - to the thousandth generation. He alone has the ability to govern generationally in this fashion. However, in the Millennial Kingdom, the Redeemed Ones will carry the same capacity to govern in this way as they rule and reign with Jesus on the new Earth.

After engaging with the twenty-four elders, Jesus, Holy Spirit, and Bethany through discerning glances,

The Father declared from His throne with love and mercy, *"Thank you precious Bethany for your time with us today. Your wisdom and insight have given us much to plan in the days ahead. You are welcome to be here as a consultant as often as you like. Your help is needed as we shape the next season of church history and move the ecclesia forward with renewed identity, purpose and destiny. The Heavenly housing emissary, at the direction of King Jesus, has your home prepared for you. Everything you need is at your fingertips. You are now empowered to create with your words, so feel free to add anything you like to your new home by speaking it into existence.. We have a few surprises for you at your eternal residence. Anything to make you smile! Welcome, home..."*

Bethany stood in astonishment at the honor and attention she was receiving. She was stunned at the meekness and kindness shown to her by the Father. She didn't even have to spend any time in Heaven's waiting area. Heaven's waiting area is primarily for groups of people who have been ushered into the Heavenly realm together and await in-processing. It is there that Jesus comes to welcome them personally and take them to their eternal living quarters. It is one of His favorite things to do...

In an instant, being overcome with gratitude, she grabbed her crown and cast it across the throne room floor - once again. Laughter and praise broke out in the throne room as the crown glided across the translucent surface towards the Father.

The Father got up from His throne, picked up Bethany's crown, walked towards her, smiled, and said, *"That never gets old, and thank you for the honor you show me. However - this is your crown.*

As He replaced Bethany's crown gently on her head, He continued, *"You are a King, Priest, and Lord forever more. Its why Jesus is the King of kings, and Lord of lords. Your rightful position is symbolized by the crown you were given. Your crown announces to all the Heavenly creatures great and small that you are Blessed and highly favored. You have been Redeemed as a Holy people, without spot or blemish. In Heaven, your word will always be appreciated and honored, just like the rest of us. You will work directly with Jesus, when the time is right, to rule and reign with Him having all power and authority to complete your assignment. Of course, there is much more revelation for you to capture. I encourage you to spend time at the Hall of Knowledge and catch up on anything you missed while on Earth. There, you will recognize the Teachers who are available for you anytime you wish to learn. The Hall of Knowledge contains information yet to be released in the Earth. This will further prepare you for the ages to come. Say Hello to Martin Luther while you are there. As you know, he went through much suffering to bring fresh revelation to the Earth concerning My grace. He is a mighty Teacher and will answer any questions you may have."*

Bethany looked at the Father with tears of Joy and said, *"Thank you Father. I never truly knew how much you loved me. My life was filled with confusion as to the depth of your love and how your sovereignty functioned. I see now. I will study and prepare for my assignment with great attentiveness."*

Responding ever so gently, the Father said, *"I know you will precious Bethany, it's how we made you... and up here, everyone calls me Abba."*

As Bethany left the meeting to spend some time at her new home, attention quickly turned to the next item on the Throne-room agenda. A day like today was always special. The release of a soul was among the most important events in Heaven. To protect the identity, purpose and destiny of the soul, this type of meeting is done in secret in accordance with Psalm 139:13-16,

"For you formed my inward parts; you knitted me together in my mother's womb. I praise you, for I am fearfully and wonderfully made. Wonderful are your works; my soul knows it very well. My frame was not hidden from you, when I was being made in secret, intricately woven in the depths of the earth. Your eyes saw my unformed substance; in your book were written, every one of them, the days that were formed for me, when as yet there was none of them." (ESV)

The secrecy isn't because the Father, Son and Holy Spirit are afraid of the demonic kingdom. It is simple compartmentalization of information. Things must be settled in accordance with the eternal plan for mankind, and how this particular soul fits into the grand scheme. This type of planning is reserved only for the Father, Son and Holy Spirit. No other creature was invited to the meeting to form man from the dust of the Earth. *"Let us make man in our image and likeness…"* was the invitation to create in the Book of Genesis. The participants for this type of meeting was to be *Elohim* alone - God in Three distinct persons. The declarations, decrees and prophetic words being recorded in the soul's Book of Destiny was to be protected at all costs until the proper time. Once the words of this book are declared openly in the Earthly realm, through Holy Spirit empowered believers, the enemy would be made aware due to the power that sweeps through the demonic kingdom.

The declarations, decrees and prophetic announcements of the Saints shake the demonic kingdom with powerful earthquake level tremors. It is only then; do they spring into action. The demonic kingdom is always behind in this regard because they do not have access to the information contained in the soul's Book of Destiny. On Earth, only the blood washed Saints of the living God have access to someone's true identity, purpose and destiny through cerebral messaging as words of wisdom, knowledge and prophecy are transmitted to their inner man.

The Father stands and declares to Jesus and Holy Spirit, *"Its time. The consummation of love is drawing near. In accordance with the word given to the Prophet Jeremiah,*

"Before I formed you in the womb I knew you, and before you were born I consecrated you; I appointed you a prophet to the nations"

we will begin the process now in order for the soul to enter into our protection and favor."

Jesus responded with an emphatic, *"I love it. Many prayers have been prayed for this child already, so his golden bowl is full of prayers, declarations, and decrees for Adriel to fight with on the soul's behalf once he is conceived."*

Holy Spirit exclaimed, *"This is great news. Are we adhering to the same process?"*

The Father replied, *"Yes. I will form him, Jesus will appoint him, and you consecrate him for my purpose in the Earth. An angelic paralegal is present to record the conversations and file them with the Courts of Heaven immediately through messenger Angels. Once the declarations and decrees are made, they are unchangeable and will remain unaltered for the duration of the soul's life on Earth. All information concerning the soul's life plan will be recorded in their Book of Destiny, which is accessible to the people of God, especially the Prophets and those to which the soul forms a covenant for discipleship. At all times they can access the book's information to direct them along their path. Usually we give some wiggle room concerning what the soul wants to do for a living. However, in cases such as this, with a five-fold ministry official, they have no choice but to pursue their appointment. Nothing else will truly satisfy because of the mantle for leadership they carry. It is written in their Book of Destiny and must be carried out because of the people they are pre-destined to meet and impact for the Kingdom. Any detour to the life-plan through self-will must be corrected through acts of grace and mercy on our behalf."*

Souls have always been released in this manner since Cain and Abel were formed, consecrated and appointed. The Father reserves the right to form a soul, because He is the designer. Jesus appoints the soul because it is His ecclesia in operation in the Earth. Jesus takes the lead in this area because He is the builder of His church, pouring over the details of the calling He wants to place on the new soul. When the appointment is made concerning the soul, Holy Spirit consecrates and devotes the soul to the purpose Jesus has declared. Holy Spirit initiates the process of depositing the gifts and talents needed to accomplish their assignment while on Earth. They work together in perfect unison.

The Father stands up from His throne and walks around for a moment. He wants to cherish the moment for a little while longer. He ponders the look and features He wants to program into the soul's Deoxyribonucleic Acid (DNA). Deoxyribonucleic acid (abbreviated DNA) is the molecule that carries genetic information for the development and functioning of an organism. DNA is made of two linked strands that wind around each other to resemble a twisted ladder — a shape known as a double helix. Each strand has a backbone made of alternating sugar (deoxyribose) and phosphate groups. Attached to each sugar is one of four bases: adenine (A), cytosine (C), guanine (G) or thymine (T). The two strands are connected by chemical bonds between the bases: adenine bonds with thymine, and cytosine bonds with guanine. The sequence of the bases along DNA's backbone encodes biological information, such as the instructions for making a protein or RNA molecule. (NHGRI,

2023)

The majority of the soul' DNA is already in place through genetics passed down from their ancestry. In this throne-room moment, The Father is simply pondering what to add to the mix to ensure their identity, purpose and destiny are achievable in their lifetime. Sometimes the gifts are undeniable and easy to recognize - like an anointing for singing, athletics or business success. Other gifts are subtle - like the anointing to write beautiful literature or develop children. The Father usually gives each new soul a hidden super-power. Something that the world will usually misunderstand and misinterpret. This hidden super-power often takes a lifetime to discover, but when its uncovered, one fully manifested soul can create havoc for the kingdom of darkness.

The Father stops, turns around to face Jesus and Holy Spirit, and begins to speak. *"Let all declarations and decrees be recorded in this soul's Book of Destiny and established this day from my throne-room, I will release the soul of a male. Let it also be established in writing in the Court of Heaven where I sit as Righteous Judge and noted in the appropriate legal documentation to include his Heavenly birth certificate - the following: his Earthly name will be called Blake which means "Shining One". He will be circumcised the eighth day after his birth and will win many souls to my Kingdom. He will grow to be 6 feet 1 inch and will carry a deep discernment in the spirit realm. His features will be handsome and will carry the ability to operate comfortably in front of people. He will have an average build, with average athletic ability but above average intelligence. He will come to know me at a very young age because we must capture his heart early due to the amount of impact he will have in the Earth for my Kingdom. Due to generational blessings already established in his bloodline, announced by his ancestors through prayer and declaration, he will have a natural ability to understand and write music, as well as books."*

The Father's portion of the declaration and decree is very concise because Jesus and Holy Spirit were commissioned to do the rest. They work in perfect unison as a team in all things. The Father forms the soul physically and establishes the basic traits through DNA already at work in the genetic code of the dot of flesh the soul will soon be knitted to in the womb of the mother. The Father can always do what He desires and change things however He wants, but He would rather work with what He has already created. DNA is His invention.

All declarations and decrees originating from the throne-room are recorded for eternity and can't be changed. All legal documentation must also be promptly filed due to the precious nature of a soul's identity, purpose and destiny. DNA sustains the generational physical recreation of humanity to include things like eye and hair color. However, this process of recording a soul's identity, purpose and destiny is the most important step. This happens prior to conception due to the top secret nature of the information contained in it. The reasoning is simple. Things will properly unfold on Earth when we are in agreement with what has already been established in Heaven. Since things of this nature are already developed, settled and established in Heaven, the Saints can call it forth through declaration, decree and prayers of agreement. Therefore, the saints have the ability to transfer the resources of Heaven into the Earth, to include identity, purpose, and destiny.

If Blake's identity is called forth by the saints as a news anchor, Heaven won't respond. This is the nature of prayer and prophetic utterance. It must align with what has already been written in a soul's Book of Destiny. This is why a saint should never come into agreement with a prayer, declaration or prophetic utterance that doesn't ring true with their spirit man through Holy Spirit corroboration. This is also why a Saint should also wait for at least 2 or 3 confirmations of the prophetic word before coming into agreement with it. In this way, a soul will mature and learn while being impacted only by prayers, declarations and prophetic utterances they themselves willfully choose to agree with. However, Decrees are different. They represent a ruling from Heaven that cannot be stopped. Most often, guardian and messenger Angels get deeply involved when Decrees are released. As was the case with John the Baptist. His name had to be *"John"* by decree from the throne-room. To ensure this happened, the messenger Angel was authorized to do whatever was necessary to protect this decree as he delivered it to John's earthly father who was Zechariah. He made a command decision, based off Zechariah's response of unbelief, to take away his ability to speak for a season. Speech can be catastrophic in the spirit realm when fueled by unbelief. The messenger Angel was given Level 1 authority to do so...

    The soul must learn, grow and transform in order to impact others for the Kingdom. Humanity often thinks in terms of personal growth or education as a process of learning scholarly things to include reading, writing and math. However, from Heaven's perspective, growth and education for a soul is simply discovering who the Father, Son and Holy Spirit made you to be. This is why it is possible to gain the whole world and lose your soul. The discovery of who Heaven made you to be should always be the chief pursuit in life. When a soul hungers and thirsts for the things of God, revelation concerning their identity, purpose and destiny can be released through dreams, visions and trances. When a soul is living in agreement with the teachings of God's Five-fold ministry officials and operate in covenant with a spiritual father or mother, they can grow at an alarming rate. However, the soul must always choose with their own will through faith to agree with Heaven's plan...

As the Father walks back to His throne and sits down, signifying that He has completed His portion of the declaration process,

Jesus springs to His feet, and begins to announce, *"Let all declarations and decrees be recorded in Blake's Book of Destiny and established this day from my Father's throne-room, Our Father will release the soul of a male. Let it also be established in writing in the Court of Heaven where I sit as Advocate for Blake and noted in the appropriate legal documentation to include his Heavenly birth certificate - the following: Blake's Earthly appointment will be as a Pastor/Teacher in the ecclesia. He will carry a deep discernment for the Word of God and will desire to study and meditate on my Word day and night. People will naturally desire to talk to him and tell him their deepest trauma. As a Pastor, he will care for many people and always desire to help them. As a Teacher, I will open his mind in extraordinary ways and deposit the science of my Word in his heart. The Bible for him will be like a five or six page book. His teachings will be deep but simple, just like mine were during my Earthly ministry."*

Jesus paused momentarily and glanced at the angelic paralegal making the entries, *"Please make sure the following is in bold letters,* **Nothing will stop this appointment, and he must always be full time in ministry***. He is being birthed in a very dangerous era in America. The spirit of Religion has taken over the region he will be birthed into, and they don't carry much revelation of scripture beyond what Oswald Chambers or other commentators have delivered to them. He will naturally end up at a Baptist Church where there are good people who love the Lord. However, when the time comes, he must encounter my Spirit and be empowered for his appointment. The Southern Baptist aren't actively teaching current* revelation concerning the Day of Pentecost or Holy Spirit empowerment. This will take some maneuvering on our part. We will simply have to work with the areas of scripture they are in agreement with. They are doing an excellent job with their youth in this season, so we can start there. Ensure his guardian angel gets a copy of his Book of Destiny and make him aware of the Decree included. As is our custom, the main copy will be available in the Court of Heaven with the records manager. This is rare but, Adriel has handled this level of information well in the past and he is a seasoned servant member of the Guardians Guild. He is actually in line to be promoted after this assignment, whether he succeeds or fails."

In the Kingdom, promotion isn't based on pass or fail. Promotion is based on attitude and effort. In the Kingdom, we yield to what God is saying and doing in our lives. We don't have to strive for advancement or increased responsibility. The Father is always looking for ways to promote His children.

Holy Spirit was ready to share His portion of the declaration process. He was always excited about the release of a soul. He loved the process of equipping the soul and devoting it to the Kingdom. He loved the way the Father involved Him in the process and encourage Him to be creative.

He walked to the center of the throne-room and addressed the Father, Son, and angelic paralegal with a loud and confident voice, "*Let all declarations and decrees be recorded in Blake's Book of Destiny and established this day from my Father's throne-room, Our Father will release the soul of a male. Let it also be established in writing in the Court of Heaven and in the Earth where I operate as Comforter for Blake and noted in the appropriate legal documentation to include his Heavenly birth certificate - the following: Blake will be set apart from birth with the following gifts*

- strong commitment to duty, communication ability and love for the arts. Blake will gravitate towards visual art and literature as a means of learning. Blake will have a natural ability to discern truth in scripture and will be a natural magnet for heartbroken people. Blake will carry a creative capacity that is above average and will see the lesson in everything. This will enable Blake to teach and preach the way Jesus did during his Earthly ministry, using everyday things to communicate the Word of God. Once empowered by my Spirit, Blake will have a strong anointing to hear words of wisdom, knowledge and prophecy. His strong sense of duty will lead him to seek deeper truth and greater anointing as a minister of the Gospel message and teacher of the Holy Scriptures. His divine gifts will enable him to be a natural lifelong learner and seeker of truth. This will protect his destiny from the spirit of Religion which seeks to keep man stuck in a fixed mindset.

With the right Pastor in his ear, Blake will always find a way to repent and adjust his thinking to align himself with what the Father is saying and doing in the Earth." The Father sprung to His feet exclaiming, *"That's what I'm talking about Holy Spirit! This is the type of declaration we need to make mandatory going forward. In the last days, I am pouring out my Spirit on all flesh. Even the religious. Therefore, this type of declaration will protect the ability to repent and adjust thinking. Brilliant!"* Holy Spirit looked at the Father with love and joy and said, *"I believe we have addressed the major hurdles Blake will need to overcome as he develops by equipping him biologically and emotionally from birth with a particular set of skills. Ministers of the Gospel are made different and therefore must always think different. Since everything man needs to bring Heaven to Earth was paid for at the cross by Jesus, thought life is crucial in the last days. The ecclesia must advance and in order to advance they must continue to repent."*

The Father paused for a moment in quiet confidence.

He thought about all the history of man up this point. The current year was 1975 and the world was being turned upside down with ideas contrary to His Word. America had already increased the worship of *Molech* by legalizing abortion as a nation. America had no idea that they were even involved in the worship of an ancient deity. They made it a political and medical issue. However, the ecclesia knew the spiritual ramifications of such an act of idolatry at the national level. Millions were to be sacrificed to this ancient god of the Ammonites in the decades to come. He wanted to intervene directly, but he knew the ecclesia would eventually take charge and cancel this unspeakable enemy contract. He also knew Jesus would stop at nothing to get Roe vs Wade reversed in the years to come. Until then, He wasn't the least bit worried. He always has a plan and a brilliant way to get that plan implemented in the Earth. He knew, even before this soul was to be released, Blake's first Pastor and Youth Minister were already being trained. Blakes wife, who wouldn't be born for another 4 years, was already being planned for by the Trinity team. He knew how much Blake's parents loved the current city they lived in and had no plans to move, because He deposited that love in their hearts to begin with.

He also thought about the situation that Blake was being born into. Blake was to be formed in the womb of someone severely addicted to dangerous man-made drugs. He was confident of Blake's future, mainly due to one variable. Blake's grandmother - Gladys, prayed… Blake's golden bowl which served as a temporary container for the prayers of the Saints was filled with enough fire power to thwart all the plans of the enemy. His heart broke at the thought of the millions who were not as fortunate to live out their days on Earth and truly know Him in that manner. A soul needs to be raised on the Earth. It is there we develop a relationship with Him through faith. In Heaven, we will see Him face to face and have everyday interactions with Him.

Our life on Earth is the setting where our mind, will and emotions are trained to appreciate the things of God. Appreciation is the key because it is the one thing Lucifer lost while serving in his ordained capacity in Heaven. Lucifer lost an appreciation for the presence of God. When a soul is raised on Earth, an appreciation of the presence and nature of God is developed that will equip us for an eternity of rulership with King Jesus. Its really no different in how a parent should raise their children when preparing them for rulership. In Earthly kingdoms, an heir apparent is trained in etiquette and awareness of duty first and foremost. They are trained to serve without selfish motive and be available to the people. They are also taught how and when to commission the military for battle. Through the years of training, with the right counsel and upbringing, they are able to carry the immense weight of rulership that will be placed on their shoulders. It is important to develop an eternal soul in this environment God calls Earth.

Since millions of identities, purposes and destinies were scheduled to be stolen by the enemy - this season of ecclesia history was pivotal. The Five-fold ministry officials being released in the Earth were to be educated, unyielding, and undeterred by the world. They were to have a grasp on technology and how to use it for the Kingdom. They were to be equipped with the revelation of scripture imparted in past generations. However, they would carry much more revelation of scripture than their predecessors. Their purpose was to prepare the way for millions of revivalists who would go forth into the Earth and recapture what was lost. All the death and piracy of man's purpose in the Earth that Roe vs Wade released, had to be restored. That would be the job of the ecclesia, which Jesus would personally involve Himself in. The Father forms us, The Holy Spirit consecrates us. Jesus appoints us to our official capacity within the ecclesia.

"Quickly!" The Father exclaimed. *"Is everything recorded and ready to be filed with the Court of Heaven?"*

The angelic paralegal, using his finger with careful examination of the declarations recorded in Blake's Book of Destiny, responded with, *"This is brilliant. Yes Abba, it is complete and ready to be filed."*

The Trinity team looked at one another and smiled. They turned to the paralegal and nodded their heads, as if to say, *"You know what to do."*

THE COURT OF HEAVEN...

It is written in the Word,

"As I looked, thrones were placed, and the Ancient of Days took his seat; his clothing was white as snow, and the hair of his head like pure wool; his throne was fiery flames; its wheels were burning fire. A stream of fire issued and came out from before him; a thousand thousands served him, and ten thousand times ten thousand stood before him; the court sat in judgment, and the books were opened."

Lael, which means *"Belonging To God"*, the angelic paralegal responsible for recording and filing declarations from the throne-room, stood up, closed Blake's Book of Destiny, picked it up and walked over to the Trinity team who were all standing in the center of the throne-room. All three placed their hands on the book and *Blessed* it. Blessing something transfers it into the Kingdom of Heaven where it is fully empowered to accomplish its purpose. This can be done in the Earthly realm as well because, Kingdom principles and prophetic acts are equally as powerful in the natural. In essence, paying *tithe* is a simple prophetic act of transferring finances into the Kingdom. The remaining 90% is empowered well beyond its actual earthly worth. Jesus used this methodology when feeding thousands of people during His earthly ministry.

He held the fish and loaves of bread up to Heaven with thanksgiving and Blessed it. The amount of fish and loaves available that day would have only fed a few people - unless Jesus openly blessed it. This empowered the earthly molecules to be used for Kingdom purpose. Now, it was whatever Jesus needed it to be. After the prophetic act of Blessing the food, the Earthly molecular structure of the fish and bread was now interwoven with spirit realm particles not currently found on the current Earthly periodic table of elements. The fish and loaves were then able to adapt and multiply into whatever Jesus needed them to be. In the case of feeding thousands, He simply needed the food molecules to multiply. God taught this concept to Aaron as he held out his staff, as an act of obedience, and the wooden molecules transformed into a snake. Elisha made an axe head swim through the prophetic act of throwing a piece of wood into the water where the axe head had sunk. This changed the non-buoyant properties of the iron axe head to become as light as a tree leaf on the water. In all these instances there is a reason Heaven responded to the prophetic act. They were all redemptive and displayed one of God's characteristics. The axe head was borrowed, so retrieving it protected a relationship. Aarons rod proved that God was superior to Egyptian magic and pagan ritual. The miracle of the fishes and loaves were even more simple than that. It's not God's will that anyone would perish, especially because of hunger…

Lael held the book firmly with one hand, as he poured hot heavenly wax on the locking mechanism of the book. It spread into a circle in preparation for the Father's seal from His signet ring.

The Father made this statement as he took off his signet ring of authority and pressed it firmly into the hot wax, thereby sealing Blake's Book of Destiny until the Judgement Seat of Christ convened,

"I Bless these declarations made today for the purpose of advancing my Kingdom. Blake will not leave the Earthly realm until all the words of this book are fulfilled. Should he die before his time, we will send him back to fulfill the conclusion of his destiny. The words of this book are hereby sealed with my signet ring of authority

and will only be accessible through faith and the gifts of the Spirit which empower my people in the Earth to communicate freely concerning identity, purpose and destiny. The seal of this book will not be broken until the appropriate time at the Judgment Seat of Christ, should Blake choose with his own will to say yes to my Son's sacrifice. Should he openly reject my Son and live out his days in sin, disobedience, self-promotion and self-will, Blake's Book of Destiny will be read aloud prior to receiving his eternal punishment at the Great White Throne Judgement. This book will be exhibit A in his trial should he reject my Son while on Earth. I Am the Lord God Almighty. I have spoken and it is hereby established with the testimony of four witnesses."

A solemn awareness of what was at stake came over the four of them. When a Book of Destiny is complete and sealed prior to the release of a soul, there is always a solemnness among them. Lael has been through this process millions of times as he has served faithfully in his assignment as Direct Paralegal to the Throne Room. He has watched as countless millions of souls have been armed with all the declarations they need to accomplish great things for the Kingdom in their Book of Destiny. He is also witness to the countless millions who refuse to follow Jesus and thereby disprove their own divine identity, purpose and destiny. In Lael's mind, he still can't understand the magnitude of love and compassion the Trinity team has for mankind. He has watched things unfold for thousands of years.

Lucifer was kicked out of Heaven in a moment described by Jesus as swiftly as a lightning strike. Of course, the Father was aware of his schemes all along and gave him a grace period to repent. The grace afforded to man was on another level all together. Lael has recorded the identity, purpose and destiny for every human since Adam was created because the Father never fires anyone who uses their will for Kingdom purpose and has a willingness to learn new things. Lael has even made a few clerical errors and included some typos when he first began recording declarations from the throneroom. He can remember, way back then, thousands of years ago, The Father just smiled and said, *"Keep working at it. I'm with you and I will help you get better at it.."* Lael loved working so closely with the Father. Lucifer is the first created being, made with a will, that the Father had to terminate from their duties with no hope of redemption. It broke the Father's heart to be forced to do this. This is why the development of a created being, made in His image, made with the mind, will and emotions of the Father had to be done differently in this age.

Lael pulled the book close to his chest, looked Abba in the eyes and declared, *"You are the Lord God Almighty. Your judgements are true and righteous."*

Jesus and Holy Spirit responded with, *"Amen. On Earth as it is in Heaven."*

Lael hurried off to the filing office located on the first floor of the Court of Heaven. As he approached the main structure it resembled the appearance of the Supreme Court located in Washington D.C. or many other Supreme Court buildings across the world. One difference is that there are 12 columns holding up the porch instead of the traditional six or eight as constructed by many Masonic builders. Lael walked up the steps and thought about the importance of this soul. He was privy to overwhelming volumes of information concerning the identity, purpose and destiny of God's greatest creation - mankind. Lucifer's jealousy for mankind is what fuels him to this day. Lael wasn't jealous at all. Lael understood his own identity, purpose and destiny and was thankful to be part of the process. In the Kingdom no one has to be jealous because we are all part of the same *Age of Grace* mission - to bring Heaven to Earth.

Even his own name, *"Lael"* prophesied the intimacy he shared with the Father. Nothing was worth losing that level of closeness. He took his job serious and wanted nothing to do with sin and iniquity. Life is always better in the Kingdom...

As he stepped in front of the main window for filing books of destiny, he was greeted by the Heavenly Director of Declaration Filing with great enthusiasm. *"So good to see you Lael. What do you have for me today?"*

Lael smiled and said, *"Another sealed and blessed Book of Destiny. Abba needs this filed with immediate effect in the Court of Heaven. He requests that, for now, only the Anointed Prophets in the Earth have access to its contents. This is a special appointment."*

The clerks face almost burst with excitement as he grabbed the book out of Lael's hands. *"Is it a Pastor?"*

Lael looked amused and said, *"You know I can't divulge that information. I would have my Heavenly Secret Clearance revoked and placed on probationary grace, and have to undergo assignment retraining, and on and on...."*

The clerk laughed and said, *"I know. I just like to mess with you. We have been at this for centuries. I know the policy."*

Lael smiled and said as he hurriedly backed away alluding to his busy schedule, *"Gotta run. Thank you my brother."*

The Director turned to the staff members, who were all working on different projects at their desks, and said, *"Who wants to file this?"*

One of the newly added inexperienced assistants stood up and said, *"I will."*

The Director glanced at another more experienced staff member and said, *"Please go with him and help him learn the process so he is trained up for the future. Remember, in Heaven everyone is honored and discipled well. If our new staff member is to succeed at his assignment, we must serve him well."*

In Heaven, everyone is trained well by those with more experienced. Knowledge is shared liberally, and everyone has a desire to see their brother and sister succeed. Promotion to Director status is based off how successful those around you have become in accomplishing their assignment.

Jesus taught this principle to His Earthly followers when he said, *"The greatest among you must be a servant."*

The culture of Heaven is a beautiful thing to observe. This culture permeates every being assigned to a Heavenly functional area. The Court of Heaven where all legal aspects involving created beings and the spirit realm are administered, The Trading Floor of Heaven where the economy of the spirit realm flows, The Mountain of God where declarations and decrees are made from the throne-room, The Hall of Knowledge which houses all technological information and biblical revelation past, present and future, are all part of the vast governance of the galaxy. Things get done faster and with more excellence than anything we can imagine here on Earth.

The less experienced staff member walked over confidently to his newly assigned partner and introduced himself. *"My Name is Abdeel, which means "Servant of God." I met you once when I was first appointed to work in the Court of Heaven in the Maintenance Department. I am so excited to explore my new area of expertise and work with you more closely. Your name is Tabeel, correct?"*

Tabeel replied, *"Yes. My name means "God is Good" and it is a pleasure to be working with you. I've heard so much about you from your prior Department. They said you were always ready to serve with your whole heart and everyone you trained succeeded in* their assignment. That is why we petitioned Jesus to give you a promotion to our department. It's a season thing. This place is getting more and more busy as we approach the 3rd Great Awakening. Much to be done on the legal side of Heaven in order to release the plans the Trinity team have been working on. I will walk you through the different sub-departments of the Court of Heaven and train you to help facilitate its functionality."

Abdeel looked excited and couldn't wait to learn. He was puzzled as to why his mistakes were not mentioned. Afterall, he made several mistakes while working in maintenance. The culture of Heaven is different than the world. Jesus declared this to His followers often. He told them in John 8:23

"He said to them, "You are from below; I am from above. You are of this world; I am not of this world." (ESV)

In Heaven, only what is true, pure and lovely is discussed concerning others. Its citizens know that only the Trinity team has the authority to judge unto condemnation. Abdeel loved working in Heaven. He marvels at the lengths the Father goes to steward His most prized possession - mankind.

Tabeel handed Abdeel the Book of Destiny and said, *"Follow me.."* He turned around and headed for the main door that led to the hallway that would lead them both to the filing room. As they walked down the main hallway he began teaching Abdeel all about the purpose of the Court of Heaven and how it functions.

"Abdeel, the Court of Heaven has always been in existence. It is there that the Father sits as Righteous Judge and Jesus serves as Advocate for mankind. Court is convened anytime one of the Redeemed request for it to be seated to handle spirit realm legal matters. One example would be if a Redeemed one were to pray on behalf of another person. It is in the Court of Heaven that a person

can make their case for forgiveness on behalf of another. It is also a place where a Redeemed one can cancel any and all enemy assignments against themselves or their loved ones. There really isn't any limit to the requests or type of requests that can be made. However, an understanding of God's Word helps them better understand the legal ramifications of their requests. They have access to the Court of Heaven only if they are in covenant with Jesus - their Advocate. Jesus taught His earthly followers to pray every day, "Forgive us our trespasses as we forgive those who have trespassed against us." This is legal terminology to be used in the Court of Heaven and serves as the foundational prayer for every believer in Jesus. Are there any questions so far?"

Abdeel was soaking it all up. He loved to learn. This was a key to his constant promotion within the Kingdom. As they walked together, he suddenly had his first question. *"I have studied the Word of God for centuries. It still amazes me to see the lengths the Father went to redeem mankind from sin. Why is there, all of a sudden, this emphasis on the legal aspects of Heaven by the Redeemed still in the Earth?"*

Tabeel said in response, *"Great question! Abba understands that it has taken many centuries to regain what was lost in the garden of Eden. Man could not handle the weight of a full revelation of His Word. It had to be unpacked, generation to generation. This protected the ecclesia from enemy attack ahead of their time. He allowed some levels of revelation to be released several times in the past, but it did not always work out. Man has a hard time seeing the big picture concerning their assignment on the Earth. In one particular generation, Abba released new manifestations of Holy Spirit presence. It seemed simple enough. Man basically experienced the manifestations around 1906 in several countries to include America."*

Abdeel politely interrupted, *"Abba loves America so much."*

Tabeel stopped in the middle of the hallway, turned to face Abdeel and said, *"Were it not for the ecclesia, America would cease to exist as we know it. As a nation, they haven't handled the Word of God well at all. Their wealth is the only reason they are still in the world-wide church picture, and that wealth is only sustained by Abba's grace and mercy. They are actually behind by at least 50 years from the rest of the world in the things of God. As a matter of fact, the prayers of the other nations have filled their golden bowl more than their own prayers. I hope they start working with each other better. I don't think they are scheduled to have their candlestick removed anytime soon. However, they are in need of revival and its happening soon."*

Abdeel shook his head from side to side and said, *"That is definitely new information to me. I had no idea they were in that condition. What is Abba's plan?"*

Tabeel answered as they opened a hallway door, amidst the bustle of a department praise break, and began walking up a flight of stairs. *"Revival... its really that simple. Through the centuries, I've served in this capacity and seen a lot of things. Abba loves to bring revival through his young ones. They aren't weighed down with erroneous theology and generally still love to have fun. They need leadership, but they don't need to be controlled. They need to be taught the Word of God, but without the religious interpretation of things."*

Abdeel asked, *"Why don't they just read the word and understand it literally?"*

Tabeel stopped before stepping on to another stair, turned to Abdeel and said, *"The Spirit of Religion works overtime in the hearts of men to convince them God's ways aren't understandable, and His word is beyond their grasp. You and I know Abba and have known Him for centuries. His ways are very practical, and His Word is quite literal. If it says, "Heal the sick and raise the dead..." that's really all they have to do. If it is says "rejoice always and pray without ceasing" that is pretty cut and dry as well. The power to do it is released on the Trading Floor of Heaven as an exchange for their obedience. Both obedience and disobedience attract the supernatural to their lives. They have to make a decision with their will - which spirit will they co-labor with?"*

Adeel's mind was once again blown away as they both continued to walk up one more flight of stairs and open a door leading them to a waiting area. He asked another question, *"Why is America so behind in the things of God? Haven't they been given the same copy of the Bible like everyone else?"*

Tabeel shook his head up and down as if to agree and said, *"Yes. However, they allowed the doctrines of devils to infiltrate their church culture. Even after the Azusa street revivals they refused to work together and combine their revelation of scripture for Kingdom purpose. They began splitting up within the same decade and formed separate denominations that further confused God's people. Jesus warned mankind about the spirit of religion and the spirit of politics in the Gospel accounts. Both have influenced the church in America for many decades now. And, what influences America, has influenced the world-wide church because the financial support they provide touches millions."*

As they both stood in the waiting area in anticipation for their filing appointment, Abdeel leaned in and asked, *"What are these doctrines of devils?"*

Tabeel answered him with absolute certainty, *"Cessationism and replacement theology are among the most damaging to the body of Christ. They aren't anything new. However, with the release of the printing press, telegraph and now the internet, within the past 300 years, these doctrines have been spread everywhere at a rapid pace. Millions have been affected by them and have allowed the enemy to steal, kill and destroy from God's redeemed ones. Cessationism teaches them that Holy Spirit empowerment was only for the original Apostles. It goes even further to declare that the Five-fold ministry officials were for another time, especially the Prophets. Replacement theology teaches them that Israel has been cutoff forever and therefore, shouldn't be included in the grand scheme of things. This teaching has released more anti-Semitism than any other teaching created by the demonic kingdom, to date."*

Abdeel looking puzzled said, *"None of what you said is verifiable in scripture. How did they come up with those ideas?"*

Tabeel responded with Holy zeal, *"The enemy of the Kingdom will stop at nothing to steal the hearts, minds, and worship of God's redeemed ones. The doctrines of devils were taught precept upon precept, as all instruction is built. Without Holy Spirit empowerment, there is no discernment as they study scripture. The Bible is a spiritual book and must be studied with spiritual empowerment. Once a person, or a congregation comes into agreement with one of these doctrines, they are destined to see catastrophic results – works of the flesh are sure to manifest among the leaders. Misinterpretation of scripture is what the Pharisees and Sadducees were known for. It was the main reason they did not recognize the Messiah. What we receive through instruction builds a construct. Revival fires deconstruct what people think they know concerning the nature of God and reestablish original precepts with fresh revelation. Ironically, revival brings to life the Word of God in fresh ways. It isn't like revival brings new information, because it has been in their bibles since it was canonized. Revival fire simply breathes new life into age old truth. God is the same, yesterday, today and forever. However, deeper understanding of who He is and what He wants to accomplished must be reestablished. In this current revival being released in the Earth, Abba has bypassed the established denominations. Sadly, they don't even know it. Many will repent and come into agreement with what Abba is saying and doing. Many will not because they live in fear. The spirit of Religion co-labors directly with the spirit of fear. Thousands upon thousands of Five-fold ministry officials have been trained in theological seminaries all over the world. Many of them will have to be retrained - if they are willing to humble themselves."*

Abdeel looked around at the busy waiting area and pondered what Tabeel was teaching him. His heart was burning within him for the redeemed. He turned to Tabeel and asked, *"What are they being retrained to do?"*

Tabeel responded with, *"First, they are being led to congregations that are shepherded well, in accordance with the whole of scripture. These leaders are special because they are retraining them to accomplish the Great Commission. They were really only taught in the seminaries to study and craft an eloquent and persuasive sermon. This is a tiny step in the process. They were never taught to heal the sick, raise the dead, cast out demons or cleanse lepers. Many of them haven't even experienced the baptism of the Holy Spirit. Therefore, they have very little spirit realm discernment. Once they are rooted and grounded in covenant with a regional Apostle, they can be retrained and released into the fullness of their identity, purpose and destiny. Abba is calling them "Revival Hubs."*

Abdeel exclaimed, *"Abba is brilliant. He always has a plan..."*

At that moment, a large digital clock located behind the registry desk flashed the message

"Now Serving BLAKE-12271975-1200."

Tabeel looked at Abdeel and said, *"That's us. You see, the first set of numbers represents the birth date of the soul, followed by another number. The second set of numbers represents the order of birth for that day. Blake is to be born on 12/27/1975 and will be the 1,200th child born on that day in history. This represents his unique filing number in the Court of Heaven and, from now on, when we administer anything on his behalf, this is the number we will use. His first name is also included for better accuracy and cooperation between departments. Many souls are birthed on the same day. However, no two souls are born at exactly the same time."*

They both stepped forward to conduct the business at hand. The filing attendant was a typical angelic paralegal ready and willing to assist them.*"*

The attendant said, *"Greetings Tabeel in the name of the Lord. Are there any unique instructions for this one?"*

Tabeel smiled and said, *"Yes. Abba wants this one kept sealed and the only ones that have access to its contents are his anointed Prophets in the Earth."*

The attendant laughed and said, *"Yep. No problem. Is there anything else I can help you with? Maybe a tour of the department for your new assistant?"*

Tabeel responded, *"Not right now my friend. I have to take him back and continue to train him for his assignment. Maybe another time."*

The attendant responded without offense, *"No worries my friend. I will get this filed immediately. The clock is ticking. I see the date and birth order for Blake. I understand that Blake's soul is set to be released soon."*

After saying this, Abdeel and Tabeel waived goodbye, turned around and left the waiting area to return to their offices downstairs.

As they walked together, Abdeel had more questions, but he restarted the conversation with an observation of sorts. *"So, all this work for one soul, who hasn't even been born yet. Does mankind have any idea how important and cherished they are to Abba?"*

Tabeel looked over at him as they continued to walk back down the stairs towards their offices, *"Not entirely. It has taken over 5,000 years to get them to this place in history. A simple awareness of the Court of Heaven wasn't released into the mainstream until a few Earth years ago through anointed Teachers. Without the internet, millions will not have access to this teaching. They have the technology to facilitate teachings such as this. However, Abba is still waiting for the internet to be made readily available to every home. He may be waiting a while because mankind always hoards and controls technology. They won't even release technological breakthroughs until they find a way to monetize it.*

They have a very selfish culture, which slows down the progress of the ecclesia. Abba would love to release technology to the ecclesia first, but the same thing would happen. They would be tempted to take credit for it and monetize it. While mankind hoards the technology and thinks of ways to monetize it, the enemy takes it and weaponizes it for his purpose. The religious spirit tells them that technology is bad and is making the church wordly. It's an endless spiral of confusion for them, but in essence, it is quite simple. Abba releases technology to advance the living conditions for his greatest creation and make life better for all mankind. They haven't yet learned the basic principle of how Abba manages mankind. It says plainly in the Word, "God so loved the world..." He loves all of them and wants them to know Him intimately."

A *Demonic Legal Delegate* (DLD) entered the waiting area as soon as Abdeel and Tabeel left to return to their offices. He was given notice that a soul was set to be released in the Earth. The demonic kingdom does not have access to the Book of Destiny, until it has been opened in the Spirit and declared verbally through the prophetic ministry of the Saints. The demonic kingdom only has access to someone's past. The Holy Spirit has access to someone's past, present and future. The Holy Spirit shares this information freely to the Saints who operate in their prophetic gift. Therefore, the delegate was there because he received information from the Earthly realm. Blake's soon to be mother has been discussing her desire to have a child for many month. She has also been speaking at length about her fears concerning the child's development in her womb to unbelievers who do not have authority over the spirit of fear. This has placed Blake's identity, purpose and destiny in the Earth at great risk. The second heaven has access to human declaration released through speech in the Earthly realm but has been cut off from all aspects of Heaven, accept to settle legal issues concerning the identity, purpose and destiny of humanity. This is accomplished in the Court of Heaven where they are only allowed a single delegate per 500 humans. This renders the case load almost unbearable for DLDs.

Satan can no longer bring accusations against the Saints like we see in the book of Job. This was a different age altogether. Jesus defeated the works of darkness for us and paid off the mounting sin debt we incurred through disobedience. Back then, Satan could bring direct accusation against humanity. This was before Jesus paid the price for our redemption. Because of His death on the cross, we have a different legal standing in the Court of Heaven. We are now forgiven and considered righteous citizens in the Kingdom of God when we surrender to Jesus through belief and declaration. When we confess with our mouth what we already believe in our hearts concerning Jesus, we become residents of a new Kingdom, and we have rights and privileges afforded to us through the blood covenant. Our past sins are purchased and expunged from our record. We are then replanted in a new Kingdom as a born again creation, in Christ. Most importantly, our legal standing in the Court of Heaven is rehabilitated. We now have an Advocate - Jesus Christ the Righteous - making arbitration and adjudication for us day and night. The Word declares this with the same legal terminology. He makes *intercession*, which also means "arbitration, mediation and adjudication". Job did not have this benefit. Job, like all Old Testament saints, were declared righteous because of their simple devotion through faith, not their legal standing in the Court of Heaven. The only reason Satan was given access to Job by the Father Himself, was because his sins had not yet been paid for. Job's legal standing in the Court of Heaven had yet to be purchased. Now, we have an *Advocate*, supporter and campaigner, and His name is Jesus. Now, under the New Covenant, all accusations must be brought to the Court of Heaven through due process in Heaven's legal department.

DLDs have to wait in the waiting area for hours to get any answers. They can request records concerning Kingdom citizens, only if he has probable cause to bring accusation. He must bring evidence to support his claim. Unbelievers, or "Pre-believers" as they are called in the court system, are often left wide open to accusation because their sin debt is still in collections. DLDs do not have actual access to the Book of Destiny filed away in the court. The Father set up the structure of the Court of Heaven to benefit the Saints. However, if generational curses are still pending, the delegate can dig a little deeper by requesting the Lineage Records. Lineage Records contain all pending contracts with demons, curses, hexes and vexes. The records also include any and all declarations made by the family members of the person in question. All words of death, to include things like, *"you are just like your father who was an alcoholic"* or *"I wish you were never born"* can be used by the demonic to wage war on a person's identity, purpose and destiny in the Earth through their thought life. Nothing can stop Abba's plan for a person to rule and reign once they are taken home to Heaven. However, in the Earthly realm, there are many variables at play to keep a person from becoming a manifested son or daughter of God. The prayers of the Saints, to include intercession for a soul are collected and stored in golden containers in the throne-room of Heaven. Guardian angels dip their sword in the bowls, which energizes the sword and equips it to slice through the plans of the enemy in the second heaven.

Blake was about to be born to a couple who were both unbelievers. This is always a problem for a new soul. Neither one of them were in covenant with Jesus. The amount of spiritual ammunition the enemy had access to, in the Court of Heaven, was placing everything at risk, to include Blake's birth. If the enemy can stop the birth of a human, they are rewarded with promotion within the kingdom of darkness above any other act of wickedness. This is what's known to them as a *"slam dunk"*. This is an all-inclusive theft of a soul's unique identity, purpose and destiny. This particular demonic delegate has been working in this position since Jesus was crucified and Satan was thus denied access to the court system. Over 1,000 years of experience and legal know how was present in his mind. He knew all the loop holes. He knew all the questions to ask. Blake's future was in danger...

The DLD approached the desk of the *Director of Lineage Records*. They both locked eyes for a moment. The humble servant assigned to lead the department had no ill will toward the DLDs. He was instructed to honor information requests made by the DLDs but was also informed that DLDs will stop at nothing to get information on a soul's identity, purpose and destiny. It was a delicate dance of sorts. The leader of the department was the only one authorized to release this level of record to a DLD. Jesus created this bureaucratic process to slow the DLDs down. It was fuel for one of the lies that Satan told his followers.

He said that he would *"...free them from the bureaucracy of Heaven."*

The very nature of the demonic kingdom is chaos and disunity from established heavenly alignment. Satan's main pitch to the angels he was influencing to disobey God was that they would be free to do what they want. This idea of DLDs was Heavens way of slowing down the demonic kingdom and burying them in so much red tape that it would frustrate their efforts to kill, steal and destroy. However, a day like today was different.

The DLD opened up with, *"You know why I'm here. I need the Lineage Records for BLAKE-12271975-1200."*

Uel, which means "Will of God", unwillingly looked behind him at the towers of lineage records for mankind. He responded with, *"My associates who usually retrieve records of that nature are out to lunch. Can we schedule you an appointment for a later date?"*

The DLD looked frustrated and impatient as he replied, *"You know full well that I have good information about this soul. I know for a fact that the parents of this soul, which is set to be released into the Earth soon, are unbelievers. I have full access to their lineage records. Don't play games with me?"*

Uel smiled calmly, *"Our game night was last night, and we had a great time. What game are you making reference to?"*

The DLD had to look at his watch and check the time. The demonic kingdom runs on a tight schedule and their work is checked for accuracy. Heaven has no time, and the court can take as long as it wishes to respond to inquiries of this nature. Heavenly servants are free to use their creativity in all things.

The DLD, after looking at his watch, said, *"You know I don't have that kind of time. I'm making my request now in accordance with the policy already established for my kingdom to operate. I will appeal to your supervisor if I'm not given the requested documents. I am within my right as a Legal Delegate of my kingdom. I won't allow the court to bury information that we want to use in our case against this new soul. This is priority one for my team right now. It's not like humanity doesn't give us enough to work with already. This soul is destined to be destroyed. We have access to his life before he even comes into the Earthly realm. It's an open-shut case for us. His parents are non-believers; therefore, he has a sin debt that is in collections. Besides that, many legally binding contracts are pending against him through generational curses. All I need are the lineage records, and I'll be on my way..."*

Uel was listening for the legal terminology the DLD was forced to reluctantly use. The DLDs had a strict protocol to follow, because mankind is Abba's greatest creation - made in Abba's image and likeness. The Court of Heaven, to include the policy, language, structure and protocol, was established by the Father as a foundational governmental entity before man was even created - as was the throne-room and the temple. It was established with several principles that believers have possibly heard of but may not thoroughly understand. Things like, *"without the shedding of blood, there is no remission for sin"* is very simply a legal declaration from the Court of Heaven. It still serves as the foundational lawful decree for humanity. Of course, when Jesus died for our sins, he wiped away the entire sin debt humanity had accrued. When a human being chooses with their will to declare what they believe in their heart concerning Jesus - they are declared righteous in the Court of

Heaven. All legal arguments against them are dismissed and expunged. The letter to the Colossians tells us,

"When you were dead in your sins and in the uncircumcision of your flesh, God made you alive with Christ. He forgave us all our sins, having canceled the charge of our legal indebtedness, which stood against us and condemned us; he has taken it away, nailing it to the cross."

However, through generational legal entanglements, the doors are open for the DLDs to dig deep into the identity, purpose, and destiny of a soul. Contracts with demons open the bloodline, at birth, to generational sickness and disease. This is the jackpot the DLD was looking for, and he would stop at nothing to sift through the bureaucracy of the lineage department to get access to what was legally his. He was there for one reason, to find a way to disrupt the identity, purpose and destiny of this soul through legal action. He had a huge case load, but this one was a priority. When the directive came across his desk from the principality over Blake's region, it was marked *"Urgent Kill. Possible Five-fold ministry official."* This type of message is automatically placed in a special in-box on his desk labeled *"Gifts to Mankind."*

The demonic kingdom works overtime to convince mankind that Apostles, Prophets, Pastors, Teachers and Evangelist aren't worthy of honor. It is true that every human is worthy of honor. However, five-fold ministry officials are worthy of double honor due to the nature of their assignment. In the worldly kingdom, respect is earned. In the Kingdom of Heaven, respect is commanded. Of course, people can choose to do whatever they want. However, Kingdom principles are superior to wordly principles in every way. In the Kingdom, *Honor* isn't earned, it is bestowed or conferred upon an individual through an act of grace from the Father. This level of respect can of course be misused or misrepresented in the earthly realm. This keeps mankind from trusting leaders. The damage the five-fold ministry officials have caused is well documented. However, the Father still demands respect for his Anointed Ones He has chosen to equip the Saints for the work of the ministry.

There is a consistent attack from the demonic kingdom aimed at degrading and accusing the Anointed Ones. Every mistake they make is broadcast to as many people as possible. Any error in parenting or business transactions conducted by the five-fold ministry is to be blasted through whatever communication means that mankind is currently using. Many years ago, it was the local newspaper. It was a little slower to develop and Heaven had the opportunity to bring a redemptive solution. In the future, through social media, accusations can gain ground immediately. Gossip and slander will run rampant like never before, feeding the blatant disrespect for God's Anointed Ones.

This will actually be the toughest time in history, since the early church persecution, to be a five-fold ministry official. Many of them will be patiently waiting for their appointment in the Earth as Jesus prepares them for their public ministry. Some of them will only be given short seasons to fully manifest - much like the earthly ministry of Jesus. With every gift of the spirit and revelation of scripture that He carried; He was still only given 3.5 years of public ministry. Jesus proved to us that every ministry season is important, no matter how little Earth years are fulfilled. The Father weaves and coordinates the ministry seasons to fill in the gaps left by unfulfilled callings. He protects His officials and warns them of what is to come through popular culture, and how it will affect the ecclesia. It would be many years until Blake would be susceptible to attack through yet to be released technology and social media outlets. However, the attack on his very identity and purpose was being launched from the second heaven through the Earthly means currently available to them in 1975. The demonic kingdom still had plenty to work with...

Uel looked up from his desk and politely said, *"Wait one moment, please."*

Uel stood up and turned to the filing cabinets. They were stacked in such a way that the top shelf could not be seen, as if to disappear into the heavens. With one swipe of Uel's hand, the cabinet sections moved swiftly upwards like a fast moving conveyor system. All at once, the filing cabinets immediately stopped moving and Uel was looking at the file for BLAKE-12271975-1200.

He reluctantly took the file, turned to the DLD, and said, *"I need to read this disclaimer to you. Its mandatory. You have 24 hours to return this file. Should you fail to return this file, you will be in contempt of court and your DLD certificate will be revoked with immediate effect. You are not allowed to copy or otherwise reproduce the contents of this file. You are not authorized to take this file beyond the Library of the Court of Heaven, which means the second heaven is off limits. Should you take this file to the second heaven....."*

The DLD impatiently interrupted, *"Yes, yes, I know, I will be in contempt of court and my DLD certificate will be revoked with immediate effect. Will you get on with it, already?"* Uel smiled and calmly said, *"I'm only doing my job sir. Now, let me continue. You are not authorized to visit any member of Blake's family currently in the earth until this investigation is complete and we have rendered a verdict in said case. You are not authorized to steal, kill, or destroy from any member of Blake's family until this investigation is complete and the court has rendered a verdict in said case......"*

At this point, the DLDs eyes were glazing over, and he lost interest in actually listening. He had heard the disclaimer from the

Director of Lineage Records for 2,000 plus years and it was getting old. Uel went on an on reading a document that was comparable to a cell phone contract or a mortgage agreement. The DLD had to stand there and listen to all of it. Jesus loves this part. He occasionally visits the Court of Heaven for a supervisory tour, just to check on the workers and bless them openly. On this day, as Uel continued to read the disclosure statement that must be read to any DLD requesting records, Jesus walked in...

Jesus was smiling as He walked in. He was eating a pomegranate and singing a new song. He even added a dance step to his walk as he greeted the workers in the Lineage Records department. They all stood to their feet and began praising Him with their hands raised high in the air. It was a full on praise break, and the DLD had to stand there and listen to every minute of it. He shook his head in disgust as the sounds of praise swept through the department. Sounds in Heaven are heard, seen, tasted, and felt. Every sense is awakened when praises to God are raised in unison. It was becoming unbearable for the DLD, who was forced to listen to the long disclosure statement still being read to him.

Finally, the Director of Lineage Records stopped and asked him, *"Do you concur?"*

The DLD said impatiently with his hand reaching out toward Blake's file, *"Yes. Now, give me the record already!"*

Uel politely handed him the file and said, *"He is the Lord Almighty. His Righteous judgements endure forever. Have a Heavenly day!"*

The DLD, with file in hand, ran out of the waiting area and headed towards the Court Library located 5 doors down. In his mind he already knew what to look for. This was an urgent case, and he would stop at nothing to uncover something to pass along to his team out in the field - in the earthly realm. DLDs are basically handlers in the demonic kingdom, much like a handler in the intelligence community. Demons can only create plans using actionable intelligence they receive from the DLDs, because the pending contracts found in lineage records give them legal precedence for their plots against individual people. Wicked spirits and street level demons only have access to this level of information through their handler. Otherwise, they run the risk of overstepping their legal authority in the spirit realm. For this, they are immediately punished by satan for their misstep, and they are usually relegated to tormenting duties in hell. This DLD wanted no part of that. He was experienced enough to recognize that legal boundaries could not be crossed in the Court of Heaven. Even his contacts who were assigned to work directly with the church of satan were not privy to this level of documentation. Like every other case he has worked over the past 2,000 plus years, he only had 24 hours to get to dig out enough legal ammunition to file an indictment against Blake.

The DLD always began with what he already knew. Information was previously collected by street level demons and included in the report, prior to it ending up on his desk. The report concluded that Blake was indeed being birthed in the natural to parents who were not in blood covenant with Jesus. The report also included several declarations made by the family of the parents, to include, *"If Sarah has a baby, it will turn out just like her."* The problem with this statement is this - it is true. Unless Heaven intervenes, Sarah's unresolved generational curses will simply pass to another generation through her DNA. Blake will be destined to battle drug addiction. Due to Sarah's lack of a father figure in her life, Blake will be susceptible to the influence of the *Orphan spirit*. It was definitely a mess. However, this was a very common situation. The DLD was experienced in handling this deadly combination. He has brought down many people in the same situation through the years. Generational curses proved to be the most covert path into the life of mankind. Unfortunately, the body of Christ has yet to fully understand this. An awareness of the function of the Court of Heaven was still being released, but at a slow rate. Like all revelation of scripture, half of the ecclesia receives it while the other half speaks against it, calling it *"new age"*. This always plays out in favor of the demonic kingdom. Even the demonic kingdom refuses to speak out against the decrees of Satan. They understand the most basic spiritual principle concerning team efficiency - *"a house divided will always fall."*

As he entered the legal library, there were many different rooms and desks. Books were organized in typical library fashion because Heaven is the blueprint for everything we see in the Earthly realm. Libraries, court houses, temples and living quarters are all shadows of what already existed in the Heavenly realm before man was created. Man usually thinks their ideas are unique. Scripture declares that there is really *"nothing new under the sun"*. All good gifts, to include witty ideas and inventions come down from Heaven - more specifically - *The Father of Lights*. These are released into the Earth through the mind, will, and emotions of mankind. Often times, through those the world would never choose to steward it. The Father, in his mercy, often releases ideas to people because He knows it will give them enough resource to provide for several generations of family members. One simple idea from Heaven gives birth to things like, electricity, the printing press, the combustion engine and the internet. These ideas, when applied to improving everyday life for humanity, pushes the entire species forward. More importantly, these ideas push the ecclesia forward.

When life improves for the whole of humanity, the ecclesia is armed with fresh weapons to fight the good fight of faith. The Spirit of Religion tries to convince the church world that technology is evil. This of course, is a lie manufactured in the demonic kingdom. The DLD took his seat, with Blake's file in hand, ready to investigate. He was sitting in the very idea the Father released to mankind thousands of years ago. A simple legal library, built to store crucial information. It is ironic how the demonic kingdom wages war with the very ideas the Father releases to improve the lives of His children. The DLD was too far gone to recognize this truth. He no longer recognizes Abba as having any say in his life or pursuit of promotion. To him, God has a record of holding back. Therefore, he no longer trusts God's processes.

The DLD opened the file and turned to the table of contents. He searched for a particular entry marked, *"Ancestry"*. Every human has an ancestry that is recorded in the lineage records. This lineage record is updated immediately when a new soul is released. Since the DLD received a tip concerning Blake's birth, and since his name was yet to be recorded, he was basically digging into the ancestry for anything he could use against him. This was a common practice for him. He was trying to stay one step ahead of Heaven. The file was just created after Blake's book of Destiny was filed. Much to the surprise of the lineage records director, he was becoming more skilled at his job than ever before. The demonic kingdom was getting bolder and more skilled than ever before. Or so they thought.

The truth is, Heaven is never behind or lacking in the stewardship of actionable intelligence. Digging through Blake's lineage would only uncover the history of Blake's family and any contracts with demons still pending payment. This is always the starting point for the DLD to set a mission in motion for his team operating in the field. They were waiting for information to act on. The DLD's job was to find it and arm them with the best intelligence he could gather. Satan had never failed to authorize a mission that originated from a DLD operating in the court of Heaven. After all, it was Satan's primary mode of operation in the Old Testament. He knew from day one, when man was created, the legal ramifications of their disobedience. He went after Eve, in the garden, with all the skill he could muster. His plan was to lure mankind into a legal battle that would rage on for centuries. After all, most of the five-fold ministry officials in the Earth were still preaching about how Jesus died for their sins. They were nowhere near ready to teach fresh revelation of scripture concerning the Court of Heaven and how it operates. This was a prime time to ramp up the efforts to steal, kill, and destroy from mankind. Especially the ecclesia. Especially the five-fold ministry officials operating throughout the world. The demonic kingdom always focuses on the area of God's Word we are most ignorant of. In this season, the legal ramification of generational curses was the ammunition being used - to its maximum effect.

  The DLD read through Blake's ancestry. He noticed a trend. Each generation, dating back to 60 A.D., was involved in the ecclesia. There were several believers in Jesus recorded during each generational phase. This finding was common. It doesn't affect the demonic kingdom's bottom line to see people say yes to Jesus. They are much more concerned with those who actually live in agreement with God's Word. Saying yes to Jesus gets you into Heaven. Living in agreement with God's Word brings Heaven to Earth. They are even more concerned about those who answer the call to preach and teach God's word. These people are dangerous to the demonic kingdom. Generations are counted in accordance with the average life-span of the fathers, whose names were recorded for eternity. The DLD noticed something he termed as *"mission critical information"* - each generation had a Pastor operating in a full time ministry assignment. This sparked his interest and began to dig deeper. Each Pastor, dating back to around 300 A.D. died prematurely. They all died from Crohn's disease. He also noticed that since around 500 A.D., they were all attacked in the area of finances, leaving them completely discouraged about their calling. They all quit the ministry and died with many unfulfilled dreams. They died having never fulfilled much of what was declared in their Book of Destiny. The DLD began to smile. This was what he needed. This would be a simple mission to steal, kill and destroy Blake's identity, purpose and destiny. He wouldn't even have to get creative. The legal library in the second heaven would now have the other pieces of the puzzle, thanks to his shrewd legal skills.

Then, something jumped off the pages at him. Around the time of Earthly existence for one of the Pastors in Blake's lineage - 240 A.D. - an agreement was made with the *spirit of religion*. This particular Pastor came into agreement with Cessationism - declared by the Apostle Paul as a *"doctrine of devils"*. It was being taught regularly as he attended Seminary in Northern Ireland. He agreed that the gifts of the Spirit and the five-fold ministry was for the book of Acts only. He came into agreement with this teaching through the influence of his Seminary professors at the time. He had no idea the chain of events that would follow, for his own life and the ministry of all who would come after him. This teaching was handed down for generations. So were the legal ramifications of it. In the spirit realm, you don't physically sign contracts with demons. Willful disobedience to God's word is treated as a breach of contract. The only way out is to repent, ask forgiveness, and live in agreement with scripture. Otherwise, the demonic kingdom has legal access to all aspects of your life. Health, finances and relationships are all accessible, much like an FBI seizer of property. When you choose with your will to agree with a lie, you have officially come into agreement with the liar and now live in opposition to God's Word. Just as Adam and Eve sold mankind into spiritual slavery and sin consciousness through one act of agreement with the enemy, so did this Pastor in Blake's lineage. It only takes two in the spirit realm to ratify any contract. This is done through the power of willful agreement.

The DLD was more than excited about this information. He could examine the actual contract in the Demonic Legal Library where contracts of this nature are kept forever. There, he would find the signature of the actual demon who originated the contract with the Pastor in question. Once a contract is endorsed by both parties, it's easy to enhance the original agreement with amendments to the contract. One lie always gives birth to more. This particular demon was skilled at his job. The DLD could see the evidence of an amendment. After 240 A.D., all following generations of Pastors began their ministry in scriptural error, making it easy to amend the agreement. What started with Cessationism, gave birth to, what the demonic kingdom laughingly calls *the theology of sickness*. The spirit of poverty, and his team, quickly moved in to seal the deal by convincing subsequent generations that poverty is God's way for increased Holiness. Their goal was to choke out the generational mantle for church leadership from Blake's lineage - and it was working.

Every Pastor in Blake's lineage died prematurely from a disease that is often healed by God's power, through the prophetic act of the laying on of hands, and releasing the anointing deposited in every believer in Jesus – its power breaks the yoke. They also died in poverty, unable to feed their families and provide an inheritance for their children's children. The basic promises found in God's word concerning provision and health were never manifested in their Earthly ministries. This left a seed of doubt for every individual called to be a Pastor in Blake's bloodline. This was just what the DLD was looking for. He had enough intelligence to commission a new team to take out Blake before he was even born.

And if that didn't work, it wasn't a big deal to him. Very few of the five-fold ministry officials he has seen born ever fulfill their destiny, anyway. The ecclesia is a mess, and the demonic kingdom knows it. The demonic kingdom isn't afraid of more humans being born. The only time they fear us is when we truly learn how to live in the Kingdom…

The DLD made mental notes, since he wasn't authorized to copy or reproduce Blake's file. In his mind, it was an open-shut case. They didn't even have to try anything new. Blake, if he was to be born at all, would live out his days trying to figure out his calling with erroneous biblical precepts. Blake would also die prematurely and never fulfill his calling at the level of his God given identity. He might operate in his purpose for a while, but he wouldn't reach the masses. He would be lucky to get 50 people to follow him as a Pastor and he would perpetuate the error he was taught to another generation. Another generation of sick and impoverished believers in Jesus was going to be the fruit of his ministry. The pressures of ministry life alone would bring Blake to his knees often as he tries to figure out how to pay the bills with an unknown pending contract originated by the spirit of poverty. The spirit of poverty would always have access to his finances, at the worst times possible. The DLD was overjoyed. He already had a plan in his mind and was ready to lay the groundwork. The DLD stood up from the research desk, picked up the file, pushed in his chair, and paused for a moment. He smiled once again and made his way back to the Lineage Records waiting area with great haste.

He had to grab the momentum and set the wheels in motion with his team on the ground. It was go time. In spirit realm fashion, he closed his eyes and envisioned where he wanted to be, and suddenly reappeared in his second heaven office. He then walked over to his desk and pushed the intercom button on his desk phone labeled, *Power of Georgia (POG)*. This gave him immediate access to the highest ranking demon in the region. A DLD has access to every branch of demonic government, to include satan himself. His function is most similar to the CIA Director in America. With one acceptation - he is not authorized to delegate the handling of five-fold ministry steal, kill, destroy missions. These were to be handled directly much in the same way the CIA Director in America was hands on with the Cuban Missile crisis in 1962. Missions of that nature are of the highest priority to the protection of the nation. Most other missions are handed down to the principality covering the region of birth for a human. In this case, the mission was to be handled directly by the DLD. He was just giving the principality a heads up concerning what was happening in his region. This often caused conflict because of the nature of the demonic kingdom. Everyone is in competition making it harder to get things done efficiently. The DLD had history with the Power of Georgia and very much disliked working with him for conducting missions in his region. He just had to put all the politics aside and get to the point with him. Afterall, they were winning, and the end seemed closer now than at any point in human history. Things were looking good for the demonic kingdom, and they were gaining ground in the US and abroad.

    The year was 1975 and several major world events positioned the demonic kingdom for advancement. Heaven was also positioning key leaders in advance of these incidents because, nothing takes Heaven by surprise. The British Conservative Party chooses its first women leader, Margaret Thatcher. This pushed society forward in its view of the role of women in leadership. Satan responded with a great victory of his own. The Vietnam War ends as Communist forces take Saigon and South Vietnam surrenders unconditionally. Heaven responded with compassion when the US carried out Vietnam "Operation Babylift" bringing Vietnamese orphans to the US. Heaven also released fresh technology when Sony introduces Betamax videotapes and Matsushita / JVC introduce VHS. One of the very first blockbuster films, Jaws, is released during June. Heaven also allowed the Suez Canal to reopen for the first time since the Six-Day War. This set the stage for commerce to pick up and function with less disruption.

Satan continued to attack the economy through the creation of damaging policy causing the Unemployment Rate in the US to reach 9.2% and recession is officially acknowledged by President Ford. US alleys felt the financial pinch as well. Britain's inflation rate jumps 25%. The First ever strike by Doctors in the US causes hospitals to reduce services. The UK implements the Sex Discrimination and Equal Pay Act which pushed humanity forward. However, 1975 marked the beginning of 15 years of civil war between Maronite Christians and Muslim militias in Lebanon. This shed doubt and unbelief through the world as to the nature of true Christianity. It also made them wonder if being a Christian was actually worth it. Bill Gates and Paul Allen develop a BASIC program for the Altair 8800 which was Heaven's plan to place new technology in the hands of humanity. Unfortunately, due to man's constant need to monetize new technology, the average household would not have access to this breakthrough for many years to come. The demonic kingdom responded with the assassination of King Faisal of Saudi Arabia and sending Baader-Meinhof guerrillas to take 11 hostages at the West German embassy in Stockholm.

It seemed as though for every blessing from Heaven for mankind, the demonic kingdom was empowered to bring chaos and destruction. It seemed like a slippery slope for the US. Just two years prior in 1973, Roe vs Wade ended in a landmark decision protecting a woman's right to have an abortion. This was the most significant demonic contract ever made by a nation. It was simply a national return to ancient idol worship. And it wasn't just any nation - it was the US Supreme Court. The contract was ratified by the *Principality* ruling over America. His name is *Molech*. Principalities rule over nations. Powers rule over states or regions. Wicked spirits serve at the commissioning of their Supervisory Power and conduct most of the one on one attacks on humans. This contract would open doors to the demonic kingdom like never before. Amendment after amendment was added to the original contract in the Court of Heaven adding curses to the land and to its people. Spirits of Homosexuality and Perversion were released into the public school system, youth groups, and youth athletics. The mainstream church received a heavy dose of influence from these spirits as well. Since the subject of the *"spirit realm"* was being ignored by the American church, the societal influences of believers in Jesus was being manipulated and abolished unwittingly. All this added up to one thing in the DLDs mind, *"We are winning..."*

The DLD thought about this as the phone rang several times. Finally, the Power of Georgia answered, *"What do you need, I'm busy."*

The DLD replied with contempt, *"If it were not for me, you would still be hustling street level steal, kill, and destroy missions. A little respect is reasonable."*

The Power of Georgia responded with even more aggression, *"Stop throwing that up in my face. That was 200 years ago when this dirt pile of a nation was founded. Half the founders weren't even Christians, they were Freemasons, which we have a strong foothold with. To be honest, I'm ready for another promotion and when it comes, I'll remember conversations like this. I don't forgive or forget."*

The DLD held the phone away from his head demonstrating the fact that he hated dealing with *Powers*. They were all power hungry and willing to do anything to get promoted.

The POG ended his outburst by saying, *"Is this in reference to today's soul release schedule?"*

The DLD, still irritated said, *"Yes. It's a steal, kill, destroy (SKD) Mission Level 1. File access code BLAKE12271975-1200. I'm sending the findings to you as a courtesy. I'll be handling this one personally while working with wicked spirits in your region. Stay out of my way, and I'll stay out of yours. I'm already the agent of record on this thing, so don't even think about taking the credit for it when it all comes down."*

The POG countered, *"I see. Always working the legal angles and getting all the credit. Lord Satan gives you way too much authority. He always has."*

The DLD replied, *"Don't worry about me and my business. I'll do my job, and you do yours. As you know, I have jurisdiction on this, and wont tolerate any mishandling of information on your part. I'm hereby taking command of any street level spirits in the field, especially in Whitfield County, GA where Blake is to be birthed into the natural realm. I'm also authorized to assign a permanent agent to this case from your region, effective immediately."*

The POG was brewing with anger at this point. He had no choice but to recognize the authority of the DLD and grant access to the requested stipulations of the SKD mission. After all, it was a Level 1 mission. These types of missions are well known in the demonic kingdom. They were to stop at nothing to erase Blake from the timeline and nullify his eventual impact on humanity as a Pastor. Level 1 missions are reserved for any five-fold ministry official being birthed into the natural realm. The POG was in full agreement with the importance of the mission. His own lust for more power is what caused him to be jealous of the DLDs authority. Every Principality knew that when the current DLD to the Court of Heaven called - it was important. It didn't help him process the call any better. A DLD is one of the highest ranks they can hold in the demonic kingdom - he just wished it was him.

The POG reluctantly said, *"Is there anything else?"* The DLD responded with, *"No that will be all. I'll be in your region at some time in the next week or so. Make sure the proper provisions are made and touch base with your disciples in the church of satan. I'll be visiting them as well through a medium in their midst. I always include them in the plan due to their knowledge of the region and proximity to earthly relationships. I'll take it from there. Are there any questions?"*

The POG responded with relief that the conversation was coming to a close, *"No, we're good."* Then he hung up.

The DLD made a mental note of this disrespectful act. This particular Power was officially on his list...

About that time, *Adriel's* spirit realm communicator rang with a notification. Notifications are sent from the Guardian Angel (GA) data monitoring station near the Holy Mountain of God. This department delivers actionable intelligence concerning humans to the GAs in the field. He glanced at his armored forearm where the display screen was located. The words were bright green, and the language was otherworldly. Portions of this same heavenly language are released into the consciousness of Holy Spirit filled believers in Jesus. It's the language of Heaven and it's been called *"tongues"* by the ecclesia for hundreds of years. In its written form, it mostly resembles a combination of Hebrew and Greek, with a touch of Japanese script. It's a powerful language with the ability to create. It's the language used by God when He *"spoke"* the worlds into existence.

Adriel recognized the message. It was a common notification to alert him of any and all activity concerning Blake's life plan. It translates in English, *"Top Secret: DLD lineage investigation complete. DLD made contact with the Power of Georgia. Set to begin official SKD mission level 1. Level 1 angelic authority granted."*

This made Adriel smile.

He had a feeling that this mission was big.

Level 1 angelic authority isn't often granted. In most cases, angels are to remain unseen and work in obscurity. In scripture, Level 1 authority is used in the case of Zechariah, also known as the father of John the Baptist. The angel had authority to use whatever means necessary to ensure the life plan of John the Baptist was fulfilled in accordance with his Book of Destiny. When the angel sensed unbelief - which negates the power of the Word of God in the natural ream - he shut down his vocal chords. This same technique is used on the vocal chords of animal life. They already possess the biological characteristics to speak. God is simply restricting their ability to speak intelligible words until the millennial reign of Christ on the Earth begins. Vocal chords were simply liberated momentarily by God when the donkey preached to Balaam. They were restricted for approximately 9 months in the case of Zechariah due to his unbelief. This was to protect the life plan of John the Baptist. The angel who was given this assignment to make a decree to Zechariah had no choice but to use his Level 1 authority...

This notification meant one thing - its game time. All the training and past experiences prepared Adriel for this assignment. It was a promotion he was graciously given after many seasons of faithful service to the Kingdom. He never failed at any of his assignments, accept for one. He didn't feel guilt or shame about it. He learned from it. In Heaven, all creatures great and small are given the freedom to grow into their function. Adriel has been discipled for thousands of years and fully understands the complexities of GA life. He is always on call. He has been given a season of rest after he successfully delivered his last human to the gates of Heaven. He was rewarded openly for this and promoted to Level 1 status. He is very excited about this new assignment and longs to see Blake fulfill his destiny. His heart burns for his assignment and wants nothing more than to please Abba. He knows that he doesn't have to earn Abba's love through performance. He already has that.

His heart burns with a deep passion for humanity. He has watched for thousands of years as humans waste time on inferior realities and commit their works to idolatry. He works tirelessly when he is on mission to help his assigned human by diligently protecting their life plan. Some of the humans he has guarded lived an entire life with no awareness of the supernatural. One human in particular, gave his life to Jesus, but sat under erroneous teaching their entire life. Time after time, Adriel intervened on his behalf without any recognition. He wished he could have done more to awaken his assigned human to the spirit realm. He simply did the best he could while operating in Level 2 authority. He simply stewarded what he was given, and Abba graciously gave him more. This is the way in the Kingdom. In the world, mistakes keep you from promotion. In the Kingdom, mistakes prepare you for promotion. Adriel never felt more prepared than he does right now.

Adriel quickly made his way - via spirit realm travel - to the Court of Heaven. Spirit realm travel is instant. All Adriel had to do was think about where he wanted to go. If he entered the Earthly realm - which is defined as anywhere inside the atmosphere of Earth - he was to remain unseen. Of course, *seers* in the Kingdom can often see his outline, stature and general appearance wherever he was located. However, Level 1 GAs have the authority to manifest completely within view of humans. The choice to do this is a very sobering responsibility. Adriel has only done this once in his 5,000 year career. In the beginning of his career, when the current canonized Bible as we know it, was not yet circulated, it was a dangerous proposition to fully manifest to a human. He ran the risk of setting off yet another religion. The Mayans and Egyptians both were culturally affected due to appearances of angels. They built belief systems around the appearance of angels. They set up idols and worshiped the image of these angels who visited them and shared technology from Heaven.

Adriel wanted no part of that. He was a soldier at heart and fought many battles in the spirit realm on behalf of mankind. He was very careful to observe and intervene using covert methods. Manifesting in full view of humans was risky. Humans cant really handle the glory that escapes from their presence. Several biblical accounts of angel visitations begin in the same way. The angel usually has to say, *"Don't be afraid."* This is because an angel has what is known as a glorified body. The earthly matter humans are made of has an expiration date. A glorified body is made of something entirely different. A glorified body is directly connected to the Father and has a different molecular structure. The elements found in a glorified body isn't on Earth's periodic table. This is why earthly scientist often mock scripture. Scripture shows us what is possible. Science simply studies what is probable in accordance with the level of innovation mankind is currently walking in. Adriel knows the level mankind is at. Even though in 1975, there are several breakthroughs being released from Heaven, Adriel is still cautious. However, with Level 1 authority, Adriel is prepared to stop at nothing to protect Blake's life plan.

Adriel quickly closed his eyes and chose with his will to reappear in the Court of Heaven - specifically the Lineage Records Department.

When he appeared by walking through the office wall, the director was pleasantly startled and jumped to his feet. *"That never gets old. I love how we make the DLD use the stairs and the doors, but Abba's Secret Service can go wherever they need to go using spirit realm travel methods. Do you think the demonic kingdom will ever understand that they are no match for us?"*

They shared a laugh as Adriel replied, *"Nope. They are truly clueless as to the power and dominion of the Kingdom of Heaven. Through the years I have witnessed the Redeemed Ones walking in this truth more and more. They are learning to see themselves the way that Abba sees them. They have been born again and filled with the Spirit of the Resurrected Savior. They have been given weapons specifically fashioned for them. Their prayer language enables them to communicate with us on a spiritual level. When they pray and fast, their spirit man is emboldened to believe for more. They have access to the Throne of Grace, The Court of Heaven, and the Exchange Market. They have access to the Books of Destiny to guide one another in the Earthly realm through prophecy. The list goes on and on as to what Jesus purchased at the Cross."*

The Lineage Records Director agreed and said, *"Amen. How can I serve you today?"*

Adriel smiled as he looked at the records and communicated with the director only with his spiritual voice. In Heaven, conversations can take place in this fashion. Words are mostly reserved for creating. Citizens of Heaven have the capacity to use both means of communication. In this instance, Adriel didn't want to alert the second heaven with his words. He was undercover in the earthly realm, but in Heaven, everyone, to include the second heaven knew who he was. He was safe to communicate anyway he wished. However, Adriel was aware that the DLD could be within earshot since he also had access to the Court of Heaven. The director heard the request,

"I need permanent access to file description BLAKE12271975-1200. Guardian Angel access code 183845732. I have Level 1 authority on this one",

with his spiritual ears.

The same ears that Jesus declared to His followers they should listen with.

The Director nodded his head up and down as if to agree, turned around and located the file cabinet for Lineage Records. After the cabinet shuffled in its usual manner, he grabbed the file and handed it to Adriel. There were no disclosure statements to read to him. That was a policy created to govern DLD access. Adriel had complete freedom to accomplish his mission. He could copy this record in order to access it later. He did just that as he waved his hand over the file. His armored forearm unit that housed his communication screen lit up with bright green script and an icon indicating that files were being copied.

Once complete, he looked up at the director and said, *"Thank you my friend. May the Lord Bless you and keep you."* The director replied, *"His Righteous Judgements endure forever."*

This was a typical reply reserved for the end of conversations in Heaven. It was as common as *"See you later"* or *"Have a great day"*. The language of Heaven is full of life and positivity. Everyone is honored and valued for who the Father made them to be. Every task is tethered to the overall mission - to co-labor with man to bring Heaven to Earth.

Adriel closed his eyes and traveled to the waiting area for

Books of Destiny. He needed to do the same thing he did with the Blake's lineage record.

After reappearing in the waiting area, the clerk immediately saw him and responded with, *"I have it right here. We received notification of your access and authority level for this one."*

He reached out and handed Adriel the book.

Adriel waved his hand over the book and copied it in the same fashion as the previous lineage record. He now had the key information he needed to begin the mission. The DLD only had access to Blake's past. Even after Blake's birth, this level of access would remain in effect. However, Adriel had access to Blake's past, present and future. The limitations placed on the demonic kingdom can't be understated. The governance, care for souls, and quality of Heaven is superior in every way. Heaven's citizens are empowered to do their jobs well. Adriel never has to piece anything together with second hand information. He knows, at all times, what the Father is saying and doing concerning Blake's destiny. Adriel understands the superiority of what has been declared in Blake's Book of Destiny. His job is to protect the life plan and ensure Blake takes another step in the right direction in each season of life. As Blake learns more and more about the Kingdom, Adriel is there to help protect the seed planted in him. Of course, the first challenge is to protect the birth of Blake's soul into the earthly realm. He is aware of the generational curses already attached to his lineage. He is also aware of the words of death declared by family members. It's a delicate dance of sorts. Adriel will need to draw strength from every experience he has had over the thousands of years he has served mankind. He isn't the least bit afraid or anxious. Fear doesn't exist in Heaven.

Adriel contemplated the declarations recorded in the Book of Destiny concerning Blake. Starting with the Father's declaration, it reads,

"*his Earthly name will be called Blake which means "Shining One". He will be circumcised the eighth day after his birth and will win many souls to my Kingdom. He will grow to be 6 feet 1 inch and will carry a deep discernment in the spirit realm. His features will be handsome and will carry the ability to operate comfortably in front of people. He will have an average build, with average athletic ability but above average intelligence. He will come to know me at a very young age because we must capture his heart early due to the amount of impact he will have in the Earth for my Kingdom. Due to generational blessings already established in his bloodline, announced by his ancestors through prayer and declaration, he will have a natural ability to understand and write music, as well as books.*"

Then he contemplated the declaration made my Jesus,

"*Blake's Earthly appointment will be as a Pastor/Teacher in the ecclesia. He will carry a deep discernment for the Word of God and will desire to study and meditate on my Word day and night. People will naturally desire to talk to him and tell him their deepest trauma. As a Pastor, he will care for many people and always desire to help them. As a Teacher, I will open his mind in extraordinary ways and deposit the science of my Word in his heart. The Bible for him will be like a five or six page book. His teachings will be deep but simple, just like mine were during my Earthly ministry.*"

Finally, Adriel meditated on the declaration made by Holy Spirit,

"*Blake will be set apart from birth with the following gifts - strong commitment to duty, communication ability and love for the arts. Blake will gravitate towards visual art and literature as a means of learning. Blake will have a natural ability to discern truth in scripture and will be a natural magnet for hurting people. Blake will carry a creative capacity that is above average and will see the lesson in everything. This will enable Blake to teach and preach the way Jesus did during his Earthly ministry, using everyday things to communicate the Word of God. Once empowered by my Spirit, Blake will have a strong anointing to hear words of wisdom, knowledge and prophecy. His strong sense of duty will lead him to seek deeper truth and greater anointing as a minister of the Gospel message and teacher of the Holy Scriptures. His divine gifts will enable him to be a natural lifelong learner and seeker of truth. This will protect his destiny from the spirit of Religion which seeks to keep man stuck in a fixed mindset. With the right Pastor in his ear, Blake will always find a way to repent and adjust his thinking to align himself with what the Father is saying and doing in the Earth."*

Adriel smiled and thought about the privilege he was given to serve Blake throughout his earthly existence. This job never gets old for him…

A SOUL IS RELEASED...

It is written in the Word,

"And the dust returns to the earth as it was, and the spirit returns to God who gave it."

The Father sat on his throne in deep reflection. The echoes of praise swept through the throne room.

"Holy, Holy, Holy, is the Lord God Almighty, who was, and is, and is to come..."

This song never gets old to the Father. It wasn't being sung on repeat for thousands of years to remind Him of His own identity. It was to remind everyone else. Much in the same way titles are used in the natural realm. A title doesn't remind the person bearing the title of anything. A title simply reminds others of their God given identity, purpose and destiny. It's an act of honor when we address one another in the earthly realm by title. It announces, *"this is how I see you. You are a Precious Saint, Woman of God, Pastor, or Teacher."* Many called Jesus *"Teacher"*, because that is how they saw him. Many did not. The enemy loves to erode the culture of honor in the earthly realm by declaring that everyone is the same. This simply isn't the case. Everyone is worthy of honor in some measure because they are made in the image of God. Even when they are a pre-believer, they are complete with many gifts deposited within them from birth. Those who labor in the Word and doctrine are worthy of double honor, in the earthly realm and in Heaven. When we honor someone in accordance with how the Father sees them, we are given access to what they carry. The sound of this song can be heard, seen and even tasted as it flows from the throne-room to the far reaches of Heaven. It reminds everyone, the Father is worthy of honor. No matter what amount of freedom is given to

Heavenly citizens, this song of praise reminds them - the Father is indeed *Holy*. He is completely set apart from anyone, yet he chooses to share his authority with man.

The release of a soul is one of the biggest events in Heaven. Even with the legal entanglements already present in Blake's lineage, Heaven isn't afraid for his future. Even with the terrible situation he is to be birthed into, Heaven doesn't trembled over earthly circumstances. Even with the small success rate for five-fold ministers in the Earth, Heaven isn't concerned about failure. Heaven is always full of faith, hope and love. Even though roughly 1% of all five-fold ministers released into the Earth ever step into a full measure of their identity, purpose and destiny - Heaven doesn't stop releasing them. Much in the same way that Jesus released 72 followers to practice healing the sick, raising the dead, casting out demons and cleansing lepers. This was after the 12 disciples were still in need of more training in the area of deliverance - Jesus released more. Heaven isn't afraid of the learning curve mankind has to overcome. Heaven stands ready to serve and facilitate the success of every citizen, no matter how many times it takes to get it right. Heaven knows full well that when a soul is released with the weighty assignment of empowering and equipping the Saints, there will be mistakes. Man holds grudges and cancels leaders. Heaven forgives and relaunches them.

There will be seasons of loneliness and feelings of inadequacy for Blake as a Pastor. As any five-fold minister develops, they will have to repent and reassess their theology. They will undergo seasons of low self-esteem and have to die to self. They may often work in a role subservient to another leader. They will have to navigate the difficulties found in Kingdom life and learn to forgive. They will not be honored in the earthly realm in accordance with how Heaven sees them. They will have to maneuver about the earthly realm, having the same stresses in life to include raising children and paying bills. On top of the normal stressors of life, they will carry the weight of their calling. The Father is aware of the challenges awaiting Blake. As always, The Father also has full confidence in the gifts the Trinity Team placed within him, and the future declared in Bake's Book of Destiny.

Suddenly, the Father stands up and makes a declaration so thunderous that it shook the Heavens, *"Let us gather once again for the release of a soul into the Earth."*

Then He sat back down awaiting the citizens of Heaven to find their places.

In that moment all of heaven began to gather. Millions upon millions of Saints rushed to the throne room. They were all robed in white. However their robes were brilliantly adorned with precious gemstones. These gemstones were so dazzling and beautiful that when the light of the father reflected off of them, it was blinding. Radiant waves of the Fathers Glory swept through every crevasse of Heaven. His light reached to the farthest reaches of the Heavenly inhabitants. Those who were in their houses were suddenly aware that something monumental was taking place. Souls are released in passionate spontaneity, just as they are conceived in the earth. It's a beautiful culmination of romance when the Father decides to release a soul. It is also a very sobering time for the Father.

He thinks back each time to when He released the soul of His son into the Earth to fulfill His purpose and destiny. He did this knowing that the world would reject Him openly and murder Him on a cross. Each time the Father releases a soul, He foresees the pain and rejection an Apostle, Prophet, Pastor, Teacher or Evangelist will endure at the hands of both believers and pre-believers. This does not stop Him from releasing more. The time has come for the ecclesia to rise up and become fully manifested sons and daughters of God. The time has come for revival in the Earth. The time has come for wrongs to be made right. Truth must be declared from the pulpits and yet to be created virtual platforms, across the Earth. After all, the year is 1975. Blake will not even have access to the internet until later in life. He will have to depend on his teachers, coaches and Pastors to direct him in the ways of the Kingdom. They won't always know what they are talking about. The Father isn't afraid of any of these obstacles in Blake's way. In time, Blake will learn the lessons needed to overcome any obstacle to his purpose and destiny…

Millions upon millions of Heaven's citizens poured in to the throne room, from every nation, tribe, and language.

The throne room enlarges to accommodate the increased attendance. In Heaven, the laws of physics are completely different. Objects can change motion even if a force doesn't act on it. Even if the force on an object isn't equal to its mass times its acceleration, it can be moved or expanded. Everything in Heaven is composed of light. Therefore all objects can be moved without an equal and opposite force acting upon it. All created beings living there have been glorified. This is not the absence of matter or physical material we would expect here on earth; it is simply the infusion of light that takes place within the matter already present. The elements humans are made of; Oxygen, hydrogen, nitrogen, carbon, calcium, and phosphorus are still present in a glorified body. However, when they are infused with the Father's Glory, they now carry the missing element that was lost in the garden when Adam and Even disobeyed the Father's command.

The Father's Glory is a measurable substance all to itself.

In Heaven, you can see, feel, hear, and taste it. The Father's Glory doesn't show up on our earthly periodic table…

All Heavenly creatures great and small rush to get a front row seat. The Father has released every soul into the Earth in the same way for thousands of years since the Trinity Team made mankind in their image for the purpose of rulership. Starting with Cain and Abel, souls have been released in this fashion - due to the failure of Adam. The declarations made by the Trinity Team, recorded in the Books of Destiny were supposed to be fashioned by Adam as the head of his family and the first human. It was why the Father had him name all the animals in an attempt to teach him to steward this power. The Old Testament demonstrated that names carry identity, purpose, and destiny all in one.

Since language is used to create in Heaven, Adam was being trained to create - it was to be his chief instrument in the dominion of Earth. This will be restored in the Millennial Kingdom. He was to rule over the earth, declare the identity, purpose and destiny of his children, and manage the landscape while giving birth to a civilization of rulers. The mechanism by which to create was through spoken word. This was modeled by the Father when He spoke the worlds into existence. Speech is the most powerful tool in the spirit realm. Through speech we pray, decree, declare and prophecy things into existence. This is the way Heaven functions. Adam had an opportunity, for a season, to walk in absolute power and authority over the Earth. His disobedience set us back thousands of years.

The roar of the crowd could have been measured on a Richter Scale at level 10. Waves of laughter and fellowship reverberated through Heaven like impressions of energy comparable to a Super Bowl touchdown or a World Cup Soccer goal being scored – but millions of times more powerful. Roars of conversation seemed to grow louder and louder.

This is the *"sound of many waters and mighty thunderings"*

spoken of by the seers who recorded their encounters with Heaven in scripture.

Heaven has many inhabitants. Therefore, when there is a gathering, the movement creates energy. Occasions such as this are pleasantly noisy and filled with joy. Many generations of people can be seen walking to the throne room while continuing their conversations. They could have simply closed their eyes and reappeared there, but there is no realization of time in Heaven. They had rather walk there with their closest friends and family so they can continue their conversations. If something needs to happen now, citizens are energized into action by the Father's voice. No one wants to miss out on what the Father is saying or doing. When He speaks, they all know it is time to come be a part of something extraordinary. The release of a soul is one of the most exciting events in Heaven.

As Heaven's citizens gather, some are within sight of the Father, and many are not. To facilitate the crowd, enormous high definition monitors are placed in full view of each section of one hundred thousand spectators. Its first come first serve seating, but there is no rush. Everyone will have an amazing view due to Heaven's technical team. They have access to technology yet to be released to Earth. Some enter the area by way of portal entry. This method is used often to get from one end of Heaven to the other. Every dwelling place in Heaven comes equipped with many portals that take a citizen anywhere they wish. All they have to do is speak it into existence. Some were busy working on a project, but when they heard the announcement from the Father, they placed their project aside, stepped through their personal portal, and reappeared in the gathering area surrounding the throne room. All this gathering takes some time because Heaven is never in a hurry.

However, Heaven moves on the Father's time, and it was

apparent that He was ready to speak.

Suddenly, The Father stood up and observed the crowd with love and excitement. He loves days like to today. A new soul means that Earth will be better empowered to bring Heaven into their reality. A new soul means that the Father's will can be made a little more manifest in the Earth. A new soul means that a blood line can continue to develop its legacy. A newly released soul means that Earth will once again be introduced to a different aspect of the Father's nature. Each new soul carries an aspect of the Father's nature yet to be realized in the Earth. The identity, purpose and destiny of a newly released soul has already been recorded and filed with the Court of Heaven. This is just the icing on the cake. All the millions of onlookers. All the millions of angelic beings. All the trees, flowers, mountains and streams, watch in awe at what is about to take place. The birth of a soul is absolutely unique to humans. The angels watch with honor and humility at this epic event. Even though it has happened many millions of times - it never gets old. The Father has a way of making each time unique and special for the ancestors of the newly released soul. Blake's great, great grandparents and others from his bloodline are all watching in the front row - their seats were previously marked with a sign that reads, *"Reserved for Blake's Ancestry"*.

The Father, with Jesus and Holy Spirit nearby, gently motions for everyone to take their seats. Then He patiently waits for Heaven's citizens to oblige while smiling at Jesus, and saying in a light hearted way, *"This usually takes a while. Our children love to talk."* They all shared a laugh as the ruckus began to die down.

For one moment, there was complete silence. This was an indicator that Heavens citizens were ready to watch and listen. The Father reaches inside Himself and retrieves one of the millions of tiny lights flowing in and out of His essence. He takes the soul, with millions upon millions of citizens watching and waiting, and holds it in his right hand. The luminosity and incandescence protruding from this single soul is radiating pure life. All souls are initially part of Him. Therefore, they carry His life. A single soul is the most beautiful thing to behold in all the universe. The Father is where souls play and exist prior to being released. This is why we miss Heaven, even if we have never visited there bodily and allowed to take in the scenery. A soul lives in the Father until He is ready to release it into the Earth. This is where the soul returns when its earthly body has ran its course. All souls, regardless of religious belief, culture or trauma, long to return to the Father. When the Father releases a soul, He is essentially releasing a part of Himself for mankind. Each soul comes complete with gifts to help it accomplish its purpose in the Earth. Each soul carries the DNA of its ancestors to help it establish legacy in the Earth. Each soul longs for the supernatural, because that is where it has existed since the foundations of the world. Each soul is so very priceless to the Father. One soul can absolutely turn the world upside down. Jesus modeled the extreme possibilities of one person, completely devoted to the Father, and filled with the Holy Spirit. The Earth never has been the same.

Jesus was only on Earth bodily for 33.5 years…

The Father, while holding Blake's soul in His right hand, begins to speak. *"All declarations and decrees concerning Blake's identity, purpose and destiny in the Earth have been recorded in his Book of Destiny and filed for safe keeping in the Court of Heaven. In accordance with the words of the Prophet Jeremiah, I formed him, Jesus appointed him, and Holy Spirit consecrated him for Kingdom service. Upon the release of this soul into the Earth, he will be entrusted to humanity. Apostles, Prophets, Pastors, Teachers and Evangelists will influence him and equip him after he* surrenders his life to my Son. His Guardian Angel, Adriel is highly skilled and experienced in protecting life plans. He has unlimited access to Blake's lineage records and Book of Destiny. He has also been given Level 1 authority."

At that moment, the citizens of Heaven were astounded. They looked at each other, as if to say, *"That's rare. Blake must be very special."*

Since there is no jealousy in Heaven, they assumed it was because Blake's book of destiny includes a decree. They were exactly right.

"Nothing will stop this appointment, and he must always be full time in ministry"

was written in bold letters.

Jonah, son of Amittai, who was among the crowd that day turned to his grandmother and laughingly said, *"Yep. I know what Blake is in for. He just has to learn to yield. He'll be fine. My guardian angel had to pull out all the tricks to get me to Nineveh. The Grace of God will be with him all the days of his life as he learns to yield to his assignment.."*

Blake's great, great, great grandfather looked at his best friend, who happened to have been his wife in the Earthly realm for 56 years, and said, *"That is the same decree that was recorded in my Book of Destiny! Blake is in for a wild ride. He will have to understand that no matter how talented and gifted he is, his assignment is to be a Pastor/Teacher in the Earthly realm. I know you remember my journey. When I realized that God's plan was the clearly designed path, rather than the interruption to my plan, I began to flourish in my purpose."*

She responded with, *"You are exactly right. You got involved with so many things before you finally settled into your God given identity. It was then that you found true happiness in your soul. I enjoyed the journey with you so much. We created so many happy memories together, chasing after the things of God and raising children. I know you remember when we first attempted to plant a church. It was a struggle, but we learned so much together. You always were a better Pastor and Teacher than you gave yourself credit for."*

As Blake's great, great, great grandfather listened to the love of his lifetime recall precious memories, a tear of joy streamed down his face. He couldn't begin to describe the appreciation he felt for her. He could not have accomplished anything in the Earthly realm without her by his side for all those years. He thought about the mighty woman of God she became. She preached the Gospel in many countries and became the first woman in her family line to graduate from college. She became a very recognizable headline speaker in the Kingdom and wrote several books. Her robe was dazzling beyond earthly comprehension and her mansion was gigantic taking up 12 earthly city blocks. She was even earmarked to rule 10 cities in the millennial kingdom. The list goes on and on concerning her charitable works on Earth. Even though official marriage isn't a Heavenly concept needed to be continued after crossing over from the Earthly realm, they still loved being together.

They simply had to talk to each other at least once per day.

We take with us - into eternity - the relationships we have built while on Earth. These are the same people we worked with while on Earth. However, then we can choose to work with them willingly. This is why it is important to learn to stay at one church and work things out with people - especially leadership. We are to advance the Kingdom on Earth together through covenant relationships. The Father leaves it up to us who we form covenants with on Earth. We then have a choice who we form covenants with in Heaven. Since Earthly covenants are until *"death do us part"*, once arriving in Heaven, we have the autonomy to reestablish old covenants, or establish new ones. Surprisingly, most citizens simply keep working with the same people. After all the ups and downs experienced together, they have learned something about themselves and choose not to establish new covenants. Often, Heaven's citizens continue to steward and develop the relationships they forged in the fire on Earth - for eternity. We are trained to settle offenses in the Earthly realm by remaining rooted within a group of people. This is one of the many reasons why grudges and offenses must be dealt with while on Earth.

His mind drifted for a moment as he thought about all the geographic moves as a family. With each move they became closer. He thought about the church drama they experienced together. With each battle, they came out on the other side much stronger in their faith. He thought about the amazing children they raised - who by now were somewhere on the front row - a few thousand seats down fellowshipping with other ancestors. The two of them just gazed at each other. You wouldn't be able to tell that they were no longer married officially. They actually live next door to each other and refuse to leave each other's company. Their children are there all the time as well. He thought about the times when the enemy tried to destroy their relationship through offense or miscommunication. He was thankful that he learned the most valuable lesson to be learned in the Earthly realm – to forgive.

His mind drifted back even further when he finally gained the upper hand on several oppressive demonic spirits that attempted to derail his life, marriage, and ministry. The *Orphan* spirit came to mind. This spirit held an asphyxiating hold on his relationships for many years after he experienced church trauma. He carried a distrust for authority and an overall inability to follow wholeheartedly. Most of his following was transactional. He was afraid for many years that his leaders did not have his best interest at heart, and they were holding him back. Once the Orphan spirit established a stronghold in his thinking, he was destined to leave any situation where he did not feel valued or appreciated. However, as he pondered the life he and his best friend lived together, he also remembered when the Orphan spirit was defeated in his life. His life was never the same after that. His relationships were deeper and more intimate. His ministry was able to reach new levels of impact in the Kingdom. He was then transformed into a better Pastor, Teacher, father and husband. All because he obtained, through growth in grace and knowledge, authority over the Orphan spirit.

He looked over at his eternal friend and said, *"Thank you for always sticking by me. I needed you then, more than I ever realized. You have always loved me well and I'm looking forward to the ages to come."*

She looked back at him and said, *"I got your back, for eternity. You always had the wisdom to repent when repentance was needed. You taught me so much about myself and how to pursue greatness. I'm the woman I am today because of you."*

After saying this, she took his hand and smiled at him. Then, they both took a moment and reflected on this momentous occasion. Another soul was being released, and it happened to be one carrying their DNA.

Souls are intimately connected through what scientists call genetic code. In Heaven, this realization is deeper and much more spiritual. Each family line exhibits a unique expression of the Father's heart. This is why churches led by families have so much to offer their communities. To see an entire family serving God in leadership is powerful. Heaven sees the abuses that stem from what the world calls *nepotism*. However, God uses entire families and ancestorial bloodlines for His purposes in the Earth. It has always been God's plan to use the entire family to advance the Kingdom. Blake's great, great, great grandparents were soaking up the moment. They knew Blake would be given a chance to make some things right. He would have the opportunity to break generational cycles brought about by demonic entities attempting to gain a foothold to derail the ancestorial plan. He would also be walking in the favor and grace afforded to him, through the prayers and declarations already made by his ancestors. Adriel would use these as weapons to fight on Blake's behalf.

The Father continued, *"Is there anyone here from Blake's bloodline who would like to make a declaration to be added to his golden bowl in the throne room?"*

As he said this, he motioned with His hand towards the millions upon millions of golden bowls displayed beautifully on shelves around the entire perimeter of the throne room. In these bowls, the prayers, declarations and decrees are stored for use by the Trinity Team and the Guardians Guild. Guardian Angels have direct access to the golden bowls in order to direct and protect the life plan of those under their care in the Earth. Ancestors can always sprinkle blessings of joy or peace from the Cloud of Witness portals available all throughout Heaven. However, the golden bowls are for the prayers of the Saints still in operation in the Earth. Guardian angels take their sword and dip it into the golden bowl, arming it with atomic power to defeat the enemy on behalf of the saint. The prayers and declarations collected in these bowls give off a sweet fragrance that is incomparable to anything on Earth. However, the Father allows one declaration to be added from one ancestor on a day like today.

Blake's great, great, great grandmother stood up and addressed the Father, and the countless millions watching on HD monitors all throughout Heaven.

She looked around at all the assembly.

It is difficult to find language for how many creatures, to include humanity, that exist there. References to this size of a gathering in scripture usually use the words *"multitude that can't be numbered"*. This is simply an understatement. It's hard to fathom what countless millions of anything looks like. Even when we gaze into the night sky, our minds cant fully grasp the enormity of what we are looking at. When we walk down a sandy beach, our unglorified consciousness can't understand just how many sand granules exist.

She was standing in front of *"a great multitude, which no man could number, out of every nation and of all tribes, peoples, and languages."*

She was going to take this opportunity to speak only if the entire bloodline was in agreement.

She looked down the first row, which had thousands of seats, before saying, *"If the Johnson bloodline agrees, I would like to declare something for the record."*

Each member of the bloodline could be seen discussing the proposal with the person next to them and nodding their head up and down as if to say, *"Amen, we are in agreement."*

Then the oldest member of the Johnson bloodline stood up and said, *"We are in agreement Precious Daughter of The Most High. Please, it's our privilege to hear and agree with your declaration."*

She smiled and bowed her head as if to say, *"Thank you."* Then she continued to speak, *"I declare, before Heaven and all its citizens, that Blake will walk in the counsel of the Godly. He will lead his family with integrity and passion. He will come to know Abba at a very young age and will grow in grace and knowledge all the days of his life. He will chase after you Abba, with all his might."*

At that moment, all of Heaven was getting energized by her declaration and subsequently shouting, *"Amen! To God be the Glory!"*

Suddenly, one section of the gathering - a few hundred thousand seated together - stood up and began dancing. The dancing continued to spread across Heaven section by section. Within a few seconds, all of Heaven was out of their seat dancing and praising God for His faithfulness. In Heaven, when a declaration is made, there is no fear or doubt to hinder its power. Pure unaltered power is released through the crowd and Heaven's citizens become undone by the force of His glory. It's called a praise break and happens all the time - but it never gets old.

With this response from the citizens, Jesus leans over to the Father and says, *"I see the anointing on her in this moment. I'm sure she has more to say."*

The Father replied to Jesus, *"No doubt. Let's call her up.."*

Since the throne is high and lifted up above the throne room floor, they both motioned her to come up the many flights of stairs to the main platform that the throne was anchored to. This had never happened to her in Heaven before, but while she was on Earth, she was a major headliner at conferences where she ministered to thousands all over the Earth. She wasn't the least bit uncomfortable speaking in front of crowds, though it took her many years to think of herself as a great speaker. She was about to bring the fire... As she made her way up the stairs, the gathering grew even more out of hand - in a good way. When she finally reached the throne platform, Jesus and the Father smiled.

Then, the Father handed her the mic and said, *"Freedom in the Spirit precious Daughter."*

She hugged both of them, turned to the multitude and said, *"Brothers and Sisters, creatures great and small.."*

With this opening statement, a new anticipation was obvious by the stillness of the crowd.

"The judgements of all mighty God are perfect, just, and true. His mercy endures forever. On this day, another precious soul is to be released. We all know the challenges that Blake will face during his life in the Earthly realm. He will have to come to the realization that Jesus died for his sins. He will then have to grow in grace and knowledge concerning his rights and privileges as an heir. He will have to overcome many demonic entities who will war against his identity, purpose and destiny. He will win many battles and will lose many more. However, he will learn the most precious lesson of them all...the battle is the Lord's"

After she completed this stanza of her message, Heaven erupted once again with dancing and shouts of *"Amen. To God be the Glory, forever and ever..."*

The Father looked at Jesus with an approving look and said, *"She is amazing. Just how we made her. Amen! Preach it!"*

She couldn't keep herself from joining in the dancing. With mic in hand, she danced around the platform enjoying the waves of Glory that worship and declaration produce in the spirit realm. Jesus grabbed the Father's hand, and they started dancing as well. Imagine the most seemingly out of control charismatic church service you have ever attended. Now imagine something a billion times bigger. That's the picture for you. Millions were slain in the spirit. Millions more were undone by the waves of Glory sweeping through like tidal waves from a tsunami. Millions more took off their crowns and cast them as far as they could towards the throne. This went on for at least 30 minutes. As things settled again, an angelic being having divine musical ability walked over to the organ located near the base platform of the throne on the sea of glass. It was enormous, having pipes that reached at least 100 stories high in Earthly measurement.

He was preparing for the next wave of Glory to be released as she kept preaching. *"Brothers and Sisters, creatures great and small. The Lord's plan for Blake's life will be accomplished. He will learn the many lessons associated with growth and promotion in the Kingdom. He will gain expertise as he walks with the Holy Spirit and serves others well. He will experience what we all experienced in the Earthly realm. Heartache mixed with joy as he navigates life and learns to yield to the Lord's purpose for his existence. I walked with the Holy Spirit for many years in the Earthly realm. I learned through many trials that He never held out on me. If He was silent for a season, He only wanted me to go back and come into agreement with what He already said. If he allowed the enemy a season to tempt me openly, it was to teach me to stand on His word, the same way Jesus did in the wilderness. As my love for His word grew, so did my understanding of my biblical identity, purpose and destiny. As he co-labored with me, He taught me that all things are possible. He taught me to think from Heaven's perspective and bring solutions to society through Holy Spirit power. He lovingly guided me through my own self-doubt. Can you believe that I once was afraid to speak in public?"*

The multitude began to chuckle at the thought of her being afraid to speak in public.

The Father looked at Jesus and said, *"I remember that season. She had no idea who she was..."*

She continued preaching passionately,

"I declare that Blake will learn every lesson the Holy Spirit walks him through. He will step into his gifts and learn to steward them for the benefit of humanity. He will stumble but will always get back up. He will serve the Lord God Almighty all the days of his life and will yield to the process as he becomes a major contributor to the advancement of the Kingdom, through his teaching, preaching, and discipleship. He will write many books, teaching the meat of God's word and his books will live on for many generations. He will be a loving husband, and a devoted father to his children. He will serve God's people in churches around the world with the compassion that Jesus carried. He will live a long, blessed and prosperous life. His life will serve as yet another testimony of God's eternal plan for every one of us. To rule and reign with Christ for all eternity. Brothers and sisters, Blake will prove once again that God makes all things beautiful in His time..."

She hung on the phrase over and over, making a demand on the anointing that was present.

She said it again and again, *"God makes all things beautiful in His time..."*

Then the multitude began to say it with her in perfect unison, over and over.

Many citizens could be seen with raised hands in worship, repeating the phrase.

She even paused with a smile and said, *"Look at your neighbor and say, God makes all things beautiful in His time."*

To which, the citizens obeyed gladly. The Father even joined in, turning to Jesus saying, *"We make all things beautiful in our time..."*

As the wave of Glory eventually lessened, it gave her an opportunity to close her message as she looked out over the sea of

Heaven's citizens.

She looked over at the Father, Son, and Holy Spirit with tears of joy and said, *"Thank you Abba for this opportunity."*

Then, she turned to the multitude and concluded with, *"All the Redeemed Ones know that the Earthly realm is the training ground for many things. It was there we learned to yield our will to Abba's plan for our lives. It was there we learned to trust each other. It was there we learned to love one another unconditionally. It was through the trials that we learned to understand our dependence on Abba. None of us got it all perfect. None of us can say we accomplished everything we wanted to. We are simply built to dream bigger than the Earthly realm's capacity to manifest it for us. We are made in the image and likeness of Abba. As Blake's soul is released into the Earthly realm, I declare blessings on his life to the thousandth generation. May he walk in favor and grace. May he take up the five-fold ministry mantle and advance the Kingdom in unique ways. And finally, May his heart burn for his own potential. May the burden for his glorious purpose drive him to pursue the things of God above all Earthly wealth or fame. May he leave a legacy of faith for all the world to see..."*

The multitude of Redeemed Ones, all Heavenly creatures great and small, the Guardians Guild, the Four creatures around the throne stood up and began clapping in appreciation for the message. The Father, Son, and Holy Spirit, all applauded while shaking their head, as if to say, *"She is amazing."*

In Heaven, everyone is valued and honored for who they are. Everyone is secure in their identity. There is no jealousy or envy. Everyone is celebrated for the unique expression of the Father they display.

She turned and handed the mic back to the Father and made

her way back to her seat.

She was still receiving a standing ovation for the message. Over the thunderous applause, her mind went back to her development in the Earthy realm. She remembered a season of crushing she experienced. She was working very hard to plant a church with her husband in the 1930s in a rural town in California. She remembered how lonely this season was. She was unsure of her calling and unaware of her gifts. She was questioning her existence in the Kingdom because women preachers were rejected openly. She would cry out to God in the secret place and ask for wisdom. Those are the moments when the Holy Spirit would visit her and minister to her. She almost left the ministry all together. In this moment, she was thankful for the grace given to her while in the Earthly realm. She was overwhelmed with gratitude. All the ancestors from the Johnson bloodline remained standing as they clapped. They all understood the journey. They all understood what Blake was going to experience. They also understood that Bake would have access to revelation of scripture and new technologies they never had the privilege to use.

Now, as they stood together in Heaven, all of it made sense. They understood things completely from Heaven's perspective. All Blake really has to do is yield to the process while growing in grace and knowledge. These are two sides to the same coin. As Blake grows in knowledge of the Kingdom, grace is released from Heaven to push his development forward. A Blake grows in grace, revelation of scripture will be poured into his heart. Throughout the Earthly process, the mind, will and emotions are trained to navigate an eternal reality all Saints are destined for. Righteous constructs will be built in his mind through biblical instruction. Understanding scripture trains the mind what to think and how to think. As the mind is renewed, the will begins to bend the knee to Jesus and His finished work on the Cross.

As Holy Spirit empowerment takes root, the emotions are trained to perceive the moving of the Holy Spirit. This process takes as long as it takes. The finished product is modeled in the life and ministry of Jesus. A fully manifested son or daughter of God is the goal. Through the process, Blake will graduate from servant, to friend, to sonship, and finally reach full maturity as a manifested son. As a servant, he will learn to serve others unselfishly. As a friend he will be positioned for entry level leadership in the Kingdom because he will understand how Jesus thinks. As a son, he will be promoted once again because he will carry an awareness of what is in account as an heir. As a manifested son, all things are inherently understood to be possible. Therefore, he will then heal the sick, raise the dead, cast out demons, cleanse lepers, rebuke storms and walk on water. This is the development of a Saint in simple terms…

The Father now turned His attention to the task at hand.

Still holding Blake's luminescent soul in His right hand, he motioned for a delivery angel to come closer.

He held the soul in the air and said these words, *"I hereby release Bake into the Earthly realm."*

With those words, he handed the soul to a winged delivery angel named *Jahdiel* - which means *"God Gives Joy"*. who stood 9 earthly feet tall. He was armored for battle from head to toe and winged for maneuverability in the spirit realm.

The delivery angel placed the soul in a locket around his neck for safe travel.

The angel got down on one knee in reverence to the Father.

The Father placed his right hand on the head of the angel

and said, *"I declare Blessings on your journey mighty Jahdiel. I appreciate your faithful service to the Kingdom."*

Jahdiel responded in Heavenly tongues, *"Yesladi Ohladee Abaa ccieda Basoh, ramandadia, ramandada hegese."*

Then he stood up and flew off with angelic power comparable to 10 jet engines. His immediate departure sent waves of energy through the multitude. They stood and praised with such passion as the angelic organ player began playing a new song. Waves of praise and worship came from the organ pipes as he played with such *"in the moment"* prophetic creativity. This particular angel has been playing music since he was created. For thousands of years he has sat down at this organ and played beautifully for the throne room inhabitants.

The angel carried so much divine creativity that he has never played the same song twice in over 5,000 earth years...

Jahdiel was flying at a rate of speed comparable to a F-16 aircraft. The glory radiating from his being left a wake comparable to a comet, screaming through space and time.

He was on a mission, and he had never failed that mission in thousands of years. His determination to deliver the package could be seen on his demeanor. As he launched himself from one speed to the next, waves of sonic booms were released into the spirit realm. It wasn't that he was traveling toward Earth - it was as if he was simply breaking through time to enter the Earthly realm. The Throne room and all the Heavenly civilization are tethered to the Earthly realm through portals. These portals provide easy access for angels to travel through. In Heaven, you can imagine you are in a place, and you can speak it into existence with your will. To crossover from Heaven to Earth is accomplished through a system of spirit realm highways. The spirit realm highway system is accessible to all

Guardian and Messenger Angels to simplify travel and accommodate their mission. With one catch - the demonic kingdom have access to the same roadways.

The reason why might surprise you. The Father loves all his creation - each and everyone. Even though the demonic kingdom is made up of Lucifer and a third of the angels who once served faithfully in Heaven, the Father still provides the method of travel they need to fulfil their purpose. Since they re-purposed themselves through disobedience, the Father refuses to judge them ahead of their time. For now, they have access to the Earth through the portal system, but only from the second Heaven where they have established dominion.

Since both Kingdoms have access to the spirit realm highway system, major choke points are where the majority of the battles take place. The portal roads are approximately 1 mile in diameter. Portals are mentioned in scripture with specific language to help God's people visualize the magnitude of these portals. Jesus was baptized in the Holy Spirit when the *"Heavens opened"* in the Gospels, and the Spirit rested on Him like a dove. Jacob saw a portal and *"angels ascending and descending"* up and down like a ladder system. The portal system is needed due to the change in physics of both realities. There has to be a bridge connecting the Heavens and the Earth. While traveling through the system, the molecular structure of the traveler changes from glorified to earthly. It's a simple physical molecular shift traveling either direction - towards Heaven or towards Earth.

The closer the spirit realm inhabitant gets to Earth; their molecular structure adapts to the Earthly environment. Demons traveling to Earth will feel themselves getting weaker. Therefore, they must inhabit a person or object as a host to be able to stay alive. Heavenly travelers actually get stronger as they come into proximity to the redeemed on Earth. The glory that each born again believer carries in the spirit realm is enough to fuel angelic beings with more than enough to survive in the Earthly reality. Since the Spirit of the Living God lives on the inside of every born again believer, angelic beings can see the location of any believer on Earth from any vantage point. The anointing that a born again believer carries explodes with a radiant glow in the spirit realm making it all the more easy to locate them. The Father refused to reward the demonic kingdom with the ability to be renewed in strength in this fashion. Angels become energized when they are near the Glory of God, to include the Glory each spirit filled believer carries. This is why they love to spend time around homes, churches and worship events. This enables them to be renewed much like a jolt of adrenaline.

Since demons aren't afforded this luxury, they must be very calculating concerning who or what they inhabit. They hate being cast out because this displaces them for a season. When they are cast out of a person or an object they are inhabiting, they are immediately hurled through the Earthly atmosphere. Where they end up is quite comical. They don't have the ability to travel instantaneously while in the Earthly atmosphere. They have to walk. It is while on this journey they enlist the help of more demons. They are hard wired to never give up. If a demon is cast out of a person, they will stop at nothing to return to the host. This response isn't because they are particularly loyal to the cause.

It's simply out of fear.

Any failure in the demonic kingdom is punishable. Any lapse in judgement is deemed a reason for retraining. None of them want retraining. None of them want to be demoted to tormenting duties in hell. They want to remain free to steal, kill and destroy the identity, purpose and destiny of any human they can. It's the highest reward in the demonic kingdom to kill a human. With the death of a human - there dies a dream - there dies a book idea - there dies a future - there dies a legacy.

Jahdiel was approaching a major intersection of spirit realm highway he was on, as he headed towards the State of Georgia, located in the south eastern United States area. Demonic patrols were tipped off by the DLD assigned to the case. The shock waves created by a messenger angel are felt throughout the entire galaxy, to include the second heaven. The demonic kingdom would follow protocol on this one. Waring demons are dispatched to stop the messenger angel at any cost. Their best chance is on the spirit realm road system, or so they think. They have tried this ambush tactic for thousands of years to no avail. This was the scene when the Prophet Daniel was waiting for his answer. On that occasion, the Principality of Persia fought personally to delay the message. He knew he couldn't win. All he was trying to do was delay the message, giving street level demons more time to counter. The *Prince of Persia* never thought about giving up on his assignment in the middle of the fight.

Demons are hard wired to never give up, because that is what the Father places in all of His creation. Every creature, great and small, on the Earth or currently residing in Heaven carries the capacity to be courageous. This why nature will always fight its way to survival. This is why the most often communicated command in scripture is, *"do not fear"*. Fear isn't part of the natural building blocks of life. Every creature, especially mankind, is built to dream big and live without fear. The demons still have that as part of their identity. This is why humans must tap into their potential by allowing God's Word to renew their minds. As humans learn to live and think in agreement with scripture, they realize the authority and power they carry. Animals know their identity and act accordingly. The only reason animals fear humans is because the fallen sinful state had to touch every creature in order to demonstrate the need for salvation. Its only in their fallen state, they fear. All of creation cries out for the sons and daughters of God to fully manifest. When mankind understands their identity, purpose and destiny in Christ, all of creation will benefit. Plants, animals, even microscopic life forms cry out for a time when their original nature is completely restored. Lions want to befriend lambs - it's their natural inclination to do so. The only thing holding back the renewal of that relationship is the plan of God for the Earth, which must be accomplished through the redeemed.

Out of nowhere, a warrior demon appears,

then another and another.

Jahdiel, though flying roughly at the speed of light, sees them and prepares mentally for the ensuing battle.

Jahdiel has the ability to predict the moves of his opponents and apply counter moves accordingly, fast enough to freeze time. The Kingdom of Heaven and all its inhabitants never become fearful in a fight. The Father has equipped them with more than enough natural ability to conquer anything the kingdom of darkness send their way. This is why scripture declares that we are *"more than conquerors"*. We are superior in every way to any demonic entity when the Spirit of the Living God inhabits us. Jahdiel has never experienced anything less than Holy Spirit empowerment and freedom from fear. He has never felt fear because, in Heaven, fear doesn't exist. He knows how to recognize fear in order to minister to his assigned redeemed one. However, he hasn't personally experienced the phenomenon. This is why the usual first words from an angel's mouth in scripture is, *"do not fear"*. They understand that a human is still navigating the effects of their fallen state. They understand that a human must be reminded that they shouldn't fear because humans never really *have* to fear. Fear is beneath the rights and privileges of a creature made in the Father's image. From an angels prospective, they have reason to fear us. After all, the redeemed will judge angels, among many other duties in the Millennial Kingdom as we rule and reign with Christ on the new Earth. Jahdiel's very existence in this season is to deliver messages, souls, and anything else the Father needs delivering, for the advancement of the ecclesia in the Earth. All of Heaven stands ready to support the ecclesia in their efforts.

Suddenly, Jahdiel could see out of the corner of his eye a flash of light.

They were using an ambush tactic he had seen many times before. In an instant, he shifted his body to avoid the sharp blade of a demonic warrior. Another blade was coming from another direction entirely - he saw that one as well and moved quickly out the way. This was all happening at the speed of light, never deviating from his course set for Dalton, Georgia. An ambush wasn't going to sway him from his course. He was headed to deliver this soul, which was still locked away in a special storage locket fashioned by the Father with technology yet to be released to mankind. Nothing was going to stop him.

About that time, as Jahdiel has done many times before, he touched his right ear with his pointer finger and said, *"Can I get some music?"*

He was speaking to his handler located at *Angel Headquarters*. Handlers were selected to support angels in the field to facilitate the missions. This enables the angels in the field to have instantaneous access to information and technologically advanced methods of spiritual warfare. They are reasonably more experienced and stand ready to coach and mentor angels in the field. They never sleep, and they stand ready to support the mission.

Jahdiel's handler responded with, *"What do you have in*

mind?"

Jahdiel said, *"Something from the Mozart era. Wait, scratch that, play my classic rock playlist from the 70's."*

He said this as he dodged enemy swords at the speed of light, never losing focus that he was in the middle of a fight. Immediately, classic rock began to play through his ear pierce. Jahdiel smiled but refined his focus on the task at hand. 70's rock gave him a boost of energy. He loved the divine creativity of mankind. He marveled at how a human can create from nothing. A song, a beautiful painting, even a remarkably engineered earthly structure all carried the fingerprint of the Father's creativity. Angels simply weren't created with this level of creative capacity. Jahdiel has always appreciated any art form established by mankind. He loves the expressed freedom and raw musical ability of the 70's rock bands. He loves how the live performances matched the studio renditions of the music produced in that era. In his opinion, nothing really tops 70's rock. Of course, he refused to listen to any song that would bring dishonor to the Father. However, when he had his 70's rock playing through his earpiece, it gave him an extra boost of motivation. He appreciated and honored mankind for their unique creativity, found only in a creature made in the image and likeness of God. His assignment was to deliver, and he planned on doing just that…

Jahdiel moved through the potential moves of his opponents in his mind.

At this time, the group of demonic warriors were seemingly gaining ground. With each one of their attempts to sink their blade into Jahdiel, he avoided it and documented another tendency in his knowledge bank.

Suddenly, he decided that he had enough of playing around.

In a moment where time seemed to stand still for Jahdiel, he dealt a fatal blow to one demon, while preparing to swing his sword toward another.

Both screamed in terror as the blade lodged swiftly in the heart and lung areas of each correspondingly.

Jahdiel moved so swiftly; several demons never knew what hit them. In mid-flight, they began to lose altitude as they grasped for their chest after feeling the effects of Jahdiel's razor sharp blade, as it pierced their armor. One after one, Jahdiel fought them and slew them on the way to his destination.

When the last demon was killed, Jahdiel paused in midair.

He was approaching the end of the portal where he could see Earth in all its beauty from space. The fight he just experienced was while traveling through the second heaven located just a few miles outside the Earth's ozone layer. He was safe now. Demons dwelling within the Earth's atmosphere are so feeble, they pose zero threat to an angel. He was now free to enter the Earth's atmosphere and deliver the package without any more delay. It had taken him all of 5 Earthly minutes to break through the second heaven.

Jahdiel rocketed towards Dalton, Georgia, breaking through the ozone layer at light speed.

As he entered Earth's atmosphere, he pressed a button on his forearm control panel that turned on his cloaking device.

As he turned it on, he thought to himself, *"I don't want to scare anyone. Better to go incognito now, even while flying at 10,000 feet."*

A clear technologically advanced reflective membrane spread itself over Jahdiel's entire body. *Seers* on the Earth could still see him, but he would be invisible to 99% of humanity. His first thought was when to make the deposit into Sarah's womb. The act of consummation had already taken place and the safest time was at night while she was a sleep. Jahdiel thought about his training in delectate situation like this. He was trained in the 3 laws of angelic interaction with humans. It was more like the 3 commandments of being an angel. They were simple, but Jahdiel was so detailed at his job, he always communicated them to himself internally at the culmination of any mission.

He thought to himself, *"Ok Jahdiel, use wisdom and remember the 3 laws; 1) Remain unseen 2) Never infringe upon human will unless to help. 3) Help only if it protects the life plan."*

These were pretty simple and straight forward and serve as the default laws of interaction. However, Jahdiel was operating with Level 1 authority. He had much more leverage to work with to accomplish his mission. Much in the same way a Special Warfare Operator has authority to make command decisions in real time. Jahdiel had earned the respect of his fellow angels and had an amazing testimony of loyalty to the Father, built over thousands of years. He wanted nothing more than to serve.

As he landed on Earth, very delicately, all 20 feet of his physique over shadowed the ground beneath him.

He walked softly towards the home where Sarah was sleeping next to her boyfriend.

He was keenly aware of any potential disturbances he might cause. He gazed across the neighborhood from the vantage point of a 20 foot tall specimen. His spiritual vision enabled him to see how many believers there were in this neighborhood. There was only one. An elderly woman was praying late into the night, and she became aware of his presence from 3 houses away. Jahdiel looked at her, and she looked at him in the Spirit. Her face began to glow with excitement, and she waved hello. There is no time or distance in the spirit realm, so this encounter was as if they were very near to one another. Jahdiel smiled and waved back.

He didn't sense any fear in this elderly woman, so after he waved, he made a gesture as if to say, *"Let's keep this one between me and you."* The elderly woman nodded in agreement and started to declare blessings on Sarah's home as she prayed.

This elderly woman was the only human interceding for this neighborhood. She was a widow who lost her husband several years prior in the Vietnam War. She is a *Seer*. However, she lost her Earthly sight after discovering the news of her husband's death.

Jahdiel pressed the communication device in his right ear and said, *"Can you download the life plan for this woman along with all applicable information regarding how I can serve her. Since I'm already in the area, and there is no fear in her, I would love to bless her."*

The Handler responded with, *"No problem my friend. You should be receiving that now."*

In an instant, Jahdiel's forearm monitor lit up with holographic forms of information. He learned that her name was Deborah and she had been in this physical condition for many years. Deborah had several children who refused to serve the Lord, and this also added to the heavy weight she carried. She wanted nothing more than to see her children serve God.

After quick examination of the data concerning her life plan, Jahdiel discovered that it would only be a few more years until she was scheduled to be promoted.

Jahdiel said to his handler, *"I'm at a loss. Do you have any ideas on how we can bless her?"*

The Handler replied, *"I think a strong prophetic decree*

concerning her children will strengthen her faith. She is living in agreement with her sickness because she was taught that disease is sent by the Father to teach people lessons... so that's an area we can't influence. She would have to be healed through the laying on of hands but there isn't a church in the area currently preaching the Gospel through miracles, signs and wonders. She is kind of stuck for now in that regard. However, we can decree concerning her children, and I believe it will increase her faith in all areas, to include her healing. The church scheduled to be planted in her area isn't for another few years. All the churches that sprung up during her childhood are now closed. She went through a lot of church trauma and likes to simply stay home and intercede for others."

Jahdiel replied, *"I see. How about I make a decree concerning her children. That's a safe bet. She has no fear or unbelief, so this will be fun. She will come into agreement with it."*

Jahdiel and his massive 20 foot tall frame moved closer to the elderly woman's home because he wanted to deliver the decree in a more intimate manner.

As he moved closer, the elderly woman noticed him and calmly locked eyes with him.

Jahdiel began to decree, *"Precious Saint and mighty Redeemed One, do not fear..."*

He paused, smiled, and continued, *"I had to say that - its protocol."*

Deborah smiled and said, *"I understand. I've witnessed angels for many years and I'm comfortable around you."*

Jahdiel was impressed at the level of anointing in this woman. He was being reenergized from his journey and short squabble with the demonic sentinels by being in proximity to the Spirit of God radiating from Deborah.

He continued, *"Dear Daughter of the Most High, your children will serve the Lord all the days of their life and will not walk in the counsel of the ungodly. The Lord will meet them where they are and open them up to powerful encounters in the days to come. They will receive dreams, visions, trances and divine encounters... Thus sayeth the Lord. I love throwing in the King James version. It sounds so epic."*

With this simple decree, the Guardian Angels assigned to Deborah's three children, ages 38, 47 and 56 all received a message on their forearm monitors. They all smiled and readied themselves for the events to follow.

When a declaration is made, the power of the declaration can only be activated by faith. Declarations must be received or acknowledged in faith. Then, the recipient must live in willful agreement with the declaration in order for it to come to pass. Large portions of scripture operate in this way. Decrees are different. They come directly from the heart of the Father. Nothing can stop a decree. *"Let there be light..."* was one of the first recorded decrees in scripture. All the demonic powers combined can't stop a decree from God or a messenger angel delivering the message on God's behalf. This was going to happen, and she knew full well what Jahdiel was doing. He was taking time from his important mission to minister to her.

She was overwhelmed with thankfulness as tears began to stream down her face.

She looked up at him and said, *"Thank you mighty servant of the Lord. You have so blessed me this evening. Now, go and finish your mission. I'll continue here in intercession for the neighborhood."*

Jahdiel stood in amazement.

He has always respected the Redeemed Ones. They believe in a reality that isn't always seen. They say yes to a savior that they haven't formally met in person, and they communicate with Heaven through prayer, rather than the in person meetings Jahdiel was accustomed to. They are expected to believe the writings of several authors whose work has been compiled into 66 books, called the Bible. They read this book in hopes of learning more about a world they haven't fully tasted of. Jahdiel admired the redeemed and considered it a privilege to serve them. Their faith inspires him to operate at the highest level of excellence in all things. With all they must endure to follow Jesus in the Earthly realm - Jahdiel took the time to bless a Redeemed One any chance afforded to him. He looked back as he was moving away from Deborah's house, towards Sarah's house located 3 houses down the street. He saw waves of prayer being released in the spirit realm. Vibrant colors and sounds streamed from Deborah's home and started a chain of glory that continued to climb, all the way to the throne-room. It was in the throne room where Deborah's prayers would be collected and stored in the golden bowls.

The Guardian Angels representing the souls Deborah was interceding for were all receiving messages on their forearm monitors around the country.

One after another, as Deborah lifted people up in prayer, by name, the stream of prayer continued on into the night sky like a ribbon of metallic alternating color streams.

This impressed Jahdiel and touched his emotions. He smiled but continued with the mission. Angels carry the basic emotional responses humans carry. This enables them to operate from compassion, rather than mere religious duty. They were trained early in their careers, the importance of the Redeemed and their place in the history of creation.

Jahdiel reached the house where Sarah was sleeping beside her boyfriend. He reached for the locket he was carrying around his neck on a beautiful gold chain. It was made of gold from the Heavenly realm. Gold in Heaven is translucent and purified from all additional elements found in earthly gold. As he was about to squeeze the locking mechanism, he heard a sonic boom. It was the sound of more demonic warriors entering the region through the same portal Jahdiel traveled to get to Sarah's house. One by one, they appeared, traveling at light speed and suddenly coming to a complete stop in the atmosphere. Jahdiel knew what was coming, a last ditch effort to abort the release of a soul. He had experienced this many times and had been training for it.

He immediately took his hand away from the locket and pressed a button on his forearm control monitor, and calmly said, *"Attention all Angels in the area, we have a Code 1 in progress, requesting backup. I just need enough time to deliver the package."*

Immediately, 10,000 angels appeared in the same fashion as their demonic counterparts.

Many of them were Guardian's Guild members having a personal stake in the delivery of this soul. The existence of one soul sets off a chain of events in the Kingdom of God. One soul carries the capacity to impact millions. However, lasting impact begins in the family. One soul can change the entire direction of a lineage. One soul can create a momentum for several generations to break free from sin and bondage to shame. One soul can change the spiritual climate in the home and produce an atmosphere of love, joy and peace. One soul can break the chains of oppression and release favor over an entire ancestorial line.

Thousands of demons ascended on Jahdiel's location.

He once again touched his earpiece and said to his handler,

"I need you to quarterback this thing. Basic Battle Protocol will suffice."

The Handler responded, *"I got your back. Proceed with the delivery."*

Jahdiel reached for the locket hanging around his neck with Blake's soul kept safe from harm during travel.

The Handler immediately took over the air waves for all communication devices in the region. *"Listen up guys, from my perspective, I believe all we need is a perimeter around Sarah's house approximately 3 blocks in diameter. We also need air coverage up to 1 mile above the neighborhood."*

Angels sprung into immediate action upon the recommendations of the handler. They moved into position creating a protective perimeter around the house, 3 blocks in diameter (712,800 square feet).

One by one, warrior angels, to include several Guardian Angels landed shoulder to shoulder to form the perimeter.

Many more flew to create the perimeter above Sarah's house, creating a dome like shape.

Street level demons were tipped off concerning the release of the soul. They didn't have specific intelligence concerning the delivery of the soul, they simply responded to the buzz of spirit realm activity happening in their region. They ran to the area where all the activity was taking place, alerting their peers as they ran.

One higher ranking demon touched his ear to activate his spirit realm communicator as he ran. *"Give us everything you got. This could be a soul delivery. Not quite sure but we are responding now."*

Within minutes, thousands of demons were within 6 blocks

of the perimeter created by the angels.

The high ranking demon told his handler through his earpiece, *"Load us up with every fiery dart you got on Sarah Johnson."*

To which the handler responded, *"I'm on it."*

Immediately the demon army, made up of street level wicked spirits of lust, greed and murder were equipped with the words of death spoken over Sarah's life as a child –

they morphed into fiery darts to be used by the demonic even though they were spoken years ago. *"You'll be just like your drug addicted sister who died of a drug overdose"* was one of the more powerful ones.

"You will never amount to anything" was yet another one.

One by one, the words of death spoken over Sarah's life by her parents, coaches, and even a few Pastors who gave up on her long ago, equipped and empowered the weapons used by the demonic army.

It was beginning to look like the angels were outnumbered.

Mathematically, they were. Fiery darts began to fly from the demonic weaponry. Technologically advanced rifles, sling shots, bow, and arrows to name a few…

the battle was raging out of control.

Under the sounds of exploding spirit realm ordinance and sword fighting, Jahdiel took a knee.

He trusted his backup fully. He could now do what he came to do and complete his mission.

He reached for the locket hanging from his neck with Blake's soul kept safely inside.

He pressed the unlock mechanism and the small locket opened to reveal a radiant beam of life.

He had to activate his eye protection visor, which slid into place originating from his helmet. The light coming from a freshly released soul is comparable to the sun. He wasn't able to stare at it very long without eye protection. He gently handled it with his thumb and pointer finger and took it out of the locket.

He gazed up for a moment to see the enormous battle taking place to protect this delivery mission.

Jahdiel always marvels at the lengths the Father will go for one soul. All of Heaven stood ready for this mission. All of Heaven prepared itself to support the mission. The entire Guardian's Guild was on alert to provide security for this mission. This mission, quite simply, was to deliver one soul, to one family, living in one house, in one town in America.

As he pondered these things in his heart, a fiery dart screamed past him and lodged itself in the house.

This was enough to awaken Sarah. Startled, she turned to her boyfriend, grabbed his arm, and said, *"Did you hear that?"*

He rubbed his eyes, looked at her and said, *"You woke me up to ask if I heard something. That makes no sense. If I heard something, it would have woke me up too. Go back to sleep, girl!"*

She laughed and did just that. She dozed off thinking nothing else about the sound she heard. There was grace resting upon the house at this time. Spirits of Fear weren't able to break through the perimeter established by the angel forces…

Jahdiel grabbed the fiery dart. On it was written, *"Addiction runs in our family."* He took the arrow and declared, *"The Blood of Jesus has broken all curses. I cancel this ridiculous statement in*

Jesus Name."

With that declaration, the fiery dart dissolved into thin air.

Finally, he reached forth, holding Bake's soul, ready to make the deposit into Sarah's womb.

He stepped through the walls of the house without moving or affecting the reality he was now superimposed upon.

He was operating in the natural, while maintaining his spirit realm molecular integrity. Jesus walked through the wall to deliver the Great Commission to the disciples in this same fashion. He was in this similar molecular state while he revealed himself to hundreds of disciples in Galilee after His resurrection. Earthly matter shifts to make room for spirit realm realities. Especially, a Glorified body operating on assignment from Heaven.

As she lay sleeping, Jahdiel places the soul meticulously in Sarah's womb.

The egg located in Sarah's ovaries had already been released and fertilized. It was a simple dot of flesh that contained the DNA for Blake's development.

As the soul touched the dot of flesh, the flesh was made alive.

All the DNA strands sprang into action, beginning the process of living and becoming. The soul began to intertwine itself to the dot of flesh, activating vital hormones for growth in Sarah's body.

Blake was now, and forever more, a living soul.

Down the street Deborah could sense the battle happening in the spirit realm. Though she could not see physically, her perception in the spirit realm was 20/20. She had gone to sleep, but sensing something happening in the spirit realm, she awoke to pray. The time was 1:11am. She knew what this meant.

It was Holy Spirit's signal for her to intercede for a person.

"Who could it be", she thought.

She didn't like it when the enemy messed with her sleep, but she didn't mind praying, especially for a soul. She arose and prayed this prayer with great conviction, *"Father, I bless your Holy name. I am thankful for all you have provided for me."*

As she prayed these words, something opened up in the spirit for her. She saw Sarah asleep in her bed. She also saw Jahdiel delivering the soul from Heaven and placing it within her womb. She then saw the demonic forces closing in on Jahdiel's location. She immediately knew what to pray.

She stood up and raised her hands to Heaven and said, *"Father, I call the Court of Heaven into session on behalf of Sarah and her entire lineage."*

Suddenly, in the Court of Heaven, angelic paralegals sprang into action, bustling about retrieving the Book of Destiny and placing it on the platform for Jesus to quickly research in preparation for the session Deborah called for. It wasn't that Heaven, or Jesus for that matter, was in a panicked frenzy. Heaven simply moves with such excellent precision; nothing catches them off guard. It was actually part of the daily briefing by Jesus to be prepared for this moment. The release of a soul into the Earthly realm is one of the biggest events in Heaven, next to a soul coming home.

As the members of the court prepared for Jesus to come in and sit as Advocate on behalf of Sarah, He smiled and greeted everyone briefly, and then sat down.

They all remained standing and exclaimed, *"The Lord is faithful and true. His mercies endure forever!"*

Jesus responded with, *"You may be seated precious heavenly creatures great and small. Let's listen to what Deborah has to say and see how we can serve her in this moment."*

Deborah lifted her voice and said, *"I lift up this precious pre-believer to you. She is not in agreement with your Word and is living in open rebellion against her mother's guidance. She is making decisions based on her own sinful nature, self-will and disobedience. I would like to repent on her behalf, of any sin held against her in your court."*

Jesus looked at the paralegal and said, *"I will permit this for a season. My grace will overshadow her and the child, and they will be safe."*

The paralegal wrote down the ruling in her Life Plan records after Jesus was finished.

Deborah continued, *"I cancel all current enemy assignments against her, in Jesus Name!"*

With great surprise and excitement, Jesus looked at the paralegal and said, *"I will permit this as well, effective immediately."*

In that moment, the prayers Deborah prayed became a decree, when they were ratified by Jesus in the Court of Heaven. All of creation has to stop and pay honor to a decree. Every creature great and small, to include the second heaven, has to stop and obey it...

Thousands of demons still waging war received messages on their forearm monitors, simultaneously.

The words read, *"Current assignment aborted. Return to current post and await further orders. Signed, Power of Georgia"*

One by one they acknowledged the message, stopped fighting, and began their journeys back to their post in disgrace.

The thunderous battle that seemed to be in the hands of the demonic was becoming a still, soft, peaceful scene.

Some demons had come from many miles away to take part in the battle. Now they would have to walk back. Street level demons aren't winged for flight. This is why being sent to a distant land is so frustrating for them when they are *"cast out"* of a person. They especially hate being cast out of a region because they will have to face the ramifications of losing territory. Since they were street level demons, they didn't really carry a full revelation of what was happening. They didn't know anything about the Courts of Heaven. Information is compartmentalized in the demonic kingdom. There isn't any trust among them. All they knew was that they had an assignment cancelation order delivered to their communication devices, and it was time to make the long journey back to their post. Another frustrating night in the demonic kingdom. All because one believer in Jesus decided to pray...

Jahdiel paused and looked around.

There was a sense of calm on the neighborhood. He knew what that meant. Heaven intervened on this one. He marveled at this weapon of warfare the Father gave to the ecclesia. He wondered why they hadn't used it more ferociously to defeat the works of darkness once and for all and eradicate them from the Earth. However, he already knew the answer. The Father is gentle and peaceable. He allows His greatest creation the freedom to grow at their own pace. He never infringes on their will and tries to stay out of their affairs, unless called upon. The Father has already left man in charge of the Earth, for a second time. It would only be a few more decades until the ecclesia would have all they need to ensure the Gospel is preached throughout the world, to every creature. The Father is patient with the process and knows the ecclesia will eventually figure out how to bring Heaven to Earth, so He can once again live among His children. The ecclesia has the keys of death, hell, and the grave, because Jesus gave them back. The ecclesia has a canonized copy of the Bible in every language on the Earth. They also have anointed Teachers to teach them what the Bible is saying, and also important, what it is not saying. They are armed with what is arguably their most cunning weapon, their mouth. With it, they are expected to pray, intercede, declare, decree and prophecy the will of God into every situation they find themselves in. If they will discover the power contained in their prayers, decrees and declarations, they will start shifting nations into Holy alignment. If they truly understand the power of the tongue, they will cancel enemy assignments, not only for individuals, but for regions. Jahdiel understood the plan and the Father's thinking concerning such things. He was now looking forward to a little time off - after a day like today.

Jahdiel took a few steps away from Sarah's house. Then, looking back, he smiled as if to say, *"What a privilege to do what I do."*

He then looked back up at the stars, knowing it was time to go home. His heart melted for the entire neighborhood. As compassion welled up inside of him, he thought to himself, *"If they only knew what the Father has planned for them. Its beyond anything they could ever pray or imagine. Ill serve them all the days of my life once the Father declares an end to the Age of Grace. I'm looking forward to it. Ill serve them then, as I have served them now. With honor, integrity, and personal courage. I'm coming home Abba!"*

As Abba looked through His personal portal located to the side of His throne, a tear of joy began to stream down His face.

Abba was hearing the message directly from Jahdiel's heart to His. The Father's heart was blessed at seeing the love, concern, and devotion of Jahdiel and the Guardians Guild members who were the first responders to this battle. He was so very proud of them and how they worked together. This was yet another successful soul release and delivery.

The Father looked up and saw Jesus enter the throne room, as He was returning from the Court of Heaven session that Deborah called for. Jesus walked in and smiled as He said, *"That was a fun one. Another successful soul delivery..."*

The demonic Kingdom was in an uproar.

They couldn't believe this happened again. The *Power of Georgia (POG)* stormed down the hallway hurling expletives at any inferior demon he could see along the way.

He knew he would have to answer for this failure. He thought he had a good enough plan to eradicate this intercessor from the neighborhood Sarah lived in prior to the delivery of this soul. He's been planning this for months feeding off excellent Intel from the street level wicked spirits under his leadership. He's gone so far as to enlist the *Church of Satan* in Dalton GA to curse this home every day for weeks. He's ordered them to attack her thought life nonstop for several days leading up to the potential delivery of this soul. The biggest problem he's faced with in this case, is the fact that Deborah loves to pray.

After retrieving the files for this case and continuing to hurl expletives to his subordinates, he storms back into his office, sits down in his lavish leather office chair, and reaches for the intercom button. *"I want to see every agent working the case 12271975 Blake-1200 in my office immediately"*.

Then he sat back in his chair in panicked reflection. He thought to himself *"What did we miss?"*

Dozens of agents began to nervously file into his office as he peered at them condescendingly one by one. He was wondering if he should fire each and every one of them and assign a completely new team to this case. He was even debating sending every one of these agents, even though they possessed thousands of years of experience collectively, to tormenting duties in hell. As they stood there awkwardly in front of his desk, he remained leaned back in his chair as he took time to look each and every agent in the eye.

Then he calmly said, *"I want answers."*

One of the agents raised his hand and said, *"Permission to speak Sir."* To which the Power of Georgia responded, *"Make sure it's good."*

The agent bravely continued, *"Sir, we followed protocol on this one to the letter. 6 months of planning is the average time spent on cases of this nature. Honestly, it should have been cut and dry. All the variables lined up. Sarah is an unbeliever, living in disobedience to her mother. She has no protection, no covenant with the Word, no one praying for her regularly all while actively using illegal drugs and living with complete reckless abandon. This type of mission is usually very easy to pull off. You of all people, Sir, know how stupid mankind is. They have no idea who they are or where they came from. On their best day, all they care about is themselves and the wordly pursuits we push them into."*

The Power of Georgia calmly replied, *"True. We followed protocol. I've worked closely on this case, as you have. I think we may be entering a season of transition. Heaven is using some new tactic or something. We have to...."*

He hung on that word as he stood up from his chair and began to walk amongst the agents. One agent finished his sentence, *"Work harder!"*

The Power of Georgia stopped, pointed at him with

excitement and said, *"That's it. That's always the answer in this kingdom. Lord Satan freed us from the bureaucracy of Heaven. A culture that holds you back from your most basic lusts. A place where there is a Father who makes you ask for things, as he lords it over us. In the kingdom of darkness, if you want something, you take it. Lord Satan freed us from having to ask anyone for anything. If you see it, and you want it, take it. Greed is good. Lust is good. Lying is acceptable if it helps you get what you want. Relationships don't matter. People are to be used for their resources and then thrown away, like garbage. Which means you have to go take it before they do. Work! Work! Work!. It's the only way."*

The agents nervously looked at each other.

Some were new to the team and were still getting to know their peers. Others had many years on the team and were hanging on his every word - this level of focus was only to collect the information to bolster their personal career plans. Intimate relationships don't exist in the kingdom of darkness. They simply listen when it applies to them and their personal goals. There is no real covenant between them. Only fear of retribution for failing their assignment.

The Power of Georgia wasn't finished.

He completed his walk around the circumference of the office and impatiently motioned for the agents to find a seat.

They nervously scrambled to find a seat. All but one. This particular demon had some respect for himself. He was ambitious and couldn't wait to share his ideas as they pressed into the next season of planning for this mission.

The POG began to speak as he sat back down in his enormous office chair. His chair looked like a gothic version of an office chair. He said, *"We all know what protocol tells us to do next.*

However, we need to think outside the box on this one. We need fresh creativity and amotion to craft a better plan to steal, kill, and destroy from Blake's life."

The ambitious agent raised his hand and said, *"Permission to speak, Sir?"*

The POG nodded his head in agreement.

The ambitious agent continued, *"Protocol tells us that Blake is the target, always. What if we expanded that target to his entire family, especially his now pregnant mother? She doesn't have much favor on her life. She is still living under the heavy influence of the spirit of Addiction. In other cases, we have simply rigged the lottery system to benefit people like this. They will usually spend it on drugs and wild parties for their friends. An overdose is bound to happen when opportunity presents itself. Since the spirit of Condemnation already bombards her thought life night and day, it doesn't take much to tip people like this over the edge. Their self-esteem is fragile, and they have no idea how loved and cherished they are by Abba."*

The other agents sneered as if to say, *"That idea sounds stupid..."*

They were only thinking this because they didn't present it to the POG first. Everything in the kingdom of darkness is a competition.

The ambitious agent continued, *"The spirit of Addiction wars against a fruit of the spirit, specifically self-control. Throughout the addiction oppression process, self-control is pushed out of the way to allow the substance to make the decisions. Once the substance has full control, self-control is no longer a variable we have to be concerned about. Humans choose with their will in their decision making process, to include saying yes to Jesus.*

Addiction, when it has become fully manifest, is in the driver's seat. Every decision pours through the filter of addiction, leaving them at the mercy of the substance."

The POG nodded his head up and down in agreement.

However, he had an immediate response, *"This is all true, and we have used this tactic many times. Giving a person large sums of money, while they are being oppressed by the spirit of Poverty is a recipe for disaster. Humans will always spend the money on indulgence and self-gratification, nullifying its value to advance the Kingdom of Heaven and bless their family with generational wealth. Most lottery winners are broke within a few years of receiving their winnings for this reason. The spirit of Poverty tells them that wealth is their ticket to getting what they want, instead of using their wealth to advance the Kingdom of Heaven. What are some more ideas? This has been done more times than I can count. Come on people, think..."*

Another agent bravely raised his hand and started to say, *"Permission to speak..."* before he was cut off by the POG motioning him to get on with it.

The agent said, *"We need an up to date behavioral reconnaissance on the boyfriend. He could be an excellent doorway to enter if we better understand his affections. Humans often think we can read their minds. We all know that we can't. What they don't know is - we don't have to. We simply read their behavior. Since every behavior begins with a thought, we already have the root to work with. Ill order another behavioral reconnaissance, but we already know that he loves to party, and he isn't all that faithful to Sarah. His porn addiction keeps him looking for more in the area of sexual perversion. Since Sarah is also being oppressed by the Orphan spirit, she will remain in this abusive relationship, rather than be alone."*

The POG smiled and said, *"Now here is an agent who is thinking outside the box. All of you can learn something from him."*

The other agents nervously readjusted themselves in their seats with jealous expressions. The POG then made the following statement with an authoritative tone as the agents feverishly began taking notes. *"Enlist the church of Satan in Sarah's region. Set up a séance with the local medium as well. We will involve them in the mission, especially since our intel is pointing to Blake's possible calling as a Five-fold ministry official. The church of satan can facilitate the street level curses and give us actionable intelligence as well. The local warlocks are hard core loyal servants and are heavily involved in the sex trafficking of children. They are also involved in the amateur porn industry. Local wicked spirits can provide the behavioral reconnaissance reports on Sarah's boyfriend, as well as all extended family. I know for a fact that the extended family members of both Sarah and her boyfriend release words of death over them often - especially the Christians in their family. Their families have pretty much given up on them, and subsequently stopped praying for them years ago. This is the main reason we have had so much access to their lives."*

The ambitious agent, sensing a pause in the POG's directive, raised his hand and waited his turn to be called upon.

The POG saw the hand and said, *"Go ahead.."*

The ambitious agent stood up and said, *"I would like to handle the behavioral reconnaissance reports, Sir. It was my area of expertise before my reassignment to your team. I served for 50 years in this region as a street level wicked spirit and know this lineage well. I'm an expert in the culture of the region and have access to the regional records."*

Regional records are kept for hundreds of years due to

generational curses still active. Only one DLD is allowed to operate in the court of heaven. Therefore, access to current lineage records is limited to the DLD. DLDs rarely release current information, unless it will help them get promoted in some way. This is the compartmentalization of information used in the kingdom of darkness. This limits the regional operation in some ways, but nothing they can't overcome with a little street smarts. The best intelligence gathering is often accomplished at the street level, where wicked spirits simply hang out and watch the behavior of humans. Much like a parent watches a toddler in a toy store - waiting to see what they gravitate towards. The affection of a human will always manifest itself openly. This is why scripture tells us to *"Guard your heart with all diligence..."* The heart is the mind, will and emotions of a human. More specifically in Hebrew culture and writing, the *heart* is the seat of affection and desire. Humans will always show their hand in some way, by simply manifesting what they desire openly. This becomes actionable intelligence for the demonic...

BEHAVIORAL RECONNAISSANCE...

Sarah and her boyfriend were sound asleep in their bed. At 12:34 am,

Sarah began to slowly stir as she gently rolled over to reestablish her position on the bed to face her sleeping boyfriend.

She opened her eyes and suddenly became aware of a hormonal shift in her body.

She heard about this from other friends who had experienced pregnancy. She knew that something was going on in her body. She just wasn't quite sure enough to jump to any conclusive ideas. As she lay next to her boyfriend, the thoughts began to bombard her. A wicked spirit present in her bedroom began his daily routine of bombarding her thought life. He simply reached into his quiver of fiery darts and released them one at a time, beginning with the first thoughts of the day.

Believers in Jesus can guard their thought life by immediately spending time in prayer, worship, and bible study to start the day. Pre-believers haven't learned this lesson quite yet. They often begin the day with a bombardment of news and political slander. This sets the course for their existence in the Earth as being unimpactful. Humans think that simply being aware of the problems happening in the Earth empowers them to bring change. Since awareness is only the first step, this is most often where humans camp out. They love to express their awareness and bombard others with their opinions on the problems facing humanity. Very few humans are willing to pay the price for change.

Simply listening to political talk shows and gorging on the latest news makes them feel better because - at least they are informed. The demonic kingdom thinks this daily cycle of news is the most brilliant idea they have ever invented. Sadly, most humans begin their day with so much bad news, they are completely unaware of the advancements of the Kingdom of Heaven. This becomes a lifestyle of bitterness, anger and offense against the world they are called to impact. It also causes believers in Jesus to further turn inward - rather than outward towards the masses of people in need of a Savior. Ironically, both pre-believers and Christians have developed the same daily routine. They both start their day with bad news, leaving them hopeless and discouraged. Sadly, Christians have completely avoided the scriptures on this topic, *"whatsoever things are lovely, pure and of a good report, think on these things..."* Humans aren't built to carry the burdens of the world. Its challenging enough to lead their families into breakthrough. The demonic kingdom has used this method for centuries. Especially since the invention of the printing press, which was primarily for Kingdom expansion. As with all technology, the demonic kingdom didn't invent the printing press, they simply know how to weaponize its use against humanity.

Sarah began her daily struggle with her thought life. It was the typical stuff. The wicked spirit, looking bored as usual, reached into his quiver of fiery darts and sent it hurling through the air, landing accurately, as it lodged itself in her cerebral cortex.

The fiery dart emitted spirit realm poison into her brain. Her brain translated the fiery dart into something very simple, but powerful. *"You should just end your life today.. You aren't worthy of love. You are a loser in every sense of the word..."* and such like.

He was positioned in the corner next to the lamp where he often hid. There was no anointing on Sarah's house, and it had never been consecrated to the Lord through prayer, declaration and decree. He had full access to every square inch of the property. There was no protection from evil for Sarah's home since they were not in covenant with Jesus and openly disregarded all religion. They were living in agreement with evil. Therefore, evil lived with them. Sarah had invited them in through declaration, unknowingly. She would often say to the Mormons who stopped by to hand out pamphlets, *"I don't believe in God, Jesus, or any other imaginary person. I live my own life on my own terms..."* This declaration opened the door to the demonic kingdom, and they have lived there ever since. Spirits of lust, anger, perversion and poverty lived there night and day attempting to steal, kill or destroy something from Sarah's life. Street level wicked spirits often get bored because they have a hard time being present. They are always dreaming of promotion, which always gives them more power in the demonic kingdom structure. Power is what they crave...

As Sarah pondered these thoughts, she looked around the room. She reached over to her dresser next to the bed and prepared a fresh needle. She used her lighter to heat up the substance in an old silver spoon. She pushed all the air out of the needle, dipped the tip into the substance and drew enough out to give her the boost she needed to get out of bed. After tying a blue latex disposable torniquet around her arm, she found a vein and injected the substance - slowly. She could feel the rush of positive emotions. She was suddenly feeling better. Sarah could muster up the energy to take on the day, as well as her thought life, as long as she had her friend, *"heroin."* This was her daily routine.

She sprung out of bed and made her way to the bathroom.

She looked in the mirror.

She examined the lines forming on her face.

She was only 27 but looked older. She already looked like she had lived many lifetimes. Sin has this effect on humans. Mental, emotional and physical health are all weakened slowly as the soul becomes darker. The heroin would only give her 6 hours of balance. She needed it in order to make it to work and seem normal and productive. She would have to take another hit prior to her shift starting at 6:00 pm. She was currently working as a bartender where she met her boyfriend. She loved the job because it required a strong work ethic, and she enjoyed serving people. The tips were pretty good as well. This was also the environment where she was introduced to illegal drugs. All it took was one dose, and she was hooked for life.

She often declared laughingly, *"I don't have a drug addiction, I have a drug affair. I love heroin and heroin loves me…"*

This declaration, of course, further fueled the onslaught of evil creeping into her home. We become what we live in agreement with. Both obedience and disobedience attract the supernatural. Sarah was attracting the onslaught to her life, her home and her unborn child.

She heard her boyfriend beginning to stir in the bed.

She reluctantly said, *"Good morning. How did you sleep?"*

He responded with, *"It would have been better without your snoring."*

Sarah defensively responded, *"I don't snore!"*

He laughed and said, *"I need to record it, so you'll believe me. You literally sound like you are sawing logs with an industrial size chain saw."*

This interaction was how they normally started their day. The day usually started out with opportunity for offense and grew from there.

Sarah thought to herself, *"Why am I in yet another relationship with a guy who doesn't know how to talk to women."* Sarah's boyfriend thought to himself, *"Why am I in yet another relationship with a woman who doesn't understand my humor?"*

Neither one of them had a successful marriage modeled for them. They both came from broken homes with one parent barely present. Neither one of them had a father present in their home to demonstrate love and leadership. They were both attempting to do something they had never seen demonstrated - a simple long term intimate relationship.

Sarah turned to him and said, *"I'm going to stop by Walgreen's and get a pregnancy test. I'm feeling a little different today."*

Her boyfriend looked at her with a tinge of fear, *"Different how?"*

Sarah responded with, *"I don't know. I've had several friends who have been pregnant. My symptoms sound similar."*

Sarah's boyfriend looked even more terrified, and said, *"This is terrible. If you're pregnant you will have to get an abortion. I'm not ready to be a father. I have my life to live, and I don't need anything distracting my plans."*

Sarah's heart sank. She held back tears as she pondered for a moment, her boyfriend's response. How on earth did she get herself in this situation. She had no idea if she was indeed pregnant yet. However, now she knew how he felt about it. In some ways, she agreed. Afterall, a child at this time in her life would be a complete distraction. She had plans as well. She wanted to own her own bar someday. She had the ability to think in numbers and manage people. She also loved the chaotic scene in a bar. It was full of life and energy. She studied how to mix the perfect drink and was well known in that arena.

She responded with, *"I see. As usual, you only think about yourself."*

Then she turned around and walked away, leaving their bedroom.

He thought to himself as she walked away, *"As usual. I've allowed a woman to dictate my future. Why do I even bother with relationships? They just hold you back from what you want to do in life..."*

A *spirit of Offense* was sitting silently taking notes as the entire scene played out.

He was preparing a behavioral reconnaissance report for his supervisor. It was a simple document. Three basic sections of the report form had to be completed and turned in weekly. Each section had a specific area to be monitored. They were *Relationships, Physical Senses,* and *Time.* These represent the three areas the kingdom of darkness considers paramount to successful steal, kill, and destroy missions. They always plan to infiltrate these areas in order to control and manipulate the human's life. In the *Relationships* section, the demon was to make notes as to the overall health of each relationship, and or potential ways to attack their relationships. In this section, every detail concerning the formation of new relationships, and the status of existing ones was to be documented. The demon was specifically instructed to make notes concerning any relationships with a believer in Jesus and how it affected the target's beliefs. Any new relationship with a believer in Jesus was to be sent up the chain immediately.

Sarah only had one known relationship with a believer in Jesus - her mother Gladys. It wasn't like Gladys was influencing her much. She swore off all religion to include Christianity. The demon assigned to document behavior made a note of this several years prior, but also remained keenly aware of any changes in behavior for Sarah. In the *Physical Senses* section, the demon was to make notes concerning the human's behavior in what they watch and listen to. This is because humans watch and listen to things they most often desire. Since Sarah loved to listen to political talk radio, it was easy to keep her in a state of anger and frustration. She loved horror movies. Therefore, it was easy for the demonic to keep her in a state of fear and anxiety. Finally, the third section to be kept up to date was *Time*. Sarah loved to be around nature, and she loved to read. Her time, when she wasn't working, was mostly spent hiking or reading. These are great activities that can be very healthy. However, Sarah pursued hiking as a spiritual experience and would often pray to the trees and streams as if they had some magical powers. She consumed books on horror, mutilation and just about anything considered deviant by most. She quite simply loved anything irreverent.

The demonic knows that humans become what they consume. They also know that every idol they expose humans to, eventually takes over these three areas of life. An idol is one of the longest running tricks of the demonic kingdom. Their plan is to highjack the human's relationships, physical senses and time. This is the deadly three strand chord used by the kingdom of darkness to steal, kill and destroy the identity, purpose and destiny of a human being. Sarah was quite comfortable because, she wasn't in agreement with anything Gladys had to say.

Afterall, *"religious belief is a crutch invented by weak humans to provide another means of coping..."At* least, that was Sarah's belief since she decided to be an atheist years ago.

The demon made a special entry in the *Relationships* section as he watched the conversation unfold between Sarah and her boyfriend. It read,

"Boyfriend would rather her have an abortion. Sarah doesn't believe in abortion. Potential to split the relationship if developed further. Another fatherless home is the goal..."

It is always the goal of the demonic kingdom to create as many fatherless homes as possible. This leaves a void in society. Most all societal ills facing humanity are caused by fatherless homes. The demonic kingdom made this a point of emphasis in the early 1960s and has continued to throw manpower and resources at the idea. It wasn't a new idea - just the rebirth of an old one. Like all ideas in the demonic kingdom, there really isn't anything new. There aren't any new spirits either. Baal, Molech and Asherah are still doing their thing, re-branded as The Stock Market, Pro-choice, and Mother Nature. Actually, in 1975, *paganism and idolatry* is at an all-time high in America.

The demon made another entry in the *Physical Senses* section. It read,

"Loves to be around nature. Feels alive after praying to the trees and mountains. Potential to expand on pagan beliefs with the right set of friends and literature. Also, a potential for demonic encounter, if done properly."

This entry was common. However, it gets tricky when the demonic decide to give someone an encounter where they manifest to a human. It can scare them off, so it has to be done carefully. They provided the same type of encounter to Joseph Smith, one of the founders of the Mormon religion. Demonic encounters change a person profoundly. If they were to manifest for Sarah, they would have to plan it out well in advance. Finally, he made an entry in the section labeled, *Time*. It read,

"Loves to spend time with people who aren't religious. Potential to influence further into humanism if introduced to the right people. Very productive and works a lot at her job."

This was also common and served as very good news. It showed her devotion to her job, which kept her too busy to think about eternity. It also showed that Sarah was fully indoctrinated into the materialist culture where the rich only provide enough wage to buy and consume on a set schedule - never releasing enough to provide the same level of generational wealth they possess. This would continue to steal her time. Since hourly workers give a portion of their time for a wage, they are actually giving away their lives one hour at a time.

After completing the behavioral reconnaissance form, the demon folded it up and placed it in his pocket. He had a meeting with his supervisor later in the day. He was excited to be on this case. Sarah served as a slam dunk in the demonic kingdom. All the cards were stacked against her. All was going precisely as planned. This would be huge for his career. To steal, kill and destroy from Sarah's life was his ticket out of Georgia. He longed to work at a higher level. He saw the privilege and power that the Power of Georgia exercised. He wanted it. All he had to do was work harder. All he had to do was keep doing his job and take advantage of those working under him in order to achieve his dreams.

It didn't matter who he had to step on to get a little higher up on the ladder. He didn't care about anyone but himself. He certainly didn't care about some human made in God's image and likeness. He believed this was his planet, given to Lord Satan many centuries prior. In his opinion, God went back on his word when he made man and gave him dominion over the Earth. This was a fight fueled by principle. This was about social justice for all demons, especially him. If he is a God of forgiveness, where was his portion? He followed Lord Satan, who was formerly called Lucifer in Heaven, because he witnessed the patriarchy first hand. In his opinion, Lord Satan was setting them free to be themselves. He set them free to live life without limits or rules.

THE EXCHANGE MARKET OF HEAVEN...

Gladys was up very late into the night. It was her time of prayer.

She loved to spend time in God's presence in worship and praise. She knew that her time was precious and decided years ago to give time to God on a consistent daily schedule. Not to be religious - simply to give a portion of each day as a sacrifice. She learned the value of this discipline early in her Christian life from her Pastor. She was taught to give God the time He deserves as an offering of friendship – because the Father longs for us to see Him this way. It wasn't that God needed to be reminded of things. She simply wanted to be with Him in an intimate moment each and every day. Through the years she has developed a hunger for God's presence. After her prayer time, she would always spend time in the Word, as well. She learned that the Bible is in fact *"Jesus in print"*. Therefore, when she spent time in the Word she was spending time with Jesus. She loved to listen to sermons on cassette tape and go to conferences. She especially loved Jimmy Swaggart and his ability to communicate the heart felt message of salvation. Among the others she deeply respected were Billy Graham and Oral Roberts. If they were on the television, she would take the time to listen to them and bask in the preaching and teaching of God's Word. Her time was consumed by prayer, study, and service in her local church. Gladys was a faithful Kingdom citizen in every way...

On this night she could feel her heart stirring for her

daughter, Sarah. She lifted her up in prayer often. She prayed specific prayers concerning Sarah's identity, purpose and destiny. She would even repent on Sarah's behalf and ask the Father to pour out mercy and grace on her life, even though Sarah was living in open disobedience to all she was taught. She knew Sarah was stubborn. Sarah had been like that since birth. It was almost comical back then, but now Sarah was 25.

Gladys thought to herself often, *"Surely Sarah is ready to yield to the purposes of God in her life. Surely she has given it some thought. Surely, she will come to her senses and realize that Jesus is the way, the truth, and the life. Did I fail her in some way through my own behavior or is she offended at how I raised her? Why won't she accept Jesus as her Lord and Savior?"*

Gladys often had these types of thoughts. She brought Sarah to church every week throughout her childhood. She encouraged Sarah to be part of the Youth Group and go to church camp. She even enrolled Sarah in the local Christian school, where she knew she would be taught about Jesus. She was fully aware of what the secular school system was attempting to impart to the children of this generation. More humanism and science. Gladys wasn't comfortable sending Sarah to public school for this reason. She didn't want Sarah exposed to anything but scripture and the subjects she would need to hold down a good job. Gladys was in fear of what was happening in the public schools since prayer was abolished in 1962.

Now, in 1975, she was beginning to see the results of this decision. More and more children were being robbed of the opportunity to see prayer demonstrated while at school. Since the daily public school schedule was a staple of American culture, the decision to remove prayer from school would cause long-term chaos beyond anything the nation could imagine. However, Gladys was among those interceding for the nation on her church intercessory team. The landmark decision to declare prayer in schools as *"unconstitutional"* was boring a hole in her soul. She as beginning to wonder if prayer even worked at all...

When we pray, God hears us. Scripture tells us to *"ask and keep asking"*. Jesus declared that whatever we ask in His name, it will be done for us". The battle rages in the mind when our prayer isn't answered. When He doesn't answer our prayer, this seemingly contradicts His Word. We are often left to wonder. We are also given a laundry list of ideas to explain why the prayer wasn't answered by others who also don't get their prayers answered. Since misery loves company, believers in Jesus often confide in one another seeking solace from the mind battle. Often, a new theological explanation is birthed to accommodate the dilemma. Believers who don't believe in divine healing almost always have one or two things in common. Their prayer for healing wasn't answered, or they were taught to yield to the sickness because it is obviously God's will. Gladys wasn't in agreement with this, but she couldn't help but feel the weight of disappointment. Her life for Jesus has been riddled with both answered and unanswered prayer. Her battle with disappointment has taken her to the *Exchange Market of Heaven* many times. It is there she makes an exchange –

her disappointment for Heaven's peace.

Her sorrow for Heaven's joy.

Her burdens for Heaven's rest.

As Gladys sat in her recliner in her living room, she gazed at the memories on the walls and shelves.

Worship music could be heard at all hours of the day and night.

She paused to reflect on the memories as she smiled and said,

"Abba, you have given me so many amazing memories. You have always provided for me and my daughter. Even when my husband decided to leave us and pursue a selfish existence, shirking his fatherly responsibilities, you were there. I am thankful for all you have done for me. However, I know there is more. I know that you are the God of recompense, restitution, and restoration. I feel a heaviness for the things that have been stolen from me. The relationship I long for with my daughter is being stolen from me, leaving me with a feeling of loneliness and heaviness. You are the God of the breakthrough. You are the Provider, Healer, Banner, and Peace for my life. I come before you tonight to make a trade on the Exchange Market of Heaven..."

Suddenly, in Heaven, a commodities broker received a message on his screen. It flashed, *"Potential exchange - Gladys Johnson - be prepared to broker on behalf of the Throne."*

The broker quickly responded with protocol. He opened Gladys' file located on his desktop to become better acquainted with her story, and any other information needed to serve her well. Since Heaven operates with technology yet to be released to humans, his desktop computer was more comparable to a holographic image. The screen seemed to float in mid-air, with all appropriate buttons and notifications also within reach. The potential exchange alerts, along with any other messages pertaining to the brokering of Heavenly commodities came with a sound notification comparable to what would later be released in the year 1992 with the invention of the smart phone. Earth wasn't quite ready for this technology yet. The desktop computer had already been invented in 1964, but it was very expensive and had yet to make its way into every home.

The Heavenly Technology Commission (HTC) was waiting for the right time to make it available to the average consumer. To be honest, they were waiting for the ecclesia to come into agreement with the purpose of technology in the first place. Many of the ecclesia expressed a fear of too much *"worldliness"* in the church. This would be an area of contention for the ecclesia for many years. *The Heavenly Technology Commission,* like all commissions formed by Heaven to help with the affairs of man, only releases what the ecclesia asks for in prayer. The only thing holding this level of technology up from being released was a firm declaration from the ecclesia, and an understanding of how to steward it for Heaven's purposes...

The broker read through Glady's history, family lineage, salvation date, baptism date, Holy Spirit empowerment date, etc... This information would help the broker form a connection with Gladys. In the Kingdom, everyone has a story. Kingdom citizens aren't simply treated as a number. Their story is fully understood by every broker, paralegal or messenger angel tasked with serving a Kingdom citizen. Notifications to serve, as well as decrees to assist are treated with the utmost care and concern. It is protocol to know the story of every human being served - first and foremost. This particular broker has 1,000 years of experience in this position.

He glanced at a motivational poster on his office wall. It was a picture of Jesus declaring to His followers during His Earthly ministry,

"Come unto me, all you who are weary and heavy ladened, and I will give you rest..."

This served as the mission statement for the Exchange Market of Heaven. Underneath this statement, it also read,

"To equip and serve the Redeemed by providing timely broker services for Heavenly Commodities."

Beneath that statement also read,

"Since the foundation of the world."

The broker understood the mission of the Exchange Market. It was very simple. When a person is redeemed, they are transferred from the kingdom of darkness to the Kingdom of Light. In the Earthly realm, it may not look like much. However, in Heaven, it's quite a profound thing - their citizenship privileges are reestablished. The benefits that were lost due to disobedience and sin are reinstated. This enables them to have access to the Kingdom, which contains their inheritance as Abba's children. This is why Jesus began his earthly ministry with a simple sermon, *"Repent, the Kingdom is at hand."* What He was trying to explain has stumped theologians for many generations. Quite simply, Jesus was telling humanity,

"Change the way you think about life itself, this Earthly reality, and the ideas you have invented for yourself through humanism and paganism. The realm of my dominion, to be released in atmospheric form, having the ability to superimpose itself onto your reality, is now within reach. Everything you need to bring Heaven to Earth is now accessible for those who choose to come into agreement with the purpose of my death, burial, and resurrection."

Once a person yields to Jesus and asks forgiveness for their sins, confessing them openly with their mouth, and believing in their heart, their citizenship is established. They are declared a righteous citizen, and all rights, privileges and honors appertaining to them are deposited into their account. More accurately, their account is unlocked. It was there all along, sitting in a dormant account, waiting to be utilized, much like a trust fund on Earth. It is actually where the idea came from. There isn't anything new under the sun because all altruistic ideas come from Heaven's Hall of Knowledge where they originate. There is no plagiarism in Heaven because all knowledge is freely shared and disseminated openly. When ideas are released to mankind, Heaven has to wait and see how the person will steward it. Usually, mankind will find a way to monetize the idea, which includes filing for a patent. A simple trust fund is an example of an idea, sent from Heaven to help mankind manage generational wealth. The proper use of a trust fund will enable earthly wealth to be maximized across several generations by establishing a protocol for the release of assets to trust find recipients.

Brokers working in the Exchange Market aren't authorized to release everything at once. They work closely with Jesus and establish a stewardship plan and release of assets schedule. However, a release of commodities is different. The broker is authorized to release commodities when the redeemed request an exchange based upon the declaration made by Jesus. He basically was saying to His followers,

"Bring me the things you aren't made to carry, and I'll give you in exchange the things you need to thrive."

Humans aren't made to carry disappointment, frustration, or regret. They aren't made to carry negative emotions at all. The Exchange Market handles the trade in real time. No extra authorization is needed. The broker looked at his commodities sheet, which he knew by heart. He also looked at the list of potential human vulnerabilities, which he also had memorized. After making preparations for the trade by catching up on Gladys' story, and once again familiarizing himself with the commodities he was authorized to trade - he waited patiently for Gladys to pray more precisely. Heaven only maneuvers in response to the specific prayers of the redeemed. This is the protocol of the Kingdom. If we don't have something, it's because we didn't ask...

Gladys continued to pray, *"Abba, I want to make an exchange. I bring you my heaviness, loneliness, isolation from my daughter, regret for not being a better example to her, and I ask for peace, in Jesus name..."*

Suddenly, the broker received a notification. It read, "*Incoming trade - GLADYS -02141954 -1345 heaviness, loneliness, isolation from my daughter, regret for not being a better example to her.*"

The broker sprang into action in accordance with protocol. He has executed millions of trades in his service to the redeemed. He was overjoyed to broker this exchange. He had a firm understanding of the human psyche. He was trained at the Broker's Academy to facilitate the exchange as fast as heavenly possible. Afterall, heaven is there to serve. His role was extremely important to the redeemed.

He thought to himself, *"How would they be able to fulfil their purpose and destiny while carrying all this weight? I'm thankful to play a role in their development. If only more of the redeemed would exercise their privilege of tapping into their divine storehouse of goods and make a simple exchange."*

He took another look at her current stewardship plan. She was due a raise in monthly finances, or *"monthly manna"* as it is called among brokers. He enjoyed facilitating this for Gladys as well. Brokers are trained in the Kingdom science of stewardship because they also manage the release of assets on behalf of Jesus - the Advocate. They don't just facilitate the exchange of emotional currency, they also handle the release of resources, to include divine wisdom, revelation of scripture, and much more. They operate as trusted Associates under the supervision of Jesus - the *Chief Resources Officer*. Holy Spirit speaks the delivery into being on behalf of the Godhead.

Jesus declared to His followers during His earthly ministry, how this works. He taught His disciples about the Holy Spirit's role in their lives, once He returned to sit at the right hand of the Father. He said,

"The Spirit will take from what is mine and declare it to you..."

This is the format for all supernatural resources being transferred into the Earthly realm. The Holy Spirit simply speaks, and it manifests for the redeemed. Words of wisdom, knowledge and prophecy are among these resources. Finances are also on the list, but most often, finance are released in accordance with co-laboring principles established by the Father. These include, *"if you don't work, you don't eat"* and such like. This ensures the redeemed are raised up with a sense of work ethic, instead of entitlement. They don't have to work to earn Abba's love. However, as in the case of the parable released by Jesus to His followers, *"Take from the man who has the least, and give it to the man with the most."* This was demonstrated in the parable because stewardship is a serious thing in the Kingdom.

The redeemed are expected to pass the stewardship test with all things - to include finances, natural gifts, and spiritual gifts. In regard to finances, *"Use what you have, or it can be taken from you"* - for your own good. This may sound harsh, but in the Kingdom there is always grace to pick yourself up and try again. It is part of the development of a Saint. Even though Spiritual gifts and callings are on the list of resources allocated by Heaven, they are never taken away in the same fashion. Their release represents an entirely different developmental progression. The redeemed need their spiritual gifts to operate effectively. The Holy Spirit baptism, which unlocks their spiritual gifts, is a down payment on their inheritance. They also need the connectivity this encounter provides for communication with Holy Spirit. Abba doesn't spiritually disconnect from the redeemed, because that association was formed by the shedding of blood. However, the administration of finances is simply called, *"The season of Stewardship."* This season of stewardship is a precursor to the season of Blessing. Brokers working in the *Exchange Market of Heaven* are there throughout the entire process of managing, forecasting, and releasing the resources for the redeemed in the Earth - all under the watchful eyes of Jesus Himself.

As an experienced Broker, he had pre-authorization for many things concerning Gladys' stewardship plan. He had preauthorization to release specific resources whenever she needed them.

THE ENEMY'S PLAN...

Lord Satan barged into the meeting room in anger.

He yelled at his assistant, *"Get me everyone assigned to case BLAKE-12271975-1200 in here, now!"*

The assistant sprang into action by pressing the nearest intercom button located on the wall of the meeting room.

He stood up, leaned towards the intercom, and spoke into the built in microphone, saying,

"All case workers assigned to BLAKE-12271975-1200 are to meet in the conference room immediately."

The intercom system fed into all offices throughout the demonic headquarters. From this particular location in the fortress, Lord Satan's assistant had the authorization to override all other activity and demand immediate attention to the matter at hand. This specific intercom was for one way communication to the entire fortress to issue commands from Lord Satan himself, or from his personal assistants. Lord Satan sat impatiently as he waited for the case workers to show up. As they filtered into the conference room, moving fast and fearful of what was coming next, he peered at them with contempt.

One by one the case workers poured in and took their seats around a large conference table. They brought with them whatever information they needed to give a detailed report on the case. They were higher level demons with experience, but Lord Satan never really honors anyone in accordance with their years of service. He governs with a different value system. His favorite saying is, *"What have you done for me lately?"*. He demands daily adherence to his authority and never takes the time to think about the work involved to carry out his commands. He only thinks about the results and how he can continue to push them to the brink of exhaustion. They scurried in looking tired, overworked, and undervalued. Each one gazed back at Lord Satan with head tilted enough to show respect and honor. Some, even with their years of experience have a hard time looking him in the eyes. Lord Satan has the tendency to accuse them of the wildest things. He once accused them of planning a plot against him. His response was to fire everyone, send them to Hades for 100 years of tormenting duty, and replace them with better case workers. His paranoia often controls his behavior.

The case workers sat around the table waiting for what was next. They all know how this could go. They were shaking in fear, but only on the inside, so as to hide their emotional weakness in his presence. They were also pouring through their documents, preparing for whatever this meeting would turn out to be. Once the meeting participants were seated, 12 in all, Lord Satan's personal assistant began to take roll. He then casually made Lord Satan aware of two empty seats. The empty seats were for the remaining members working on the case.

Lord Satan barked in anger, *"What part of "All case workers assigned to BLAKE-12271975-1200 are to meet in the conference room immediately, don't we understand?"*

The demons already in attendance, seated and ready to meet looked at each other with fearful glances, just hoping those who were missing would show up so they could get this meeting over with.

And then, in walked the DLD assigned to the case and the *Power of Georgia* following closely behind.

As they took their seats, each one looked at Lord Satan apologetically.

The DLD said, *"My apologies Lord Satan. We were working on the case and had to wrap up our meeting. It took a little longer than expected."*

Lord Satan responded with, *"You are here now, so let's get on with it. What do you have for me?"*

The DLD addressed Lord Satan, but also the entire team assembled for the meeting. He began his briefing with a smile, and said, *"It's a pretty cut and dry case. I've got signed and sealed generational contracts dating back thousands of years on this human. I don't see any hope of Blake ever stepping into his identity, purpose, and destiny in the Earth."*

It was a bold statement, but everyone seated at the table nodded their heads up and down in agreement. The DLD was the lead on the case, and he already sent briefing summaries to each of their personal assistants.

The *Power of Georgia* sat in disdain and acted as if the meeting was an interruption to his already busy day.

Lord Satan glanced at the Power of Georgia and said, *"Do you have somewhere more important to be."*

The Power of Georgia answered with false humility, *"My Lord, this is in no way an interruption. I was just thinking about the case and the detailed needed to carry out the assignment. It seems as though it's a little overboard for one soul. I mean, I've read the file but, why all the extra attention?"*

Lord Satan looked back at him with no response and proceeded to look around the room at each case worker individually with an intense pressurized glare, *"I'm ramping up efforts to wipe out the Five-Fold Ministry in the Earth. The favor and love the old man shows for these people makes me sick. They are difficult to get rid of, and I'm putting the pressure on you to make this happen.*

From here on out, this is the level of detail we will put into every case concerning a Five-Fold Minister. Their influence is what is dangerous to my kingdom. They declare from pulpits the love of God. They feed the homeless and care for widows. They are always praying and declaring the old man's purpose in the earth. Originally, we were focused on Israel. They are still here. When the Apostle Paul was commissioned to declare the old man's purpose to the gentiles, our focus shifted again. Now, with the eventual release of new technology slated for this generation, we had better ramp up efforts to destroy anyone carrying the anointing to govern the redeemed. I don't care how we do it. I want results......"

Each demon assigned to Blake's case looked at each other with edgy expectancy. It was as if they were waiting on one another to respond. At the same time they were nervously mulling over ideas in their head so they could be the first to bring a clear cut direction to the table and impress Lord Satan.

About that time, the DLD spoke up and said, *"It's been proven that we can't stop the old man's message from being broadcast on the current technology platforms. The viewing audience numbers show that Billy Graham and Jimmy Swaggart are watched more than any other show on television. Our plan was to hijack the television stations and flood humanity with depictions of fleshly behavior. Since they are born spiritually dead, they would naturally yield to their sinful behavior depicted on the television because, through skillful writing, whatever form of behavior they see regularly would become normalized. Stories of homosexual partnerships and parents raising their children without the knowledge of God will become the normal prime time programming for millions. The plan is to ensure they never hear the message about forgiveness of sins and so on. This plan has flaws and should be adjusted as the results are documented."*

Lord Satan replied, *"What kind of flaws are you alluding to?"*

The DLD relished the opportunity to responded with, *"All creativity originates from Heaven's library and the Hall of Knowledge. Artists carry the anointing to create stories and film makers carry the anointing to produce cinematic depictions of those stories for public consumption. We must ramp up efforts to influence the artists to write and produce kingdom of darkness content for public consumption. With the right amount of unresolved trauma, a writer is easily influenced to produce damaging imagery. Seducing spirits are often put to work for this type of thing. This will flood the airwaves with our message of humanism and paganism. Horror movies will flood the cinemas with death and desensitize human sentiment on a new level. Several stories are slated to be released in the coming decades. The story of Harry Potter, for example, will place basic witchcraft principles in the hands of millions of children. That story isn't scheduled for release until later in the early 2000s. My point is that with each release of new viewing platforms, we must work harder to influence the artists."*

Lord Satan looked at the DLD and said, *"How can we get more horror movies into the homes?"*

The DLD responded, *"The TV stations aren't budging quite yet. Cable television has them available, but not all families have cable television, currently. I think we just need to make it cheaper. We just have to hold fast until the release of the internet. That's when the efforts for kingdom of darkness programming will be ramped up to its maximum potential. As is our custom, we simply hijack the ideas released from the Hall of Knowledge and put our spin on them, for our purpose."*

Lord Satan smiled. It was rare that he smiled, but this particular DLD was on a fast promotional track due to his performance. Lord Satan discipled him personally and has always seen his potential. However, what the DLD doesn't know is that Lord Satan has had several disciples he has used for their talents and then, when he is done with them, he throws them away. Lord Satan looked at the rest of the case workers and said in disdain, *"Is he the only one here with a brain? Anyone else want to contribute to the discussion, or do I need to fire all of you and assemble a more competent team?"*

The Power of Georgia sat up in his seat and said, *"In my region, I already have oppressed humans working in entertainment. The stuff they write is filled with works of the flesh, on full display. However, It hasn't stopped the evangelism efforts of the local ecclesia. I see your point but, how do we ramp up efforts in our regions. I have some ideas from my discussions with the Power of California. He called for all hands on deck after the Azusa street revivals in 1904 and basically hijacked the creativity poured out in the region. Members of his team inhabit several writers, directors, and cinematic producers already. That's where the majority of the content is currently being produced and distributed from."*

Lord Satan chimed in, *"Exactly."*

The DLD looked at them both and continued to share his vision, *"I have gathered actionable intelligence on the release of something the humans will call the "internet" and, as of 1975, it has already been invented. With the release of this technology, the world as we know it will be changed forever, ushering in the last era prior to the rapture of the ecclesia. Humans will be able to communicate worldwide in seconds. Of course, this invention comes from the Hall of Knowledge to push humans closer to their destiny, and like all inventions of this magnitude, they will only release it to the public when they have found a way to monetize it for selfish purposes. At some point, every human on earth will have the ability to broadcast themselves, with whatever message they choose to deliver."*

Suddenly, everyone in the room readjusted themselves in their chairs due to the discomfort they were feeling.

This type of power of expression being given to humans could do irreparable damage to the kingdom of darkness. They were imagining every born again believer on earth with the ability to publish content instantaneously. Not even the movie producers had that kind of power in 1975. It was a long production process to bring content to the public that often took months, even years of planning. Even Lord Satan looked uncomfortable...

Lord Satan, trying not to look disturbed by this new piece of information addressed all in attendance, *"Lets table that discussion for another time. We are here to discuss the SKD plan concerning Blake."* The DLD replied to Lord Satan while casually addressing all in attendance, *"Yes my Lord, about that... I've been doing a lot of research since this case came across my desk. I want to use the simple approach with a touch of creativity on this one. America is changing rapidly, and many new technologies are being released from the Hall of Knowledge. If we play this thing right, we can get Blake hooked on porn early in life and when the internet is officially released, he will have no chance of beating the urge. He will have access to porn magazines by age 7 and VHS recordings of porn by age 12. The agencies responsible for managing television content would never consider this type of material suitable for prime time. However, if we are patient, there will be a season of humanity where there will be no regulation of content whatsoever. At some point, they will invent the smart phone and have the internet in their hands at all times. We just have to work a solid plan to get porn in the hands of Blake as soon as he is able to process the desire cognitively."*

One of the case workers raised his hand as if he was

requesting permission to speak.

The DLD glanced his way and said, *"What's your question?"*

The case worker responded, *"Why is exposure to porn such a vital piece of the plan for Blake?"*

The DLD then addressed the entire board room, *"The human soul is the heart of man, and is layered. Because of this structure, we can make lasting deposits into the soul through the senses. The soul serves as the gas tank for the mind, will and emotions. It is written, "Out of the abundance of the heart, the mouth speaks..." It is also true that from the heart all behavior originates. Since it's a natural desire within the humans to procreate through the act of sex, we attack this area heavily. It's their strongest natural desire, next to food of course. It's actually a very normal act meant to be shared by two consenting adult humans who are in covenant with one another. When a human becomes addicted to the visual pleasure of watching others take part in it, we can easily oppress them. The spirit of Lust can operate freely within the mind, will and emotions of the human. This is important because the one fruit of the Spirit we all know is most important to the development of a human is self-control. As we erode the level of self-control within the mind, will and emotions of the human, doors begin to fly open. This serves as the foundation, and we can continue to up the temptation for other things. After a while, looking at pictures isn't enough. They will seek opportunities to be promiscuous. This always plays in our favor concerning their standing in the court of Heaven. I've taken many Pastors out with this simple tactic. It all starts with making it accessible at an early age. It most often can be made accessible by their earthly fathers. I once used a street level wicked spirit to whisper in the ear of a child and told him exactly where his dad kept the porn in his home."*

Another case worker raised his hand and asked, *"With all due respect, I still don't understand why this is one of the first tactics we would use for Blake."*

The DLD impatiently gazed at the case worker and said, *"Addiction to porn will erode Blake's self-confidence, bombard his conscience with guilt and shame. It will jeopardize his legal standing in the court of Heaven and give liberty to the spirit of Lust to terminate his ability to self-regulate natural desires. The world will teach him that it's not a big deal and that sex is just a simple physical act. This is one of the biggest lies we feed humanity. Sex isn't just a physical act, its uniquely spiritual. Through the act of sex, each party receives a layer of their sexual partner's soul. This creates what we call a soul tie. This soul tie creates a problem for them in the court of Heaven. Now, they share in the curses, hexes, vexes and contracts already established in their lineage. It literally doubles their vulnerability to spiritual attack. It's meant to do the opposite as well. When two born again believers consummate their love through the act of sex, it doubles their blessings and favor. The two become one..."*

The last case worker to ask a question began to nod his head in agreement and said, *"That makes sense now. I'm still in training and have been studying several subjects to include Spiritual Law. I desire to be a DLD someday."*

The DLD looked at him with respect and replied, *"I remember those days. Make sure you thoroughly understand Spiritual Law. Through the act of sex, humans create legally binding agreements in the spirit realm. The ecclesia isn't quite up to speed in this area, especially in America. The Cessationist doctrine we have released has stifled all interest in the spirit realm. They are clueless concerning the actual effect of blood covenants."*

The case worker made a note on his legal pad as the DLD

was speaking.

Lord Satan looked around the room as the conversation began to get deeper. Then he said, *"You have all memorized the Word. You also understand that I was the one who originally tempted Adam and Eve in the garden. The DLD is trying to get you to understand humans better by making you aware of their most common weaknesses. We begin with the basic weaknesses all humans are born with. Since they are all born disconnected from the old man, we work hard to make our own connections and create footholds as early as possible. From the time they are conceived in the womb they are a living soul. This is why abortion is a slam dunk for us. They never even have the chance to impact anyone on Earth by stepping into their identity, purpose, and destiny. If we can snuff them out during that season of life, all the better. However, if they make it to birth, we know that our window of opportunity has opened, and we must take full advantage of their human frailty.*

When Adam and Eve were formed, I knew I had to act fast. My tactic back then is the same tactic we use now. Offer them what they were born for, now. Offer them what they want, now. I like to feed on their desires and offer them something that they won't have to wait for. The old man loves to develop them through the seasons of stewardship he establishes for them. He patiently gives them with more, only when they have proven they can steward what they have been given. This is how he develops self-control in them. He does this because humans have a tendency to want things they aren't ready for. This is why one of my favorite tactics is to dump enormous amounts of money on humans and watch them destroy themselves. The old man would never do this. He cares for them too much. I offered Adam and Eve what they were born for - autonomy and freedom to take what they want. I know how the old man thinks. He loves his creation and develops them with established principles –

all of which I am well versed in."

All those in attendance were taking notes as Lord Satan spoke.

Partially because it was the culture. He expected them to hang on his every word. After all, he was the one who coerced them into rebelling with him to begin with. They were loyal and dutiful demonic workers, not necessarily out of respect, but out of fear.

He continued on, *"Sex, food, self-preservation, acquisition, and dominance are the five basic human desires the old man placed within them when they became a living soul. What the old man calls "sin" is simply when humans decide to satisfy these desires outside of his will. His will for sex is for the act to only take place within the boundaries of marriage. His will for food is that they eat what they need to maintain healthy levels of weight and nutrition. His will for self-preservation is for them to take care of themselves and each other. His will for acquisition is for them to acquire the things they need to accomplish bringing Heaven to Earth, while enjoying the convenience of having cars, houses, and basic things of this nature. He equips them with special talents to not only make a living in whatever economy mankind decides to establish, but also to contribute to his kingdom expansion on Earth. His will for dominance is for them to establish dominion, not only geographically but inside the mountains of influence established by Heaven to create Heaven's culture on Earth. The mountains of influence are where the battle rages for the culture. Its where I operate the most by influencing them to bombard these pillars of culture with demonic inspiration. The mountains of entertainment, business, education, family, media, and government is where I operate. Most revivals die because they fail to influence the influencers. The 1% of humanity operate at this level and they are fairly easy to manipulate."*

One case worker looked up from taking notes and raised his hand.

Lord Satan said with unusual politeness, *"Go ahead. What's your question?"*

The case worker looked puzzled, and said, *"What does all this have to do with Blake?"*

Lord Satan and everyone else seated around the table shook their heads as if to say, *"This one must not be very bright..."*

After a condescending glare Lord Satan continued, *"I'm trying to give you some context. The open doors we seek to influence humanity starts with their basic desires. What they desire is innate to their being. It's how the old man made them. He made them in his image and likeness. However, they have no awareness of this when they are born. It is only when they are introduced to the Word that they learn about their true identity, purpose, and destiny. Most of what they learn is formed through instruction. The become what they are instructed to become. This is why it is written, "Train up a child in the way they should go..." Children are extremely pliable. If we can make lasting deposits in their soul at a young age, they will carry fragments of trauma and bad theology their whole life. They will build an entire life on poorly fashioned principles. My favorite thing to see happen is when they grow up with such a stubbornness to change the way they think, it becomes almost impossible for them to repent. The first sermon Jesus ever preached was because of this tactic. Jesus told people to, "Repent, the Kingdom of Heaven is at hand..." What he was imparting to humanity was a different way of thinking. In his sermon on the Mount he released teachings that did great damage to my kingdom. People left the sermon that day understanding that what they thought they knew was erroneous. I successfully imbedded my way of thinking within their own religion, but his teachings released* truth. Even his own people didn't recognize him after many years of prophetic declaration describing him in detail. You see, the true battle ground for humans is in their mind. Within the mind we can build constructs that manipulate their behavior – in whatever way we desire. I use false religion to gather them in groups and teach them error. I use the media to spread fear. I use entertainment to bombard them with temptation. I infiltrate government by influencing leaders to make decisions for mankind contrary to his Kingdom principles. I infiltrate families to create chaos in the one place a child should be safely trained. There isn't anything I won't do to steal, kill, and destroy from these despicable creatures."

The case worker once again looked up from taking notes and nodded his head as if to say, "I understand."

Lord Satan stood up from his chair and continued with a sense of urgency because he realized he was scheduled for another meeting,

"At the lowest level is where you operate. I commission teams for SKD missions so I can concentrate on higher level work. I'm only directly involved at this level due to the nature of what Blake may be called to accomplish in the Earth according to the intelligence collected by the DLD. We must eradicate the 5-Fold Ministry from the face of the Earth. If Blake is another one of these favored individuals, I had better see some progress with this case. 5-Fold Ministers carry revelation of scripture and favor that seems invincible. I'm telling you that it should be easy, and I expect to see consistent reports detailing the outcome of seasonal attacks on his family, his mind, his microsystem of support and anything else that contributes to his development. Follow protocol and we should never have to worry about Blake starting a church, writing a book, or winning anyone to Jesus in his lifetime. As you all know, there is punishment for failure. Your authority in my kingdom is only on loan *to fulfill my purposes. Ill strip you of it and send you to Hades for 100 years if you test me...."* Everyone looked at Lord Satan with fear. They also finished whatever note they were taking in preparation for his departure from the meeting. They were to stand and declare, *"All hail Lord Satan, rightful king of heaven and earth!"*

As Lord Satan stood up and made his exit with his personal assistant scrambling behind him, they made that declaration...

As Lord Satan left the meeting room, there was an awkward calm for a moment.

Since angels were the first creatures made with a self-determined will, they all had their own thoughts on what just took place.

Some case workers thought about all they had to endure working for someone like Satan. They thought about what it was like in Heaven when they were free. They thought back to the times they could run and play in the Father's love. Their minds drifted for a moment back to a better time and place. Had they thought things through, it's quite possible they would have never left. Satan made it sound so simple, as he always did. He made the Father out to be some control freak who only cared about His plans and purposes. He painted the picture that the Father was about control and manipulation. He even taught them about the beginning before things got complicated. They served alongside him for centuries as worship angels. Satan, who was then called *Lucifer*, was the anointed cherub that covered the Father's heart as all of Heaven cried out in praise. Lucifer would feel the waves of Glory flood his soul as the worshipers in Heaven and on Earth gave glory to the Father for His goodness and His kindness. He became intoxicated with the waves of Glory flooding his soul during worship. He simply made the decision, over a period of time, that he wanted it for himself...

It was a more simple time when *Lucifer* and his worship angels were serving in Heaven. Prior to the recording of the *Book of Genesis*, the story had never truly been told concerning the chaotic state Lucifer left Earth in. The formlessness and voided reality he left for the Father to piece back together was a testimony of his self-will. The beautiful creatures that existed, only to be left to the hands of Lucifer as he ruled with fear and animosity over the Earth. On that day, Michael the Archangel held him up with one arm while the Father hit him with several million volts of Holy Spirit charged love lightning, casting him out of Heaven. The Prophet Isaiah made reference to this when he declared,

"How art thou fallen from heaven, O Lucifer, son of the morning! how art thou cut down to the ground, which didst weaken the nations! For thou hast said in thine heart, I will ascend into heaven, I will exalt my throne above the stars of God: I will sit also upon the mount of the congregation, in the sides of the north: I will ascend above the heights of the clouds; I will be like the most High. Yet thou shalt be brought down to hell, to the sides of the pit."

Lucifer wanted to be like God. His hatred for man is rooted in this desire. Only man is made in God's image. Therefore, we are *like* God. The one thing he wanted more than anything else, man displays it completely.

Since that moment, things have never been the same for this group of angels. They were stuck, with no hope of redemption. They made their decision – many of them regret it. As Lucifer lived out that season for thousands of Earth years, the third of the Angels that followed him were used and abused. Lucifer ordered them to pollute the bloodline of the Earthly priests known as the *Melchizedekian Tribe*, by having intimate relations with their women. This action gave birth to the giants in the land that King David would have to deal with later in his journey as the Father developed him into the leader he was born to be. This beautiful tribe of Kings and Priests were originally charged with the stewardship of Earth prior to it becoming *"formless and void"*. The last of this tribe was found alive when Abraham paid tribute to *Melchizedek* by giving a tenth of all his goods, having secured a victory over militant factions set to destroy mankind throughout the region.

As of 1975, there were no members of the tribe left. At every turn, Lucifer was determined to corrupt anything the Father created – at any cost – to include the worship Angels who followed him. If they had it to do over, many would have refused to follow Lucifer. It was difficult for them not to be influenced by his charm and deception, having worked so closely with him over thousands of years…

Lucifer was the most beautiful creature in Heaven. *Ezekiel* prophesied as much when he spoke under the inspiration of the Holy Spirit concerning Lucifer,

"You were the signet of perfection, full of wisdom and perfect in beauty. You were in Eden, the garden of God; every precious stone was your covering, sardius, topaz, and diamond, beryl, onyx, and jasper, sapphire, emerald, and carbuncle; and crafted in gold were your settings and your engravings. On the day that you were created they were prepared. You were an anointed guardian cherub. I placed you; you were on the holy mountain of God; in the midst of the stones of fire you walked. You were blameless in your ways from the day you were created, till unrighteousness was found in you. In the abundance of your trade you were filled with violence in your midst, and you sinned; so I cast you as a profane thing from the mountain of God, and I destroyed you, O guardian cherub, from the midst of the stones of fire. Your heart was proud because of your beauty; you corrupted your

wisdom for the sake of your splendor. I cast you to the ground; I exposed you before kings, to feast their eyes on you. By the multitude of your iniquities, in the unrighteousness of your trade you profaned your sanctuaries; so I brought fire out from your midst; it consumed you, and I turned you to ashes on the earth in the sight of all who saw you."

The case workers refocused their attention to the DLD as he shuffled through his stack of information on Blake's case.

He paused and looked puzzled for a moment.

He looked at his paralegal, who was sitting to his right, and asked, *"Did you grab the notes I took concerning BLAKE-12271975-1200 Book of Destiny?"*

The paralegal said, *"Yes sir, its right here."*

Taking the notes, which were scribbled in demonic script on several pieces of paper, he repositioned himself in his chair, and prepared to continue the briefing with those present. As he quickly glanced around the table, ensuring the entire team was present and accounted for, he swiftly checked them off one by one in his head.

They were the Power of Georgia and his administrative assistant, a high ranking regional Church of Satan Warlock representative, who was there only in the spirit to receive orders for his region. His actual physical location was in his office on Earth in a drug induced trance. He was fully present in the meeting, but only to listen to instruction. There were 7 prior to the departure of Lord Satan and his assistant. Now there were 5 left. They would carry the authority to do whatever needed to be done to carry out the SKD mission.

They were a seasoned team and, up to this point had never been fired. Since the culture of the demonic kingdom is quite frankly, *"What have you done for me lately?"* none of their past triumphs really mattered much. They were never honored for their time in service, loyalty, or devotion to the cause. Even though they operated at the highest level of demonic authority, and this meeting was filled with officials operating in what scripture calls *"high places"*, the *Prince of America* would be briefed later when there were any developments on the case through official memorandum. Principalities are mainly involved in the politics of a State. They work tirelessly to find ways to influence state policy concerning just about everything. Since state level decisions trickle down to cities, if they can influence the voting on issues such as education, transportation, commerce, and such like, they can release kingdom of darkness policy to govern the affairs of men rather easily.

A Principality's greatest triumph is to place evil in office. Someone who has already been trained in occult practices and demonic rituals. This type of political puppet can cause havoc for generations. It takes decades to heal and refocus an entire nation. The former *Principality of Germany*, who was responsible for the training and manipulation of Adolf Hitler was promoted to *Chief Principality of Earth* and works directly with Lord Satan to this day. He co-labors with Spirits of Religion and Politics to bring about destruction in the Earth but operates through the demonic protocols and policies set in place to facilitate the communication of orders. Principalities seldom do the grunt work. This is why the Prince of Persia's response to the prophetic word being delivered to Daniel was so rare. Sometimes, the Principality of a nation has to get their hands dirty, especially when their job is in jeopardy. That particular Principality was fired immediately for his incompetence and relegated to tormenting duties in hades. He is still there to this day.

Allowing that level of correspondence to be delivered from Heaven to Earth is unacceptable. He should have had a plan in place to shut down the prophetic in his nation. However, Daniel's prayer life was so detailed and robust, the Father sent this word with a messenger angel – and not just any messenger angel. It was Gabriel himself. This is why the DLD position is one of the highest rungs on the ladder of promotion. Facilitating the details governing the SKD missions coming down from the top and working with Powers responsible for state and city level regions, is the last stop before being promoted to a Power. The DLD position prepares them for promotion to a Principality much like being the American CIA Director would prepare someone for Presidency. Serving as a DLD places a demon in direct proximity to governance at the highest level in the demonic kingdom. He was going to stop at nothing to destroy Blake from the face of the Earth, along with any dominion he would have been given by the Father in the *Kingdom of Light*.

The DLD finished taking roll with his eyes and began his briefing, *"My plan is to follow protocol, but sprinkle in some things that commonly work against humanity. We will begin with a question for the Warlock who is present in spirit. Is Sarah in agreement with abortion?"*

This particular Warlock who is responsible for the entire district of Satanic churches in the State of Georgia has been in this situation before. Even though he was generally present to receive orders, it was considered a privilege to be asked questions.

The Warlock replied, *"Your Highness, She is not in agreement with abortion at this time. I can commission a Spirit of Infirmity to attack her from this day forward if that would jar her fear response to abort the fetus. If the medical condition is bad enough, humans are known to give up hope for healing of any kind."*

The DLD looked at him and said, *"Her mother would cancel this assignment through prayer and declaration with no problem as soon as it begins to take root. We have to think of something more complex. Something that even Gladys wouldn't have faith for. The lineage records indicate several generational curses still active and binding, to include Crohn's disease, but that won't manifest until later in life. Bi-polar disorder has a predetermined onset between the ages of 19-23, so that's out of the picture right now. Conception has already taken place and Blake is an official living soul, so everything we decide now has to be accomplished through earthly means. Get me an (OBIB) Official Behavioral Intelligence Briefing on Sarah's boyfriend, his immediate circle of friends, and his family."*

The DLD's paralegal raised his hand and said with pride in his own diligence, *"Done sir. Its right here."*

After passing the information to the DLD, he continued to rummage through the stack of file folders and hand written notes from his own research on the case.

The DLD began to read aloud the briefing prepared by the paralegal. It read, *"Official Behavioral Intelligence Briefing (OBIB): Greg Williams is currently living in agreement with Paganism, Humanism, and practices willful disobedience to the Word. His lineage does not include anyone who has surrendered to Jesus and therefore several generational curses exist to include premature death, cancer, and alcoholism. His spirit is completely disconnected from the Father and therefore susceptible to manipulation by lower level wicked spirits in the region through music and entertainment. Greg is open to just about anything due to his naive nature and loves to dabble with witchcraft. He was raised in foster care and carries soul wounds deposited at a very young age. He was abused physically by his caretakers and locked in closets as a toddler by oppressed humans. He is easily manipulated through fear, anxiety, and an overall feeling of worthlessness. He is currently being oppressed by spirits of poverty; therefore he has trouble learning and struggles to maintain suitable employment."*

The DLD stopped reading as if to find a clear direction to take this SKD mission, and said, *"That's it. We found the catalyst. We can use this guy to the maximum. I've used so many boyfriends in the past to influence pregnant women to abort. We can go that route as soon as possible..."*

After declaring this, he looked around the room intolerantly one more time as if to say, *"What are you all waiting for?"* The meeting participants sprang up from their seats as if to recognize the temperature of the room. That was as plain as it gets from the DLD. Protocol for such things has already been written, and they were expected to spring into action. The demonic kingdom doesn't carry the creativity that flows from the Father. They simply recycle the same tactics over and over. It's unfortunate that they don't have to change their methods. As of 1975, the ecclesia had yet to fully understand how they operate. Therefore, they didn't have to change all that much. In America, only *Derick Prince* and a handful of Five-Fold ministers were even attempting to go near topics such as the spirit realm or explanations concerning the structure and strategy of the demonic kingdom.

This was the season to go all out, before America would be awakened to spirit realm realities all around them...

HEAVEN'S PLAN...

The Father, Son and Holy Spirit were enjoying a moment of fellowship. Actually, Jesus and the Holy Spirit had stepped inside the Father for this.

Their ability to do this is why they are considered to be *"three in one"*.

The Father, in essence - is Heaven. Nothing is separate from Him and He encompasses all of what's known as the Heavenly reality. If you could envision someone being bigger on the inside than they are on the outside, it would help paint an accurate picture of what this phenomenon looks like. Its beyond human comprehension and only those who have been taken to Heaven to witness the splendor and Heavenly physics involved in that dimension, can even begin to make sense of it.

The *Seers* have a unique ability to see these things clearly in the spirit realm. The only problem is, with the onset of Cessationism in the world, the spirit realm isn't addressed in the current ecclesial culture. John, the writer of the Book of Revelation was given liberty to see into the spirit realm. Several of God's Anointed Ones mentioned in scripture were given liberty as well - to include Ezekiel and Isaiah. The problem with Cessationism is that, like the Sadducees, supernaturality is dismissed as spiritism. As the ecclesia is awakened to the reality that the spirit realm is more real than the natural world around them, the warfare on the mind of humans will increase. This will be the beginning of the 3rd Great Awakening to take place in the Earth. God's people won't simply have access to their next meal. They will be given inventions from the Hall of Knowledge to eradicate hunger altogether. God's Five-Fold Officials won't simply be given ample tithe and offerings that barely support their ministry on the Earth. They will be given enough financial wealth to bail out the entire city they minister in. They wont simply be living off one event offering that barely gets them to the next engagement they are scheduled to preach at. Their bank accounts will have more than enough to pay their own travel years in advance, regardless of what is collected at the meeting. The number of private jets among God's people will outnumber the rich by a landslide. God's people will sit at the gates of the city they serve and influence policy. God's people will write and produce some of the greatest cinema and television ever witnessed in the Earth. Their stories will influence people to think different and understand that they are valued by the Father - far above anything the world can declare to them. It's hard to believe all this, considering the state of the world in 1975, but Heaven always has a plan. Heaven is always a step ahead of the demonic kingdom. It's not even close...

Jesus stepped into the private meeting area from His location inside the Father. Following directly behind Jesus was the Holy Spirit. They were laughing at a story Jesus was telling about a time in His childhood.

Looking directly at Holy Spirit, He finished the story as he was chewing a bite of pomegranate,

"Then, out of the blue, I decided to try to walk on water. I wasn't sure if it was going to work. I was in a season where You were teaching me about my abilities as the Son of Man, having been baptized in You. I felt empowered and inspired beyond anything prior to that. This of course was after the enemy took me in the spirit to tempt me for a season."

Holy Spirit said, *"Yes I remember. I had to get you up to speed quickly. Your public ministry was starting to take off and you needed to be able to demonstrate the gifts of the Spirit as you ministered to the public."*

The Father chimed in and said, *"I do desire for the ecclesia to step more fully into their Holy Spirit empowerment. This will set the stage for the 3rd Great Awakening. My people carry demonstratable solutions for society, not just a sermon."*

Jesus and Holy Spirit replied with, *"Amen!"*

Then Holy Spirit continued, *"We have an outpouring scheduled for Toronto in January 1994. That will push the ecclesia forward a bit. Of course, it will cause controversy with the nominal established church, but it has to be sent, for the sake of those crying out for more."*

Jesus nodded His head in agreement and replied, *"Amen. Cessationism must be rooted out completely. That teaching was released so long ago in The Apostle Paul's day, and still has deep roots in the religious theological community. It's still taught in seminaries for an entire semester. An entire generation of Pastors and Teachers have been trained to teach the people of God that spiritual gifts are no longer for us. This has to be eradicated through the release of fresh demonstrations of the Power of God."*

The Father also nodded His head in agreement and said, *"We will root that doctrine of devils out, in part, with worship music. There is a generation of worship leaders being raised up as we speak. Keith and Melody Green were led to a small bible study just a few months ago where they surrendered their lives to Jesus. I have called Keith Green to write some of the most influential worship music of all time. His style and approach to worship music will give birth to the kind of creativity needed to push the ecclesia forward in that area. Next year, he will actually sign with Sparrow Records and begin producing the kind of music the ecclesia needs to hear in this season. He has no idea how much his music will influence a generation of believers. Unfortunately, the established nominal church will reject it. However, as my people seek my face, and things become more clear for them, they will open their hearts to what I have planned in the Earth."*

Holy Spirit replied with, *"Amen! Blake will be introduced to this music early in his development by his Youth Minister. Even though his Youth Minister will be primarily a Cessationist believer, he won't push the theology on him, so Blake will be safe from that. Besides, the amount of anointing for teaching we plan on placing on Blake for ministry, he would have a hard time even believing that parts of the Bible aren't true."*

Jesus replied with, *"Exactly. Cessationism won't even make sense to him."* Then, they all openly shared a laugh...

The Father sat down at the head of the meeting table.

Jesus sat down at His right hand.

The Holy Spirit sat down to his left.

The Father continued, *"Our meeting today is to finalize the plan for BLAKE-12271975-1200. As you know, once we declare these things, the demonic kingdom will have access to the information through the spirit realm airwaves through their many scouts and intelligence agencies located in the second heaven. For the most part we will follow protocol on this one and make adjustments along the way. Oh, I just remembered, we need Blake's life plan team here at the meeting. Have either of you let them know about the meeting?"* Jesus said, *"Yes, I just spoke with them yesterday. Adriel was involved in a skirmish surrounding the time of Blake's conception. Nothing major. He acted heroically as usual and even blessed a local believer in the process."* The Father smiled and said, *"Oh, good for him. He's such an amazing servant. One of our best. He will need to hand select his assistant Guardians, one for each of Blake's gifts. We will get into that once he arrives."*

Immediately, Adriel was seen hurling through the air many

Earth miles away, moving at an intensely high speed towards the meeting area.

He landed just outside the beautiful garden scenery that enveloped the meeting area in an open field.

When he landed in a crouched position, the ground absorbed the impact and sent a spirit realm shock wave that was both seen and heard all throughout Heaven.

As he slowly stood up to reveal all 20 feet of his majestic frame, he looked at the Father, Son and Holy spirit with a smile that communicated the confidence to say, *"Did you see that?"*

Just then, the Father got up from His seat and ran to meet Adriel.

The Father loves to overwhelm his creation with appreciation for the part they play in the overall plans of Heaven. No creature in Heaven is considered unimportant or irrelevant. It's the Father's custom to run towards his creation, big or small, and greet them with a hug and a kiss on the cheek. Everyone feels important in Heaven because the Father treats every creature, big or small with respect and gratitude for what they carry. There are billions of Guardian Angels in the service of the Father, under the direction of Gabriel. Everyone of them feel the same level of love and appreciation when the Father greets them. The Father threw His arms around one of Adriel's massive calf muscles. The Father chooses to operate in Heaven, the size of a normal human being – around 5'11". This is to accommodate living among the billions of humans who have come home and now inhabit the mansions and travel road systems there. He would never want to make humans feel intimidated by his true size. Even with this adjustment, He is immeasurable in size on the inside and has the capacity to hold the entire galaxy in his being, all while remaining 5'11".

As he hugged Adriel, he said with a smile that grew to a chuckle as he finished, *"I love you my friend. I'm so excited for this season of your life. You have guarded the life plan for so many redeemed ones through the centuries with love, joy, peace, patience, kindness, goodness, faithfulness, and self-control. Except for that time you stepped in the middle of a race riot and accidently stepped on a human. They were born again so, it was a simple explanation of why they died, and I immediately sent their spirit back to their body. They have shared that story with millions – so it all worked out."*

Then the Father looked up to see Adriel towering over him with magnificent beauty and strength.

Then, Adriel stepped away gently, so as to be completely honoring of the Father's personal space and bowed down in worship.

The Father placed His hand on Adriel's head and declared a blessing, *"I bless your ministry. I bless your coming and going. I bless your future in the millennial kingdom, and I bless your current assignment."*

With that blessing, tears of joy streamed down Adriel's face.

Guardian Angels carry the capacity to exhibit a full range of human emotion. This enables them to operate from compassion – the way Jesus operated among humans during His Earthly ministry.

The Father finished blessing Adriel and stood there with a gentle smile.

Adriel, with tears still flowing down his face, lifted his head from his bowed position, and locked eyes with the Father. He said, *"I receive it. Thank you Abba."*

The Father reached out and placed his hand on Adriel's face, and while looking intently at him, said, *"This is a very special boy you are assigned to look after. There is mighty calling on his life. He will carry revelation of scripture for an entire generation. He will walk in favor and blessing all the days of his life. Your assignment is simple, but there will be challenges. I have full confidence in you and in your ministry to him. You have always been very loyal and dutiful, Adriel. As always, Heaven stands ready to assist you as you travel back and forth between the Earthly and Heavenly realms. I expect this season of your ministry to be full of surprises, but nothing you haven't experienced at some point in your many years of service. Are there any fears or concerns that I can help you with?"*

Adriel changed positions and carefully sat with his legs crossed so as to be as close to the Father as possible without invading his space with his massive frame. Even while sitting with his legs crossed like a child in an earthly kindergarten classroom room, he was every bit as massive. From the ground to the top of his head was at least 10 feet in height, even while sitting.

The Father leaned in while placing his right hand on his knee, expecting the conversation to further develop, and said, *"You can be vulnerable in this moment. I'm here for you."*

Adriel wiped the remaining tears from his eyes and began to share his heart…

The Father turned around to address Jesus and the Holy Spirit from about 50 feet away, who could be heard laughing at the latest story Jesus was telling to the Guardian Team now arriving one at a time and taking their seat at the meeting table. The Father said to all who were currently in attendance, *"We won't be long. It will be just a moment."*

Adriel, collecting his thoughts and readjusting himself after being undone by the Father's blessing on his life, said almost apologetically, *"I'm afraid."*

The Father looked at him with a look that could only be described as compassion mixed with hope. The Father has a look that both encourages and inspires. His voice and His gaze impart the same things in the spirit realm. His eyes burn with love and empathy and when He looks at one of his creatures, they are energized and strengthened with all of Heaven's power behind it.

Adriel continued, *"This is the most important assignment of my ministry. I feel overwhelmed that you would ask me to be part of the journey for this young man. I see the mess he is to be born into. The world is so malicious and cruel, Abba. I long for the day when you usher in the Millennial Reign of Christ. I long for the day when you call your children home and take them out of the Earthly realm to be with you for eternity. I long for the day when mankind is finally free from the effects of sin and shame. I long for the day when you bring judgement to Lucifer and place his kingdom under your feet."*

The Father repositioned His hand and placed it on Adriel's hands, which were folded, fingers interlaced in his lap, and said, *"I understand, Adriel. It has been a long and tedious season for you. You see, when my son gave His life to redeem mankind, that's exactly what He accomplished. The ecclesia has been given power and authority to root out evil from the Earth. They were commissioned to heal the sick, raise the dead, cast out demons and cleanse lepers. They were told by my Son to go into all the world, to include the mountains of influence, to bring Heaven to Earth, by establishing my Kingdom. You see, we are in the beginning stages of the 3rd Great Awakening. This is where you will see the ecclesia begin to do these things. They are learning to work together and put aside doctrinal disputes. They are being repositioned for influence and reestablished at the gates of the cities to bring about change. I* *have so many Apostles, Prophets, Teachers, Evangelists, and Pastors being trained in this season to facilitate my plans. I know it may seem dark, but there is hope…"*

Adriel was beginning to look encouraged. Since there is no insecurity in Heaven, one would be astonished at how vulnerable, even the mightiest creatures are in the presence of the Father. From Him all life flows. To be separated from this life giving force is the eternal punishment spoken of in scripture. Adriel could not imagine a world where he would be separated from this life giving vitality. This is why, when faced with the season where Bake will be in proximity to the Gospel message, he will work overtime to ensure the message is delivered loud and clear. At the spiritual age of accountability, often around 11 years old, a human is susceptible to all kinds of ideas. It was Adriel's job to ensure Blake is present and within ear shot of the Gospel, wherever that may take place.

There are other methods of delivery to include supernatural dreams and visions. However, Blake was to carry a supreme love for scripture. People with this kind of gift often surrender to Jesus by simply reading or hearing the Gospel. Something burns within them when its heard or read. They generally make a decision in the moment due to the power of the Word declared openly through speech or lodged in their subconscious when they read it. It doesn't take a supernatural encounter for people like Blake to surrender to Jesus. He will be hardwired to respond to the declared Word. It's indicative of a teaching gift, placed within his soul from conception.

The Father continued, *"You will do well. I created you with your own unique abilities, for such a time as this. I know 1975 is pretty chaotic and the political environment, as well as the ecclesia in America is divided. I'm fully aware, and I have a plan for Blake in all of it. You don't have to worry or carry any anxiety concerning this assignment. You are fully equipped to handle anything that will come your way. Today we will assemble your team and discuss the plan. All declarations, decrees, words of wisdom, knowledge and prophecy will be released on a predetermined schedule throughout his life span, as protocol dictates, through my servants on the ground in the Earthly realm. Your biggest role is protection and clearing a path for Blake to be where he is supposed to be at the appointed times. We will discuss this in detail in the meeting. I love you Adriel and I'm excited for this season of life for you."*

Adriel, looking more confident, began to broaden his massive shoulders as if to say, *"It's going to be just fine."*

The Father turned around and began to walk towards the meeting area.

He then stopped, turned around and motioned to Adriel, as if to say, *"Follow me."*

Adriel stood up to reveal his majestic 20 foot tall frame and walked towards the meeting area where Jesus, The Holy Spirit and the life plan management team was waiting around a large table, holding the Father's hand. It was more like the Father holding one of Adriel's fingers. It was a precious site to see how gentle and kind the Father is in moments like this. Even giants struggle with confidence. This is why the Father ensured that His Word would be packed with declarations concerning fear and anxiety. It's no accident that the most declared command in scripture is, *"Do not fear..."*

The meeting area was now pulsating with energy and faith. The attendees were seated around the table and the Guardian Angels were sitting with their legs folded and ready to receive instruction from the Trinity Team. Seated around the table was the Father, Son, and Holy Spirit - one paralegal to record all declarations, decrees, words of wisdom, knowledge, and prophecy – and one representative from Blake's lineage. Seated in the courtyard surrounding the table, since the chairs were human size and they simply occupied more space and were not able to fit - one representative from the Host of Heaven, Adriel, and his team to include a separate Guardian Angel for each of Blake's gifts. His gifts were teaching, musical ability, writing, artistic expression, and leadership.

As everyone found their seat, or place to sit in the courtyard, Jesus stood up and opened up the meeting with the following, *"I welcome each of you to this meeting concerning Blake. I haven't seen this large of a life plan team assembled since Billy Graham's days on Earth were being planned. I have full confidence in this team and look forward to working with all of you. Now that I take a closer look, this team more closely resembles King David's team – and we all know the ups and downs he endured in the Earth. I look forward to seeing how you handle the challenges Blake will face and operating in your empowerment to bring about the desired outcome – to become like me. It's the purpose of it all. The Earthly realm is a training ground for Kings and Priests of the Most High God. In order to prepare mankind for the Millennial Kingdom, they must be developed to represent Me well in the Earth. Since they take their personalities with them into eternity, your role is to work closely with Holy Spirit, who is the active facilitator of their development. All works of the flesh must be trained out of them. The work I have for them to do, ruling and reigning with me for 1,000 years, serves as the foundation for the ages to come. Since we are approximately 175 years from the Rapture of the Church, things will be ramped up a bit in the next 50 years. Blake's role in all of this, as with every human being, is very specific. Are there any question so far?"*

Since everyone can read the thoughts of one another in Heaven, there is no insecurity when it comes to open communication in meetings. It's one of the many reasons Heaven is so efficient.

Adriel raised his giant hand and waited for Jesus to acknowledge his apparent question. *"Go ahead Mighty Adriel."*

Adriel smiled and said, *"This is definitely a different time to be born into. Prayer doesn't exist in schools right now. What's the plan to ensure that Blake will be introduced to the importance of prayer?"* Jesus nodded his head up and down and waited for an opportunity to answer. Then Jesus said, *"The town Blake will move to is filled with Baptist churches. He won't grow up in the city he will be born in. I have a place in mind and the location will be released later. As you all know, we love to give people options, especially in America where there are so many amazing places to grow up. Blake's mom will eventually give her life to me. However, Gladys will provide the majority of Blake's parenting during his childhood. I have just the right Youth Minister for him as he enters Middle School. I actually have several depending on the city he actually gets planted in. His Youth Minister will be the first to teach him how to do a simple daily devotion, which will draw him closer to the power of the Word."*

The paralegal raised his hand, Jesus pointed at him, making it apparent that it was his turn to speak, and the paralegal said, *"This part gets me every time. Humans have the idea that they don't have options. Religion teaches them to be afraid of their every decision concerning where to live and what job to do and so on. Scripture clearly communicates that "God is with them wherever they go."*

Jesus agreed and said, *"Yes. It's one of the tricks of the Spirit of Religion. To make mankind feel guilty and shameful for all sorts of things. Religion teaches them that their desires are evil. What we are in the process of releasing, through the Teachers operating in the ecclesia, is that they already carry the desires of God in their* soul. It was deposited in them at conception. Religion stifles these desires to sing, dance, create cinema, play professional sports, and even pursue a career in politics. The basis for the erroneous teachings concerning what a human being decides to pursue is of course partially rooted in scripture. Many teachers preach from the Gospels and point out the calling of the twelve apostles and use it as a theoretical underpinning to bolster their doctrine. They teach that every human being must abandon all of their desires and follow me. This is true. However, many are called to operate in the mountains of influence. I had several friends during my Earthly ministry, to include Lazarus and his family who were considered wealthy. I didn't tell him to sell all he had and give to the poor. We need more Holy Spirit filled believers operating in business, medicine, the arts, and politics. They are already built to thrive in these environments. After all, when I issued the Great Commission to my original followers, to include the 500 I appeared to in Galilee, I said – "Go into all the world." This includes business, government, the arts, entertainment, and medicine. I even have a million souls marked to operate as Mental Health Counselors in the coming decades. You can see how this could have been misinterpreted?"

The paralegal politely said, "Yes, I can see that. In an attempt to live in agreement with scripture, human beings often fail to truly understand the essence of the Word."

Jesus replied, "Exactly. It's been a process of working with the ecclesia for the last 2,000 years to produce anointed translations of the original text. In the coming decades, there will be several translations released in order to bring about a clearer understanding of what scripture tells them. That is a great observation."

As everyone was absorbed in the atmosphere of the meeting, and hanging on Jesus' every Word, Abba looked around the table and eventually locked eyes with each participant – one by one.

His eyes expressed the deepest compassion and appreciation for their work.

God's creatures never have to work to earn His love. God's heart swells with gratitude when He sees teams working in unison, focused on the one thing that needs to happen. The efficiency of Heaven is fueled by one characteristic – unity. It's a level of unity that only exists in His presence. What is being demonstrated at this meeting doesn't happen all that often on the Earth. It's a level of unity that, even after 2,000 years of ecclesial leadership in the Earth, has yet to fully manifest. The ecclesia is still trying to wrap their minds around Holy Spirit and how to co-labor with Him. What the Father wants to see is unity in the ecclesia, *"on Earth as it is in Heaven."* Life Plan Teams embody this characteristic. There is a clear cut leader – Adriel. However, he has been trained to demonstrate the Father in all his behavior. Adriel knows how to make command decisions in the field, as well as solicit advice from his team in real time.

Adriel has been trained to think big picture in all his decisions concerning the protection of Blake's life plan. He's also been trained to ask questions when clarification is needed. Once this meeting adjourns, he will be launched into a lifelong relationship with Blake. He will watch over him as he is developed in the womb. He will be present when Blake breathes his first breath of oxygen. He will be there when Blake takes his first steps as a toddler. And of course when Blake takes his first spin in an automobile. When Blake cries out for help, Adriel will be there to provide last minute protection from danger. Holy Spirit is there to develop Blake on the inside – his mind, will, and emotions. Adriel is there to operate in the seen and unseen realms. With Level 1 Authority, he will be able to manifest physically if need be to provide protection from dangers present on Earth, as well as wage war on unseen realities threatening his life. Adriel will be expected to memorize Blake's Book of Destiny. It will serve as the compass on Blake's journey, should Blake fail to recognize the voice of the Holy Spirit, or ignore the gentle leading he will receive from predetermined words of wisdom, knowledge and prophecy released through God's people.

The Father felt it was time to move the meeting along.

He paused for a moment,

looked at Adriel with a look that communicated His confidence in him, and then said, *"Adriel, are you prepared to recite the official record concerning Blake's identity, purpose and destiny?"*

Adriel said, *"Yes Abba, I'm ready."*

Then suddenly, all meeting participants stood up. Its customary to stand when official decrees and declarations are made concerning mankind.

Adriel, now standing, took a deep breath and made the official declaration taken directly from Blake's Book of Destiny. He said, *"His Earthly name will be called Blake which means "Shining One". He will be circumcised the eighth day after his birth and will win many souls to the Kingdom. He will grow to be 6 feet 1 inch tall and will carry a deep discernment in the spirit realm. His features will be handsome and will carry the ability to operate comfortably in front of people. He will have an average build, with average athletic ability but above average intelligence. He will come to know me at a very young age because we must capture his heart early due to the amount of impact he will have in the Earth for my Kingdom. Due to generational blessings already established in his bloodline, announced by his ancestors through prayer and declaration, he will have a natural ability to understand and write music, as well as books. Blake's Earthly appointment will be as a Pastor/Teacher in the ecclesia. He will carry a deep discernment for the Word of God and will desire to study and meditate on God's Word day and night. People will naturally desire to talk to him and tell him their deepest trauma. As a Pastor, he will care for many people and always desire to help them. As a Teacher, God will open his mind in extraordinary ways and deposit the science of His Word in his heart. The Bible for him will be like a five or six page book. His teachings will be deep but simple, just like Jesus during His Earthly ministry.* **Nothing will stop this appointment, and he must always be full time in ministry.** *Blake will be set apart from birth with the following gifts - strong commitment to duty, communication ability and love for the arts.*

Blake will gravitate towards visual art and literature as a means of learning. Blake will have a natural ability to discern truth in scripture and will be a natural magnet for heartbroken people. Blake will carry a creative capacity that is above average and will see the lesson in everything. This will enable Blake to teach and preach the way Jesus did during his Earthly ministry, using everyday things to communicate the Word of God. Once empowered by Holy Spirit, Blake will have a strong anointing to hear words of wisdom, knowledge, and prophecy. His strong sense of duty will lead him to seek deeper truth and greater anointing as a minister of the Gospel message and teacher of the Holy Scriptures. His divine gifts will enable him to be a natural lifelong learner and seeker of truth. This will protect his destiny from the spirit of Religion which seeks to keep man stuck in a fixed mindset. With the right Pastor in his ear, Blake will always find a way to repent and adjust his thinking to align himself with what the Father is saying and doing in the Earth."

The Father looked at Jesus and the Holy Spirit, specifically and said, *"This part never gets old. I'm looking forward to seeing the development of this young man. He is one of many positioned to bring about change in the Earth. His generation is unique. They will be raised without much technology but will live in the midst of a major technological shift in the Earth. His generation will be present to see the 3rd Great Awakening. As he develops, his test will be to embrace what I am saying and doing, as it will confront what he thinks he knows about me and my Word. He will have to repent often and humble himself as my plan for his life unfolds. The team we have surrounded him with are some of the best. I'm expecting big things..."*

Jesus nodded His head and replied, *"If he will surrender to me, and allow me to walk with him, I can use his life to reach millions."*

Holy Spirit added, *"The months ahead are crucial to the plan. Blake has the support he needs and I'm also expecting big things."* The Father stood up, which was the customary end to meetings such as this, and said, *"Thank you and Bless you all for your time and service to this precious soul. There will be challenges ahead, but nothing Heaven can't handle. I have full confidence in the work you all have put in already."*

Then, suddenly, Adriel received a notification on his arm band communicator. The message said,

"IMPENDING THREAT: BLAKE-12271975-1200."

Adriel looked down and acknowledged the message. Then, he said to the team with coolness, *"We must be going...."*

LITERARY REFERENCES

Adler, P. A., & Adler, P. (2012). *Constructions of deviance: Social power, context, and interaction* (7th ed.). Belmont, CA: Wadswort

American Psychological Association. (2015) (n.d.). *Ethical principles of psychologists and code of conduct.* Retrieved from http://www.apa.org/ethics/code/index.aspx

Ando, J., Ono, Y., & Wright, M. J. (2001). Genetic structure of spatial and Verbal working memory. *Behavior Genetics*, 31, 615-624.

Anxiety and Depression Association of America, (2013), *Facts and Statistics; Did you know?,* Retrieved from: http://www.adaa.org/about-adaa/press-room/facts-statistics

Apter, M. J. (1982). *The experience of motivation: Theory of psychological reversals.* New York: Academic Press. (Franken, 2006-05-22, p. 409)

Balaam, Retrieved from: https://en.wikipedia.org/wiki/Balaam#

Bandura, A. (1977) Bandura, A., *Self-efficacy: Toward a Unifying Theory of Behavioral Change*, Psychological Review 1977, Vol. 84, No. 2, 191-215

Baumeister, R. F., & Bushman, B. J. (2011). *Social psychology & human nature* (2nd ed.). Belmont, CA: Thomson Wadsworth. ISBN: 9.7805E+12

Berk, L. E. (2010). *Exploring lifespan development* (2nd ed.). Boston, MA: Allyn & Bacon. ISBN: 9780205748594.

Butcher, J. N., Mineka, S., Hooley, J. M. (2012). *Abnormal Psychology*, Retrieved from http://online.vitalsource.com/books/9781256815037

Crandell, T. L., Crandell, C. H., & Vander Zanden, J. W. (2012). *Human development* (10th ed.). Boston, MA: McGraw-Hill Higher Education. ISBN: 9780073532189.

Dictionary, (2019), Google Online Dictionary https://www.google.com/search?source=hp&ei=-

Erikson, E., (2015) *Social & Emotional Development*, Retrieved from: http://bjspt2014.weebly.com/social--emotional.html

Erikson, J.M. (1997). *The Lifecycle Completed* (exp. Version). New York: Norton.

Ford, Donald H. & Urban, Hugh B. (1965), *Systems of Psychotherapy: A Comparative Study*. New York, John Wiley & Sons, Inc, 1965, p.109.

Franken, R. E. (2006). *Human Motivation*, 6th Edition, Retrieved from http://online.vitalsource.com/books/1111898472

Freud, S. (1987). Psychopathology.

Garrett, B. (2010). *Brain & Behavior: An Introduction to Biological Psychology*, 3rd Edition, Retrieved from: http://online.vitalsource.com/books/9781452268651

Hayford, Jack W.; Moore, S. David (2006). *The Charismatic Century: The Enduring Impact of the Azusa Street Revival* (August 2006 ed.). Warner Faith. ISBN 978-0-446-57813-4.

Henderson, R., (2016) *Operating in the Courts of Heaven*

Hertel, P. T., & Rude, S. S. (1991). Depressive deficits in memory: Focusing attention improves subsequent recall. *Journal of Experimental Psychology*: General, 120, 301- 309.

Hewitt, P. L., Flett, G. L., & Ediger, E. (1996). Perfectionism and depression: Longitudinal assessment of a specific vulnerability hypothesis. *Journal of Abnormal Psychology*, 105, 276- 280.

Hirsch, E.G., Price, I.M., (1906) Othniel, *Jewish Encyclopedia*, retrieved from: http://www.jewishencyclopedia.com/articles/11800-othniel

Hirsch, E.G., Ryssel, V., (1906) Othniel, *Jewish Encyclopedia*, retrieved from: http://www.jewishencyclopedia.com/articles/11800-othniel

Hunt, M. (2007). *The Story of Psychology*. New York, NY: Anchor Books. ISBN: 9780307278074.

Jacobs, J., Price, I.M., (1906) Samson, *Jewish Encyclopedia*, retrieved from: http://www.jewishencyclopedia.com/articles/13071-samson

James Strong, S. (1890). *Strong's Exhaustive Concordance*.

James, K. (1611). *The Holy Bible*.

Jastrow, M. & Price, I.M., (1906) Balaam, *Jewish Encyclopedia*, retrieved from: http://www.jewishencyclopedia.com/articles/2395-balaam

Jaycox, L. H., Foa, E. B., & Morral, A. R. (1998). Influence of emotional engagement and habituation on exposure therapy for PTSD. *Journal of Consulting and Clinical Psychology*, 66(1), 185-192. doi:10.1037/0022-006X.66.1.185

Jérémiee Gilbert, Nomadic Peoples and Human Rights (2014), p. 73:

Jutta Joormann, Marco Dkane, Ian H. Gotlib. (2006). Adaptive and maladaptive components of rumination? Diagnostic specificity and relation to depressive biases. *"Behavior Therapy"*, 37, 269- 280.,

Johnson, B. (2015) *The Power that Changes the World*

Johnson, B., Clark, R. (2017) *Anointed to Heal*

"King James' Parliament: The succession of William and Mary – begins 13/2/1689" The History and Proceedings of the House of Commons: volume 2: 1680–1695 (1742), pp. 255–277. Accessed: 16 February 2007.

Liadorn, R. (1996) *God's Generals*

Levens, S. M, & Muhtadie, 1. (2009). Rumination and impaired resource allocation in depression. *Journal of Abnormal Psychology,* 118(4), 757-766.

Levesque, C., Copeland, K. J., & Sutcliffe, R. A. (2008). Conscious and nonconscious processes: Implications for self-determination theory. *Canadian Psychology/Psychologie Canadienne,* 49(3), 218- 224

Livescience (2019), Retrieved from, Livescience.com

Locke, J. (1689). *An Essay Concerning Human Understanding.* London

Luszczynska, A., & Schwarzer, R. (2005). *Social cognitive theory.* In, Conner & P. Norman (Eds.), Predicting health behavior (2nd ed. rev., pp. 127-169). Buckingham, England: Open University Press.

Markus, H., & Kitayama, S. (1991). Culture and self: Implications for cognition, emotion and motivation. *Psychological Review,* 98, 224- 253

Markus, H., & Kitayama, S. (1991). Culture and self: Implications for cognition, emotion and motivation. *Psychological Review,* 98, 224- 253

Maslow, A., (2015) *Maslow's Hierarchy of Needs*, Retrieved from: http://en.wikipedia.org/wiki/Abraham_Maslow

McCullough, M. E., & Willoughby, B. L. B. (2009). Religion, self-regulation, and self-control: Associations, explanations, and implications. *Psychological Bulletin*, 135(1), 69-93.

Morris Jastrow, Jr., Charles J. Mendelsohn, Marcus Jastrow, Isaac Husik, Duncan B. McDonald, George A. Barton, (2020) The Ark of the Covenant, *Jewish Encyclopedia*, Retrieved from: http://www.jewishencyclopedia.com/articles/1777-ark-of-the-covenant

Newberg A, Pourdehnad M, Alavi A, d'Aquili E. (2003) Cerebral blood flow during meditative prayer: Preliminary findings and methodological issues. *Perceptual and Motor Skills* 97: 625-630, 2003.

Newberg, D. A. (2010), *Principles of Neurotheology*. . ISBN 978-1409408109. Farnham, Surrey, England:: Ashgate Publishing.

Newburg, A. B. (2012). *Andrew Newburg Research*, http://www.andrewnewberg.com/. Retrieved from http://www.andrewnewberg.com/

Niiya, Y., Crocker, J., & Bartmess, E. N. (2004). From Vulnerability to Resilience. *Psychological Science* (Wiley-Blackwell), 15(12), 801-   805. doi:10.1111/j.0956-7976.2004.00759.x

Orr, J. (1915), *International Standard Bible Encyclopedia*, Howard-Severance Co., Chicago, Retrieved from e-Sword X Bible Software, iMac version

Oyserman, D., Fryberg, S. A., & Yoder, N. (2007). Identity-based motivation and health. *Journal of Personality and Social Psychology*, 93(6), 1011-1027.

Pavlov, I. P. (1927). *Conditioned Reflexes: An Investigation of the Physiological Activity of the Cerebral Cortex*. Translated and Edited by G. V. Anrep. London: Oxford University Press. p. 142.

PCOG, (2020) *Pentecostal Church of God General Bylaws*, Historical Perspective, Section 3 and History. Retrieved from: https://en.wikipedia.org/wiki/Azusa_Street_Revival#cite_note-2

Plomin, R. (1990). The role of inheritance in behavior. *Science*, 248, 183- 188

Ramirez, J. (2019), *Out of the Devils Cauldron*, Retrieved from: https://www.goodreads.com/author/quotes/4775993.John_Ramirez

Schmidt, R. F. (1989). *Behavior Memory* (Learning by Conditioning) In Schmidt, Robert F.; Thews, Gerhard. Human Physiology. Translated by Marguerite A. Biederman-Thorson (Second, completely revised ed.). Berlin etc.: Springer-Verlag. ISBN 3-540-19432-0.

Schur, Edwin. 1979. *Interpreting Deviance*. New York: Harper and Row.

Science (1993), This is your brain on stress. *Science*, 262(5137), 1211-1211.

Science of Psychotherapy (2019), *Prefrontal Cortex Definition*, Retrieved from https://www.thescienceofpsychotherapy.com/prefrontal-cortex/

Stark E., (2020) *The Prophetic Warrior*

Strong (1890), *Strong's Concordance*, E-sword Edition

Synan, Vinson (2001). *The Century of the Holy Spirit: 100 years of Pentecostal and Charismatic Renewal*, 1901-2001. Nashville: Thomas Nelson Publishers. pp. 42-45. ISBN 0-7852-4550-2.

Thio, A., Calhoun, T. C., & Conyers, A. (2010). *Readings in deviant behavior* (6th ed.). Boston, MA: Allyn & Bacon. ISBN: 9780205695577.

Tobias, S. (1979). Anxiety research in educational psychology. *Journal of Educational Psychology*, 71(5), 573-582. doi:10.1037/0022- 0663.71.5.573

Truity, (2015) *Personality Types Explained*, Retrieved from: http://www.truity.com/

United Nations, (1948) "Universal Declaration of Human Rights", Retrieved from: un.org

US Census Bureau, (2017) *Data representing children living without a step, biological, or adoptive father*. Retrieved from: https://www.fatherhood.org/fatherhood-data-statistics

Vallotton, K. (2007), *Basic Training for the Prophetic*, Retrieved from: https://www.goodreads.com/work/quotes/1395616-basic-training-for-the-prophetic-ministry-a-call-to-spiritual-warfare--

Watson, J.B. and Rayner, R. (1920). Conditioned emotional reactions. *Journal of Experimental Psychology*, 3, 1, pp. 1-14

Wei, M., Heppner, P., Mallen, M., Ku, T.-Y, Liao, K. Y.-H., & Wu, T.-F. (2007). Acculturative stress, perfectionism, years in the United States, and depression among Chinese international students. *Journal of Counseling Psychology*, 54,(4), 385-394.

Whiteley, P. (2002). *Motivation*. Oxford, UK: Capstone Publishing, Ltd.

VIDEO REFERENCES

2022 Dr. Myles Munroe *Keys of the Kingdom* (Parts 1-4)

2010 Bill Johnson *The Contrary Presence of God*

2012 Bill Johnson *Divine Favor*

2013 Bill Johnson *Fulfilling the Dream*

2013 Bill Johnson *Heavenly Dominion*

2015 Reinhard Bonnke, *Faith and Fire*

2016 Your World with Creflo, *Exposing the Dark Side, Part 1*

2016 Your World with Creflo, *Exposing the Dark Side Part 2*

2017 Kris Vallotton, *Basic Training for the Prophetic Ministry*

2018 Kris Vallotton, *Bethel School of Prophets*, Session 1

2019 John Ramirez - Rock Church - *Spiritual Warfare*

2019 Tony Evans, *The Authority of Binding and Loosing*

2019 Tony Evans, *Understanding Spiritual Authority*

2019 Robert Morris, *What's My Part?*

2020 Emma Stark, *Power Hour*

2021 Bill Johnson, *The Power of the Gospel*

2022 Danny Silk, *Unpunishable*, BSSM Online

2022 Bill Johnson, *Faith and the Renewed Mind*, BSSM Online

2022 Bill Johnson, *Is Your Heart Healthy*

2021 Kat Kerr, *Inhabiting Heaven Conference*

2023 Kat Kerr, *Talking About Heaven*

BIBLE REFERENCES

English Standard Version

New Living Translation

New King James Version

King James Version

New International Version

The Passion Translation

BULK ORDERS FOR CHURCHES AND MEN'S GROUPS

Please email me at ronniecdallen@gmail.com for bulk orders of 50 or more.

CREATIVE TEAM

Scott Richardson

Anderson Grandini

Made in the USA
Columbia, SC
10 March 2024